"Out of print for a full half-century. . .this book is as swift, hard-edged and suspenseful as any crime novel written in the 1980's. . .deftly characterized and always surprising. The plot relentlessly propels the reader forward as it twists and turns like a roller coaster, providing a breathless and exciting ride from first page to last. . .a sheer delight"

– William F. Nolan

(from his new Introduction)

MAX BRAND

THE NIGHT FLOWER

With a new introduction by William F. Nolan.

INTERNATIONAL POLYGONICS, LTD.
NEW YORK CITY

THE NIGHT FLOWER

First serialized by *Flynn's Detective Fiction Weekly* in six installments from December 16, 1933 through January 20, 1934, under the title THE DARK PERIL by Max Brand. First book publication 1936 by The Macaulay Company as THE NIGHT FLOWER by Walter C. Butler.

Library of Congress Card Catalog No. 87-80308
ISBN 0-930330-48-X

Printed and manufactured in the United States of America by Guinn Printing.
First IPL printing June 1987.
10 9 8 7 6 5 4 3 2 1

INTRODUCTION

Today's mystery reader may be surprised to encounter the byline of "Max Brand" on a crime-suspense thriller. This author (whose real name was Frederick Faust) achieved his impressive mass-market fiction reputation as the creator of *Destry Rides Again* and more than 170 other hard-galloping Westerns. Yet, working mainly as Max Brand, Faust wrote some two-dozen full length crime thrillers for a wide variety of pulp and slick paper magazines, including *Black Mask, Dime Detective, Detective Story Magazine, McCall's* and *Cosmopolitan.* Ten of these crime novels have been published in book format—from *Six Golden Angels* to *The Granduca.* And with such books as *Spy Meets Spy* and *The Bamboo Whistle,* Faust was writing about glamorous, fast-shooting, international secret agents in the mid-1930s, long before Ian Fleming dreamed up James Bond.

Including serials, short stories and novelettes, Faust sold more than 600 fiction pieces between 1917, when he began his career, and 1944, when he was killed in Italy as a 52-year-old war correspondent. More than 70 of these fall into the crime genre, and (as Max Brand) he was a major contributor to *Detective Fiction Weekly* from 1933 into 1937, where *The Night Flower* saw first publication.

Of course, as the legendary "King of the Pulps," Faust wrote a staggering amount of wordage (under 20 pen names) in many genres—producing pirate tales, sagas of the frozen Klondike, fantasies, South Seas adventures, boxing stories, horse-racing dramas, romances, tales of war and revolution, and medical suspense novels—the famous Dr. Kildare series for films, radio and television.

Eclipsed by his widespread fame in the Western genre, Max Brand's work in the field of crime-suspense has been unjustly neglected, and it is a great pleasure for me, as a long-time Faust enthusiast, to introduce *The Night Flower* to modern mystery readers.

One is tempted to speculate that when Faust wrote this novel, in the spring of 1933, he was influenced by Dashiell Hammett's *The Glass Key,* published two years earlier. Both treat the basic theme of a strong and ultimately shattered friendship between a big-city political boss and his hanger-on. Like Hammett's Ned Beaumont, Faust's Charles Pursivant is a product of the underworld, whose loyalty to his corrupt mentor is deep and unquestioning, a loyalty which leads both characters into a world of pain and personal revelation. And while Faust's treatment of this theme is far different than that of Hammett, both novels share this fascinating conceptual base.

Did Faust read Hammett? We'll never know.

First printed as a Max Brand serial titled "The Dark Peril," in six 1933 issues of *Detective Fiction Weekly,* the story surfaced in the form of a hardcover book from Macaulay in 1936 as *The Night Flower,* under a new pen name invented by the publisher: "Walter C. Butler." (Macaulay published one other Faust crime novel under the Butler name; then it was dropped.) Unlike hardcover Brand Westerns, which automatically appear in softcover reprint editions (148 of his Westerns have been paperbacked), *The Night Flower* was never reprinted in softcover. It has remained out of print for a full half-century, yet it has not "dated." Along with such gifted contemporaries as Cain, Hammett and Chandler, Faust was a storyteller whose best work transcends a given period; it is timeless, an adventure for the ages. Aside from a rather charming aura of period romance, this book is as swift, hard-edged and suspenseful as any crime novel written in the 1980s.

The Night Flower is deftly characterized and always surprising. The plot relentlessly propels the reader forward as it twists and turns like a roller coaster, providing a breathless and exciting ride from first page to last. As a mystery novel, this one is a sheer delight.

Beyond its elements of action and adventure, the book's poetic images resonate in the mind. This is certainly not out of character for Fred Faust, since a classical poet wore the pulp-fiction mask of Max Brand. From his earliest years, Faust was a lifelong disciple of Homer and Dante. His epic verse (dating back to his high school days in Modesto, California) celebrated ancient Greek gods and noble Arthurian knights. Myth and legend colored all of his prose fiction.

The Night Flower artfully reflects these poetic roots. In its pages we encounter haunting word pictures that only a dedicated poet could achieve:

> "They ran on easily towards the city [of New York] while the glow of the town spread wider and wider before them and burned upwards into the rain."

> "The wise old Greeks had worked glorious statues in ivory and gold, and the girl was in silver and gold – red gold for the hair and the paler gold of the sun on her face and throat."

> "The night was struggling to be fair and whole continents of stars appeared...but clouds would close in...and the squalls of rain kept moving about like tall ghosts between earth and heaven. There were dark ghosts toward the moon, but away from it they had a sheen and their trailing skirts raised a glimmering dust over the water. The landscape, too, was tarnished whenever a shadow fell, but big patterns of trees and shrubs and grass were always in high relief, polished by...moonshine."

This novel was written in a period of transition. Faust was at a creative turning point with his fiction, moving out of the pulps into the higher-paying, more demanding slick paper markets, such as *Collier's* and the *Saturday Evening Post*.*

Eventually, in 1938, Faust would enter Hollywood, beginning the Kildare years at MGM. An Italian battlefield in World War II would claim his life in May of 1944, ending a career which produced thirty million words of commercial fiction. A total equal to 500 books. Duc to the sheer mass of his work, it has taken critics many years to access Faust's place in the field of popular fiction. But the verdict has finally come in:

> "No man ever lived who could invent so many plots...or so crowd a few thousand words with action. Max Brand's best work may well become a permanent part of [our] folklore."
>
> Quentin Reynolds

> "Brand was a genius, a major event in the pulps...His stories exist at a singularly pure level, free of time's limits, in a world more open, more dangerous, more intense than our familiar present."
>
> Robert Sampson

> "Among that notable cluster of American writers born in the decade between 1890 and 1900, which included...Fitzgerald, Faulkner, Wilder, Hemingway, Benet, and Wolfe—Faust can reasonably be called the unknown giant. In various guises, he filled the empty spaces among his illustrious contemporaries

*Faust had originally aimed *The Night Flower* at the *Post*, then edited by Thomas Costain, who reluctantly rejected it with the comment that it contained "a lot of fine writing." Later, Faust would place several of his best stories with the *Post*.

and in a way embraced them all. He was serious and popular, highbrow and lowbrow, American and cosmopolitan. None of them performed on a more gigantic scale and...none reached a larger audience. Faust was to the writing of his era what Babe Ruth and Red Grange were to sports, Charles Lindbergh to flying, Henry Ford to industry: the expression of an expansive time, when horizons seemed larger and possibilities less limited."

Robert Easton

Here, then, back in print at last, is one of Max Brand's finest novels, creating a vivid atmospheric portrait of New York in the early 1930s, of three-horse drays, gas lamps in seedy apartment buildings, thugs in long dustcoats, cradling Thompson machine guns inside swift black limousines with curtained windows – of buried treasure, of car chases through rain-black night streets, and shootouts in castled forts above storming seas.

Here is a high-risk saga of adventure, of life beyond the edge, of characters boldly seeking what Faust called "the bright face of danger" in a novel that truly deserves the overused descriptive label of "a lost classic."

Here is Max Brand at his best.

William Nolan
Agoura Hills, Calif.
1987

William F. Nolan has edited three volumes of *Max Brand's Best Western Stories* (Dodd, Mead), and wrote the recently published *Max Brand: Western Giant* (Bowling Green Popular Press). Two of his novels, *Space for Hire* and *Look Out for Space,* are available in Crime Classic editions.

PROLOGUE

AT ten in the morning, the armored truck backed up to the pavement in front of the Weaver Trust Building. At that time, the first twelve stories along the street were rubbed over with shadow. There were people in upper windows who had to lean out in order to look down through the dimness, as through water, at the picture of the removal. The Weaver Trust had prospered to such a degree that it was going to seek more spacious quarters, where it could have Doric pillars across its face and envelope itself in that religious atmosphere which seems so near to the heart of the American banker.

Into this truck, porters carried bundle after bundle of ledgers and papers of various sorts. They carried, finally, two sacks which were neither very large nor very heavy. But one contained almost a million in currency and the other contained well over a million in negotiable securities.

That was why the president of the Weaver Trust came out on the sidewalk and maintained an anxious frown until the stuff was shut behind the heavy steel doors of the truck. There was a guard inside the truck. He had a good fighting face that was a comfort to the banker; also, he had a pair of automatic rifles and loop-holes through which he could command all directions except the driver's seat. On that seat were two more men with fighting faces; the banker approved of them thoroughly; he knew their first names and their last names and their records. One was a mastiff, bulky and grim; the other was a hungry-faced little terrier with a blood-stain in his eyes.

But most of all the banker was pleased by the truck itself. It was not over large, but it was painted at battleship grey and he knew it was sufficiently armored to turn steel-jacketed machine-gun bullets as though they were brittle hailstones. So, when he had seen the door of the truck closed, he turned and sauntered through the revolving door into his bank, holding his head high and a bit tilted so as to bring out the strong lines of his chin. It was the attitude which he always assumed when he faced the cameraman of a newspaper.

Now that the truck was closed and the sidewalk cleared, the hungry-faced little man at the wheel touched the self-starter. It whined small and high; then the motor caught hold with a subdued purring but the truck had not yet started when a closed car slid around the next corner and stopped right in front of the truck.

A big fellow, a great, wide, ponderous bulk of a man made still more huge by the long dust coat he wore, stepped out of the machine and turned a little as though he was only casually interested in the curses of the truck driver. After that, he stepped to the side of the big car, pulled a bantamweight machine-gun from under his coat, and put a burst of four bullets through the body of the man at the wheel. The second burst fairly smashed the center out of the fighting face of the other fellow on the driver's seat.

In the meantime, out of the closed car had stepped another figure, likewise in a long dustcoat, a tall and somewhat leaning gentleman, with head and shoulders inclined at the angle which long study produces. At the side of the truck he paused and said: "Mustard gas, Tony. Just hop out of there and it will be all right."

He drew himself up on the front step of the truck and rested his hand on the shoulder of one of the dead men, as he spoke.

Tony cried out rapid words that sounded like the barking of a dog. The rear door of the truck opened. Tony hit the pavement running and kept on sprinting until he dissolved in the crowd that was piling up half a block away.

The fellow of the studious head and shoulders, stepped in through the open doors and dragged out the two sacks. He carried them towards the closed car, while his companion discouraged an attack from the bank by shattering the glass of its revolving front door with a third small burst of fire.

There were two hundred people looking on before the closed car moved away in leisurely fashion, skimmed past the shrinking crowds at the next corner, slowed for the turn, sounded its horn carefully, and then continued without haste down the cross-street.

CHAPTER I

THE repeated sound of the telephone pressed a finger against the brain of Pursivant harder and harder and his consciousness began to run forward in him through glimmering doorways and corridors of shadow. The glitter of real daylight entered his eyes. He puckered them and saw Gregory, his man, at the foot of his bed. The sunken cheeks and temples of his valet gave him more the look of death than ever. The beard and moustache barely parted over the drop of the grey lips but most of the weariness was in the eyes and the long, triangular shadows under them. One could have guessed that something had happened to him and that afterwards nothing mattered. Only Pursivant knew that Gregory was younger and in other ways different from what he seemed.

"Good morning, sir," said Gregory. "Mr. Richard Franklin is telephoning."

He came around to the head of the bed and held the pillows while Pursivant pushed his shoulders and head up against them, then reached for the telephone.

"Well?" he said into it.

"Good morning, Mr. Pursivant," said the sharp, clear voice of Sammy McGuire. "The chief wants to speak to you."

Pursivant looked into the blankness of his mind and the darkness of the opposite wall until his eyes found his ivory statue of the old Chinese mounted archer. The rounded top of the soldier's target seemed more than ever to complete the top of the circle that was started by the round of the horse's belly; so Pursivant looked suddenly askance through the

French doors, over the little balcony at the towers of the lower city that rushed up into the sky and seemed to be still growing as he watched. They were pale in the morning dazzle. If one could step away to a sufficient mental distance, they would be no more than they seemed to the eye—just a picture to be framed in the grasp of a hand, to be picked up between thumb and forefinger. That's what artists can do. That's where they have the edge. They can spread out life on the flat of the hand. But artists are such long-haired bastards.

Over the telephone he heard the deep voice of Richard Franklin. He felt the vibration of it all through his body, to his heart.

"Bill, come on over."

"I'm sunk," said Pursivant. "I'm not stepping out this morning."

"I need you. Come fast," said Franklin, and hung up.

"Damn it, I won't go," said Pursivant. "That's the trouble with friends."

"Yes," said Gregory. He had put a tray of toast and coffee on the table beside the telephone. He was stirring the coffee that he had poured into a cup so that it would cool more rapidly. "Yes, they make you a slave."

"What friend ever made a slave of you?" asked Pursivant, almost angrily. "Put the coffee down. Go out and leave me alone. Ring up Franklin and tell him that I've gone back to sleep."

"Yes, sir," said Gregory. He held out the cup of coffee. He was smiling a little as he offered it.

"Makes you feel smug, eh?" said Pursivant. "You've been up for an hour. It gives you a height and you can look down on me. Start that shower, then."

He took the coffee, sipped it, felt the acrid heat of it work down his throat. He lighted a cigarette. The fumes of it reached his brain at once, like the distillation of a fine poison. His heart gave a ragged flutter; there was a stirring of revulsion through him; but now he knew that the day had commenced. Already he could hear, behind the closed door of the bathroom, the cool rushing noise of the shower. He slipped a leg out of bed, swallowed half the cup of coffee, and sat up, looking down at the ugliness of his foot and the shoemarks on it.

He stood up. From this higher level he could look into the back yard at the yellow-green fire of sunlight that burned in the tree. A long, black slant of shadow cut across the flame. That was the way life was, the golden fire and the black pressed together like two hands.

He went into the bathroom and walked up to his enlarging image in the big mirror. Nothing about the picture pleased him. The big line that came down from his nose past his mouth was deeper than ever; his skin was more swarthy, his brow more darkly gathered. There were too many things that a painter likes to get hold of. He was only thirty-five but he was full of what a painter calls "character." Other men named it "life" but he felt that most of it was simply the booze. If a fellow could get into happiness, right into it, there would be no need of booze. He looked down at the slight sag of his belly. With the tips of his fingers he pushed the loose outer flesh into a pouch. He glanced back into the mirror and saw his elbows sticking out, sharp and thin. But his shoulders were still a comfort.

He stepped under the shower, scrubbed. Franklin wanted him. Nothing matters in this world except a man's friend. He got out of the shower. Bathrooms are too damned white; tiles are too slippery underfoot.

Gregory helped to dry him, working with a big, rough towel and a slow, heavy touch. He washed his face, rubbed on some French paste that takes the place of lather and pulled and puffed and distorted his face while he shaved.

He drank another cup of coffee, munched toast in great mouthfuls as he stepped into a grey flannel suit and a pair of black low shoes, specially made for him of the thinnest and softest calf. He had been a sprinter, once, and he kept on giving his foot comfort a good deal of thought.

Before he left the house, at the front door he turned to Gregory and said: "I'm sorry, Gregory."

The old eyes of Gregory looked straight into his, bright and soft with understanding.

"Certainly, sir," said he. "Every day has to have a morning."

He pulled open the door and Pursivant went down the steps in front of the old brown-stone house to the closed car that was waiting. Vasco, cap in hand, held the door. To have a chauffeur was a good deal of swagger. So was having one of these old houses with its back yard and trees, and all that; but to Pursivant such things meant more comfort than swagger.

A tall, thin, blond man stepped quickly up while Pursivant was leaning to get into his car. The fellow took off his hat and showed hair so thin that the pink of the scalp showed through.

"Beg your pardon, Mr. Pursivant," he said, "will you listen to me for one minute?"

"No," said Pursivant.

"You can give me my life as easily as you can give away a cigarette," said the other. "Will you listen for one minute?"

"No," said Pursivant, and got into the car.

His machine started at once, rolling him softly past the stranger who stood with open eyes. They were like the eyes of a statue; they held the blank of a terrible future. Pursivant gritted his teeth before he tapped on the glass behind the driver's seat and then motioned over his shoulder. They stopped and backed up, Pursivant opening the door to say: "Get in here, will you?"

The blond fellow slid in like a snake. He sat in the corner with his knees and feet pressed together, his fingers turning his felt hat into a rag. "Go on. And make it quick," commanded Pursivant. But desperate hope was shaking the other like fear; he could only mouth, soundlessly. Pursivant pulled a small flask out of a side pocket of the car and passed it across. He looked before him at the square shoulders of his chauffeur and down the long glimmer of the street as he said: "Take a drink of this. Then start with your name and try to get ahead." There was no kindness in his voice. It was dry and hard and everything was in it except the disgust which he was fighting down.

"My name is Tom Holden," said the other, gasping over the sting of the brandy. "I've been up the river. I did five years. I got out. I was going straight. I hit a hard bit and went wrong again. I got another chance to go right and I took it. But the dicks are after me. They're going to get me. They're going to shove me up the river. Mr. Pursivant, what I mean is—for God's sake! You can say one word to Mr. Franklin. What I mean is—"

His voice shook to pieces. "Take another drink," ordered Pursivant, still keeping his eyes straight ahead. He was full of a loathing that was like hate, because there was fear in him. These years and years he had been out of the criminal world but still the shadow reached for him now and then. Generally he could shake it away; it seldom had the eyes of this poor devil.

"If I should help you," said Pursivant, "you'd spread the news around, and a crowd of sneaking thugs would come with their hands out."

"I'd never tell," said Holden. "I swear to the dear God! I'll kiss the Bible and—"

"Stop it!" said Pursivant. The voice shut off, but there was still the sound of the frightened breathing, and that was even worse. "Are you broke?"

"I've got some money. I'm all right. I'll get along. I'm not begging for money," said Holden.

"Here's a hundred for you," said Pursivant. "Better get out of town. You won't be followed, if that's what you want to know. You'll have your second chance—I suppose it's really your hundredth chance. Goodbye."

The man got one shuddering hand against his breast. The other hand he held out in farewell. Pursivant wanted to take it, but a great disgust prevented him. "Goodbye, sir," Holden was saying, "and God be good to you. I'm going to be a new man and—"

"Ah, quit it—and get out!" said Pursivant, as a savage impulse came bursting up in his throat beyond his command.

Holden dropped his extended hand and slid out backwards onto the pavement. Pursivant, as the car started again, would not turn his head, but out of the corner of his eye he saw the shadow standing there, hat in hand, and he wanted wings of magic that would put both time and distance between him and this memory.

The morning was very fresh. Gasoline fumes had not yet begun to choke the air like blue dust. The tires of the big car made a rapid, crackling sound something like dry grass when it burns. The streets were polished black with wetness, here and there. Sometimes the sun rippled its fire over a thousand windows. Sometimes they ran through tunnels of twilight that pointed at some distant brightness. So they came to the Wheeler Building. Without bending the head far back, one could see no higher than the ankles of it, so to speak. The entrance doors kept drawing people in and whirling them out again in scatterings.

Pursivant went over to the tower elevator—Franklin's tower—and the wise mug of the elevator man stretched in a smile.

Other people were hurrying towards the elevator but the door was closed in their faces. Pursivant was started up at half speed, leaning on his walking stick. The elevator man faced him, still grinning.

"Anything for Saturday, sir?" he asked.

Pursivant touched the glass and iron grill of the door with his eyes.

"Try 'Fetch and Carry' and in the third," he said.

"Thanks," said the other. "Is it pretty hot?"

"Nothing is very hot," said Pursivant.

"That's right, too. Nothing is very hot. It's the hot stuff that gives you the sock in the eye."

The elevator picked up speed until the feet of Pursivant pressed more heavily against the floor. It came to a soft, air-cushioned stop. The door clicked open.

"Thank you very much, Mr. Pursivant," the man was saying.

"You'll probably drop your whole wad on *Fetch and Carry,*" said Pursivant, stepping out into the entrance hall of the tower suite. The elevator dropped down from behind the closing door with a whine and a moan.

A girl came towards him, stiff with official dignity, brittle to the smiling point with consciousness that she had a pretty face. As she came, he felt her glance on the sour swarthiness of his features, then dropping 'till it ran down the glimmering of his stick.

"Yes?" she said, briskly.

He gave her his card. "I want to see Mr. Franklin," he told her.

She opened her eyes at the card, flushing, unable to lift her glance all the way to his face. "Excuse me, Mr. Pursivant," she said. "I didn't know—"

She went off in haste, while Pursivant looked over the furnishings of the room and did not know whether to approve or to sneer. There was a big green tapestry on one wall, a forest scene with a strange-looking hunting dog in a corner of it. It looked like money that was out of place in an office building; it looked like such a lot of money that one could not laugh at it. That was the way with Franklin.

Pursivant went to the first window. He glanced down at the buildings that leaned away from his eye at various angles, and on to the harbor where boats seemed to be standing still, with their wakes streaming out behind them. White puffs of steam rose silently from their whistle-pipes. Franklin sat up here above the city at the height of a hawk waiting on, and he had eyes that could mark his prey in the confusion of the crowds of little people beneath him. Franklin *was* a hawk. But in our country, what are you going to say? You can't throw all the grafters out the window. You can't throw the Richard Franklins out.

The girl came back for him. She was able to look in his eyes, now, and keep on smiling as she opened the doors for him. Pretty girls ease the way through life. You always half want them; enough to make you feel a bit foolish.

"Here is Mr. Pursivant," said the girl, from the threshold.

Harry Lefton—once Leffwitz—was just leaving from a conference with Franklin. His face was the white of the underside of a stone, or rather, the under side of Broadway. The fire was in his eyes and the dirt was in his smile.

"Hello, Bill," said Franklin. "You know Harry Lefton."

"Do I?" asked Pursivant, without moving a hand to answer the gesture of Lefton.

Lefton pulled back a step and bowed over his hat: "My Lord Pursivant," he said, "has filled up his eye with polo ponies, lately, and so he can't remember old friends." Lefton went out on the heels of that.

Pursivant said: "Hello, Dick!" and went over to a window as though for the view but really because anger was in his teeth and disgust in his throat when he saw the great stony brow and the soft jowls of Richard Franklin. Behind his big desk, with his lips pressed together and his eyes fixed on a stern future, he looked as though he were posing for a political photograph.

"That was a bad play you just made," said Franklin. "You know Lefton is a fellow with a lot of power in both hands."

"Particularly the hand that's behind his back," answered Pursivant. "I never wanted to know his kind and now I don't have to. Rat-catching isn't in my line."

Pursivant leaned on a steel window frame and kept on looking at the city because he wanted to postpone seeing that face again. It was full of the Italian sallowness, this morning. He kept thinking of the real name, Riccardo Francolini. What right have the damn Dagoes to come over to our country and hit the high spots? But in this case there was the other side of the occasion to be considered. There was nothing in his life that matched his affection for Riccardo Francolini; there was no affection which was so solidly based on reason, for it was Richard Franklin who had given him the chance to close the door in the face of his old life and enter a new career. Rum-running and various other activities of his early years had seemed rather adventures than crimes, at the moment, but just when he found that the sea he had embarked on was a danger and a vice that should be abandoned, he discovered that he needed help to get back to the honest shore. Richard Franklin had given him the chance he wanted.

He was thinking of this and waiting for Franklin to speak again, when he realized that his friend was so deeply offended that the silence might be prolonged. It was the moment to make some ingratiating or light remark, but Pursivant did not need to use a social diplomacy with Franklin because the friendship between them was of pure steel, without flaw. There was only one fact that could snap the chains, and that fact was buried in a past which Franklin, surely, could never know. Instead of bridging over the difficult moment, Pursivant continued to look out the window as he said: "There's a poor devil called Tom Holden. He's been up the river. The police are going to give him another ride. Tell them to let Holden alone. He'll leave town; pull the hounds off his tracks, Dick."

After a moment Franklin cleared his throat and answered: "Very well." Then he added: "Why do you do it, Bill? Kick people in the face like that, I mean."

"Like Lefton? Well, think it over. He makes his money out of women. The highest thing he does is to put on bedroom plays. I'm through with him and I'm through with all the rest of it. All the dirt, I mean."

"A man can't cut himself adrift from his past," answered Franklin. "Turn around here."

Pursivant turned, bracing himself against the grasp and the burden of that big, luminous eye. But the weight of it told on him at once.

"Sit down and talk about yourself," said Franklin.

"I'm glad you've changed the subject," replied Pursivant.

"I haven't changed it. I'm going back to it," nodded Franklin. "But tell me what you've been doing. More polo, eh? Wait a minute."

He picked a scrap of paper out of a drawer. "You were out on Long Island riding with the pack of—"

"Why do you keep notes on me, Dick?" asked Pursivant.

"Because you are out of my ken a lot of the time," said Franklin, finally folding the paper and putting it back in the drawer. "I don't even know half the schemes you're promoting. I have to look in the newspaper to find out that you're in Florida, fishing, or hunting in Virginia or Long Island or somewhere else, or at a race meet, or spending a week-end with a steel magnate who's also entertaining my lord What-not. You're away from me most of the time. We're pulling apart."

Pursivant went to him and put a hand on his shoulder. "Old Dick!" he said, and Franklin looked up at him with a sudden smile, saying: "I know nothing matters between us, but you're getting damned upstage with a lot of people who are useful to me."

"Because I'm not the man you are," replied Pursivant. "I'm small time. You use all sorts of people from thugs to gentlemen, to make your picture, and it's a good picture before you finish. You run this town with graft, but you keep it pretty decent and you give the people a better government than they can remember. But I can't use so many colors. When I was a hunting cat, I was that and nothing else. You showed me that I was being a fool. You made me face about. Don't hold it against me if I've kept on going in the new way, until I'm outside the underworld, Dick. It has no hold on me any more. That poor devil Holden—it made me sick to talk to him, because I could feel the reek of the old life come out of him—guns and crooks and night-work and the whole dirty business. I'm through with it forever. It's hell."

"You'll never go back to it?"

"Never!"

"You're wrong," remarked the boss. "You're going back to that hell because I'm asking you to."

CHAPTER II

PURSIVANT merely sat down and crossed his legs. Now and then he tapped ashes from his cigarette. One thing he knew was that he was not going back to the world of mugs and yeggs, but he waited curiously to see how Franklin would work on him.

The big Italian got out of his chair, pulled off his coat, started walking up and down. He drew up his belt a notch so that it pressed still deeper into the fat of his stomach. The cuffs of his shirt fell far down on his hands. The hands looked a little unclean; that was the Italian stain.

"I'm going bust," he said. "I had too much in the Weaver Trust Company. The boys that robbed the armored truck during the removal, yesterday, were robbing me."

"Is it straight that they got two million?" asked Pursivant.

"And a half," said Franklin.

"How much was yours?"

"I'm not rich. But what they got of mine was my blood."

"Sell some of your stuff. Look at this flock of green tapestries."

Franklin made a quick turn in his pacing. "Are you going to stay outside?" he asked.

"Talk a little," said Pursivant. "Who did the job? Inside stuff?"

"I've got a theory. Cappen and Merrill did the job."

"Arthur Cappen is out of the game. Merrill quit when Cappen got cold feet, years ago."

"Cappen and Merrill did the job," said Franklin.

"All right," said Pursivant. "Grab the pair, then. That's easy."

"Merrill is on the sea, bound for Europe. I tipped the police. They went through Merrill with a fine comb when he pretended he wasn't looking, but there's not a penny of the stuff on him. That means that he and Cappen have hidden the money, somewhere. They've been lying low for years, planning one last big stroke. They've made the stroke. They've got their stuff. They've put it away. They'll let it rest and ripen till things have cooled down a little. Then, in a year or so, they'll open up the cache and be fat the rest of their lives."

"All you have to do is to find where they made the cache."

"I'm not a fool," said Franklin. "We've tried Merrill. There's nothing on him. There's probably something on Cappen, though. The police haven't brains enough to get at him. That's where you come in, Bill. You're going to get at Cappen."

"What's on him?"

"In that armored truck, there was a lot of stuff out of safe deposit boxes. One of those boxes was mine. It had some rubies in it. Cappen began his work in Burma; and jewels have always been his specialty. That stuff of mine is not big but it's the perfect color. No matter what happened to the rest of the loot, Cappen has one or two of those rubies in a vest pocket. They're only a couple of carats at the biggest, but that's enough for a man to look into. Listen to me—Cappen spent five years at a jeweller's. He went straight for five years because he loved to handle the stuff. He has one of my rubies in his vest pocket right now."

"You're excited," answered Pursivant. "Besides, if you jail Cappen, if you send him up for a long term, Merrill will simply come back and get the whole cache."

"The fear of that is what will make Cappen squeal. He'll turn state's evidence, get himself out of the pen, and take a good slice from me. That's all rgiht. He can have the slice but I need the rest of the meat that belongs to me."

"You've got the whole police force to work for you," remarked Pursivant. "Set them on the job."

"Cappen knows the whole police force—the whole brains of it. That's why you're going to try the job for me."

"You're crazy, Dick. Cappen isn't carrying around any of your stuff. He's not such a fool. Besides, the trail might go clear to hell and back."

"You're the only man I could ask to go that far."

"You're not asking me. You know that if I take another dip into the shady stuff some of it will stick to my hands. If I follow Cappen, I'll cross twenty trails. If I hunt them to-day, they'll hunt me to-morrow."

"You're Charles William Pursivant, the celebrated young promoter with the racing stable. Nobody has anything on you."

"If they haven't anything on me, they'll put something on me. Dick, if I tackle this job, they'll get me as sure as hell. They'll find out that I was once outside the law. They'll tie me down with that or with something else."

Franklin put his hands on his hips, looked at space, and began to nod.

"Maybe you're right," he said. "I didn't think of it all the way. When a man's afraid, he puts his teeth in his first idea and keeps on swallowing till it chokes him. Here—have a shot of this with me."

He took out a brandy flask and a pair of glasses and filled them.

"Here's to two of us that's all of us," said Franklin.

Pursivant nodded. He kept looking at the soft jowls and

the thick neck into which the necktie was squeezed a good bit. He felt the eyes of Franklin right on his own but he lowered his own glance into the tawny brightness of the brandy he was drinking. The oil of age smoothed over the fire of the cognac. When he put down the glass and watched the film of liquid ebb down towards the bottom, he was breathing the fragrance of France.

"I'm going out to your place, pretty soon, and do some riding," said Franklin. "There may be some man left under the fat. Goodbye, Bill. I've got to start the wheels of the machine rolling, again."

Pursivant went to the door. When he opened it, he heard a bell buzz softly in the distance. It reminded him of the fear of the ante-room and of all the other fears that he had ever known—the first day of school, the first jump at a fence, and the facing of angry men.

The girl from the waiting room came towards him.

"Go back again," said Pursivant. "He doesn't need you yet."

He closed the door, turning slowly back into the room.

"What's the matter?" asked Franklin. "Forget something?"

"Almost," said Pursivant. "I almost forgot quite a lot. Give me another shot of that stuff."

"You were right," said Franklin, scowling. "Get out of here before you change your mind like a fool."

Pursivant filled one glass and took it. "Now go on," he said. "Where do I find Cappen?"

He was able to look up, at last, and right into Franklin's eyes. He was glad that he had come back.

"You damned pirate, it's all right," said Pursivant.

"It's not all right," said Franklin. "You stood by Alberto in the big pinch and now it's my turn to—"

"Quit it!" snapped Pursviant. "I can't stand that. Quit it, will you? And talk sense!"

But he kept on seeing the yellow run of the Rio Grande, the huddled Chinamen in the boat, the beautiful, reckless face of Alberto Francolini in the stern sheets.

"Well, you're asking for it, and now you can take it," said Franklin. "But you're a fool, Bill. If you step outside the law again, you're right—maybe you'll never be able to get back inside the frame again. But—if you want to know—Cappen is going to Christopher Verney's house. There's a party at Verney's, to-night. You know Verney? He has some horses."

"He has some real horses. Only the fellows with the piles of coin have anything real. They have the real horses. They have green tapestries that are real. Well—give me a gun, will you?"

Franklin pulled open a drawer and laid a big flat-sided automatic on the desk. "Don't you go heeled any more?" he asked.

"Starting right now, I'll go heeled the rest of my life," said Pursivant, his fingers wandering over the gun as though he were seeing it by touch. He pulled back the flap of his coat and fitted the automatic away. "So long," he said, without looking at Franklin. He received no answer, and walking across the office without another glance behind him, he opened the door and let it jerk back against its air-brake and went straight on into the waiting-room.

Half a dozen men were there. He knew most of them because they were important; but the girl ran away from the cluster to ring the elevator bell for him. She glanced up at Pursivant with frightened eyes. Some of the group came around him. They asked him if the Old Man had been giving him a bad time. They wanted to know how he was betting that afternoon. The opening of the elevator door gave him his chance to get away, and then he fell in one long, heart-taking drop to the street level.

He sent Vasco home and walked after him because he wanted to stretch his leg muscles. If he sat still in the car he would start in cursing himself for the way he had left Franklin. It would have been better if he had hit Riccardo Francolini in the face.

He walked so hard that he could feel the tobacco taste rising out of his lungs. As he turned up the steps of his house he said to himself: "He's only a damned Dago, anyway, damn him!"

He was reaching for his keys when Gregory pulled the door open and stood aside. It startled him and angered him just a little, as though he had been inside Gregory's mind ever since he left, and that was why his man had been so ready to hand the door for him when he returned.

He went up the stairs. The door clicked gently, shutting away the rushing street noises that sounded like hurrying waters; behind him, Gregory was coming up, also.

If Gregory followed him into the upstairs library, he would give the damned, impertinent rascal a piece of his mind.

He went into the library and threw his hat and stick on a couch. Gregory came rustling in after him to put a bowl of flowers in the sun, to lean and straighten a rug.

"What do you want?" demanded Pursivant.

"Nothing, sir," said Gregory.

"Get out, then."

"Yes, sir," said Gregory. But he stood at the door, running his hand hastily over his pointed grey beard, looking like a frightened minister of state in the presence of his king.

"What's the matter with you?" asked Pursivant.

"As you came up the stairs, it only occurred to me—" said Gregory, making a slight gesture, "that it might be put in a less apparent place, if—if—"

Pursivant threw the gun on the couch.

"All right," he said. "Fix a sling that will hang it under the pit of my arm."

Gregory took a small, silver tray, put the gun on it, and went out of the room holding the tray in both hands, seeming to stoop over it a bit, with reverence. But that wasn't reverence, Pursivant knew. Perhaps it was fear. Perhaps it was grief.

He telephoned to Christopher Verney, looking the while at the sun on the flowers and on the big bronze Chinese bowl. The bowl threw back the sunlight; the yellow flowers drank it up.

"I want to come out this evening and look at the Irish hunters you bought the other day," he said to Verney. "I'll be out some time before sunset; that's all I know. Is it all right?"

"I want you to see 'em, Charlie," said Verney. "There's a seventeen hand gelding with his bones all wrapped up in silk velvet. Wait a minute. I'm having a party and the party needs Charles William Pursivant. You come out and stay for it."

"No," said Pursivant. "I'm tired. I want to see horses, not people."

"You spend the night here and rest. A whisk of country air will do you good. Don't argue. It's finished."

But Pursivant knew it had only begun.

CHAPTER III

LATE that afternoon, Pursivant took the car out through the city traffic towards the country with Vasco sitting by preference in the rear of the machine; from that point he could better endure the perils which his master was sure to brush with one fender or the other. And the more Pursivant considered the snaky ease with which Vasco always picked his way through the traffic tangles, the more he had to twist and jerk and jump the machine. Now and then he could see, on the edges of his field of vision, the frantic gestures of Vasco to the sides or soaring overhead.

Through the turmoil of his mind he was able to see the events of the moment only as figures in a mist, while doors to the past kept opening, and showing him clear pictures. There was that death-scene of Alberto Francolini, on the bank of the Rio Grande, which recurred to him more than anything else. The main claim upon the affection of Richard Franklin, in the beginning, had been that he had been Alberto's friend, and had remained with him to the death. And that was true, in a sense, though the facts were that as he lay bleeding, wounded by the attack of that madman of an Alberto, it was a bullet out of Pursivant's revolver that had killed Franklin's brother.

Yet the friendship was based on more than a lie. He had done much for Richard Franklin but never so much as Franklin had done for him on that day when the plainclothes men were hemming him in at the race-track. Franklin had simply said to him: "They want you for the Willett diamond theft.

You may have done worse things, but you're not a sneak-thief. I'm going to send these fellows about their business."

And from that moment the police vanished out of the life of Pursivant. It was years ago, but the cold dread of that day at the race meet was still a thing that puckered the back of his throat. And as they sat in the stands and watched the next race, Franklin had talked to him, quietly, gently. For Alberto's friend, he said, he would always do his utmost; but a crooked life was sure to lead to a crooked end. Facts were more moving than words; Pursivant from that day was a changed man, because he had had the gun held at his head.

The car passed the rim of the city as though issuing from a noisy room into the outer quiet. The road looped through hills and Pursivant kept the car shuddering with speed at every corner until they slid over a hilltop into view of the Verney place. It was a big, rounded promontory that sloped out into the sunlight between the shadows of two valleys that joined in a long furrow pointing towards the sea. The end of that furrow was filled with the horizon sheen, mostly, and a small wedge of heavy blue at the bottom. This was riding country, and Pursivant looked away over it with an eye of loving judgment before he glanced back at the red roofs of the Verney estate, the main house pushing back the sea of woodland and the cottages making little islands which were sometimes all awash with the green of climbing vines. The bronze on the gates was glittering; the whole place was gilded with money; the whole lives of fellows like Verney are overlaid with gold. He was all right, but he had to hold up his fortune for the world to look at; he had to build his house on a hill where it *must* shine. He had to have his meadows fitted smooth as lawns over the round of the promontory, like a short-cropped wig on a very bald head. Well, money can buy horses but it takes brains to breed them, brains and a few acres of blue grass and a jockey sitting on a ragged fence. That was the way Pursivant bred and raised Logician, which would have made him famous if the stallion had not died in the middle of his three-year-old form. But Verney had to do things in style before an audience. Even his woods were scarlet maples, now unfolding in crimson and purple like clouds that are stained by a sunset. But Verney was all right and he kept on trying to get the full taste of life. That was why it was not surprising to meet at his table a fellow like Cappen with a known prison record and present-day fame as a gambler. Jockeys drank with judges across Christopher Verney's board.

Pursivant turned down the drive with the gravel crinkling softly under the tires. The bright mist of the maples swept over his head; he saw a silver birch here and there, like a thin ghost in the midst of the glory. And ten minutes later he was in riding clothes, walking beside Verney towards the stables. Verney's fat, pale face was twitching with excitement. "I'm going to show you something more than horses!" he said.

"That's what Irishmen say about their hunters," remarked Pursivant.

"I'm not talking about horses. I'm talking about the party to-night. You know Cappen. You know what he is. But I'm going to show you something that he's done for the world. A lot of people here to-night but you'll only be able to see one. Someone that you've never met. Cappen did it, too. That's why I've got him here. He's down there in the little cottage. You're going to stay, Charlie? I *want* you to stay."

"Unless I get a call. I might have to make a quick start."

"That's the trouble with you fellows," complained Verney. "You're always rushing. Life needs leisure. Wine, horses, women, you've got to spend time on 'em. Otherwise, you can't get the full taste."

Pursivant, listening to the pouring of the words and the crassness of them, said nothing. From behind the stable he could hear the bumping of hoofs on the soft, deeply worked earth of the schooling ground; he could hear the squeaking of saddle leather. So they walked around and he saw a skinny ape of a stable boy upon a heavyweight hunter. Verney called, and the boy brought the horse over to them. There was no fidget in the big brown gelding. He simply stretched his head once against the reins and then regarded the two men with wise, fearless eyes.

"That's the one I told you about. Tumble off, Jerry. Lengthen those stirrups for Mr. Pursivant."

The lad whipped out of the saddle. He gave Pursivant one shining look as he laid hands on the knot of the cinch-strap.

"I saw Logician once, sir," said he. "The Domino strain. They can say what they want, but the best ones are long and low!"

Pursivant got up on the horse, fitted his feet in the stirrups, his knees against the vast pads of muscle behind the shoulders. His legs had a foolish spread to encompass that mighty barrel, but the long rein and the shoulder slope promised him a gallop. He was right. The gelding had cat's feet under him and the lift of a swallow in the air. He jumped so big that every time he cleared an obstacle, Pursivant had a look at the horizon and the bright hills running towards it. His mouth was all silk, too; a child's hand could steady him and let him out at the height of his jump.

Pursivant, for one joyful moment, forgot Cappen and the rubies which had been haunting him like savage red eyes. He forgot Richard Franklin and pulled up the brown horse with a smile that did the heart of Verney a great deal of good.

"This fellow ought to have his legs stretched, Verney," said he. "Hop on another horse and go over the hill with me."

They went over the hill, and the next beyond it, until the clean taste of the sea air had blown the city dust out of the brain of Pursivant. He pulled up to look for a moment at the clear outline of Duck Island, and the long, finger-shaped peninsula that stepped out into the point of it.

Then he was willing to ride back with Verney, and say pleasant things about the horse all the way to the stables.

"What's more," said Verney, "you're going to hunt him. I know the pace you like, and all that; but one of these days you're going to forget thoroughbreds and hellfire and try the cushions of this cross-country bus."

There was a trip through the stables, after that, and a good deal of fingering of cannons and stroking of silken shoulders.

"Now what do you say to the lot of 'em?" asked Verney, anxiously, as they walked out into the wide red stain of the sunset.

"All I say is: Damn you, Christopher!" said Pursivant.

Verney laughed, his mouth opening small and the fat shaking under his chin. "Well, you ought to know," he said. "If anybody knows you ought to. But you're going to see something better than horses, tonight. Don't say anything. Don't ask any questions. You're going to see something better than horses!"

Rubies would be better to see than horses, that night, thought Pursivant as he dressed for dinner. He kept telling himself that Cappen would never be fool enough to carry about with him any part of the loot, and yet he continued to see the lean fingers of Cappen fumbling at something small in the pocket of his vest. The main thing was that in important matters Franklin was never wrong.

When his tie was knotted and his dinner jacket on, he stepped out onto the balcony that ran across one side of his room. It was built over the roof of the big southern portico and every room on that side of the house enjoyed a private section walled away from the others by a hedge of potted shrubs. Besides, all the guests were apt to be dressing and there was little danger that he could be spied upon; nevertheless he softened his footfall on the tiles. From the stone railing he saw that it would be an easy drop to the lawn beneath and right away among the trees a triangle of three lights shone like a signal from the cottage where Cappen was staying. He stared at them so fixedly that he could see the paths of the lights over the moist lawn, like ghostly star-trails over water. He had one corner of the terrace so that he could easily look into the east where the hills were rolling up against bright stippling of the sky. The lighthouse, that flashed and darkened beyond the hills, seemed to be beyond the stars, also.

Automobiles were arriving one after another. As they took the bendings of the entrance drive, their headlamps shone far among the tree trunks and waved away from them again. He listened to the stoppings of the cars. Clear voices were continually sounding through the open, dying, being reborn again very faintly inside the house. After a while he went downstairs, conscious of the weight that pulled from beneath the pit of his left arm. It was not that he expected to need a weapon until later on but it was better to have the gun with him than to leave it to be found in his room. After all, when Cappen knew that he was there, that room might receive a pretty thorough rummaging. When it came to putting two and two together, Arthur Cappen was a lightning calculator.

In the rooms below, he found the sort of a crowd he had

expected, a good many pretty girls, a few middle aged women, and all the men chosen because they were interesting rather than important. In such surroundings he felt that his own stature grew; but for the work he had on hand this evening, he would have preferred a mask over his lean face. He went idling from group to group. Time ran on slowly; people began to look away from their conversations for cocktails. Then Christopher Verney came rapidly on him with his eyes pinched into slits. He shouldered Pursivant to the side, breathing: "Hell's to pay. That Stan Wiley—that bounder, that drunken puppy—he's taken the girl away. He was going to give her a spin around through the hills till twilight. They're not back. She has to change. Everything's held up. There's her aunt over in the corner turning to stone. My brain's turning to ice."

"What girl is it?" asked Pursivant.

"*The* girl. The one the party's all about. Come over here and talk to her aunt. Keep her happy. What am I to do?"

He dragged Pursivant up to a woman of fifty something. The years had dried her and tanned her and loosened her eyelids, but she wore no make-up to attract unnecessary attention to her face and the rest of her seemed sound and strong.

"Mrs. Leigh, this is Pursivant. He'll talk to you. You know—Charles William Pursivant. Wiley hasn't brought her back, yet. I don't know what to do," said Verney. He hunched up his narrow shoulders as he poured out his soul.

"Mr. Pursivant will know what to do," she said.

"Serve the cocktails and get hold of yourself," said Pursivant. "Are you afraid that they've run away?"

He saw the head of Mrs. Leigh go back a bit but she kept her expression steady enough.

"*They* haven't run away," answered Verney. "But Wiley—

he's a young fool. Something came over me when I saw him drive off with her but then it was too late."

"Look here," said Pursivant. "This is the Twentieth Century."

"He doesn't know," complained Verney to Mrs. Leigh. "He's never seen her. He doesn't know anything about her. I'm going crazy. I'll lose my wits in another five minutes. I've got to go out and wait for her. Pursivant, be a good fellow and come along. The rest of 'em can sop up cocktails in the meanwhile."

He grabbed Pursivant's arm. Mrs. Leigh was looking straight at Pursivant and he said: "It's going to be all right. Verney's having a panic but I know Stan Wiley."

"I've got to tell Cappen, too," said Verney. "He'll go out of his wits too, when he hears. If only she'd show up! I'm going to tell Wiley what I think of him. Oh, the rotten bounder! Hurry, Charlie!"

He gave orders for the cocktails as he scurried out of the house and across the lawn. Pursivant could feel the dampness of the grass above the tops of his shoes.

"Suppose that Wiley's gone out of his wits? Suppose he's lost control of himself? Suppose he's gone batty?" groaned Verney.

"Oh, Stan Wiley's no dope fiend," said Pursivant. "Why are you heading for Cappen's cottage? Is he still down there?"

"That's where Wiley will bring her—if he ever comes back! That's where she's staying with her aunt. And Cappen's her guardian."

"Cappen? Guardian?" said Pursivant.

"You know Cappen's past but you don't know what he's done for the girl. Worships her. She worships him. A beautiful relationship, Charlie. One good thing in a rotten life.

When you see her and think of Cappen, you'll pity her. But you'll pity Cappen, too. Educated her and everything. And one day she's got to know—"

He ran out of breath as they came to the entrance of the cottage. They were pushing the door open when a pair of headlights swung over towards them from the main driveway and a car rushed down on them behind a great cone of brilliance that narrowed suddenly, flashed past, and the automobile skidded to a stop. Stan Wiley got out from behind the wheel and came around to help the girl down. There was not much light, but Pursivant recognized the great shoulders and head of Wiley and he could see that the girl had some sort of a mannish cap over red or golden hair.

Pursivant reached for Verney's shoulder but his fingers slipped off the fat of it as Verney charged into action.

"I want an accounting for this, Wiley," he said. "I'm not going to stand it! We've been waiting—"

"I'll talk to you in a minute," said Wiley in a voice that was a great deal too quiet.

He went on towards the open door, walking himself and the girl into the wedge of light that came out from it. Wiley's bulk got in the way so that Pursivant had only a glimpse of the girl's face; but a touch is as good as a handhold when the electric charge is great enough. Then he heard her voice speaking slowly, and he knew that she always spoke slowly. If a man were blind, the voice would be enough; one sound of it.

She was saying: "Goodnight, Mr. Wiley."

Wiley pulled his hat off the wild tangle of his hair which always looked as though he had just come through a football melée. He was as rough and fierce as a mustang but Pursivant saw him take the girl's hand and bend over it and kiss it. That act of bending allowed Pursivant to see the girl clearly enough, and he could believe that Wiley was kissing her hand.

As Wiley straightened, she looked down at her hand and then gradually up at the big fellow. "I'm sorry," she said. "Goodnight."

"*You* are sorry?" said Wiley. "Goodbye, Miss Leigh."

She turned her troubled face to Verney. She was sorry to be late, she said. She would rush into her dinner clothes. They had—lost the way! Then she went quickly through the door, across the hall, and ran up the stairs into the freshening light. She had on a loose tweed coat, but that could not hide her.

The sense of something important seemed to have penetrated Verney in spite of his fat and his excitement; he had been quiet after his first outburst, but now he exploded again. He wanted an explanation. He would have an explanation at once. The girl had said that they had lost their way. She was only trying to cover up some abominable thing that Stan Wiley had done and Verney intended to find out what it was.

Pursivant looked into the face of Wiley, all newly worked with pain. Then he put a hand on Verney's arm and said: "You've done enough and talked too much, Chris. Leave Wiley alone."

But Wiley answered slowly, getting his voice past his teeth in pauses.

"No, because Verney is right. People might think things—about her. I kept her out late because I lost my wits. I've been asking her to marry me. Is that enough for you, Chris?"

He got into his automobile and drove away. Verney, all the wind and storm of anger gone, observed naively: "I don't think he's going to come to dinner. Poor old Stan! Listen to me—he never met her before this evening. He gets her into his car; there's a look in his eye at the time; then he doesn't come back. My God, but I was worried."

Then he began to laugh, weakly, leaning a hand against the wall while his body shook up and down: "What'll happen when she walks into that crowd and they all get the injection in the center of the brain. They won't feel any pain till they come out of the trance. Wiley—he's going to Darkest Africa to be a missionary or pull out the front teeth of lions, or something like that. Wait here. I've got to get back to the guests and keep the cocktails going. You bring her along when she's ready. Thank God for the man of chilled steel. *You* won't lose the way."

CHAPTER IV

THE cottage was small. There might be four master bedrooms, Pursivant decided. The girl was moving about in a chamber to the left of the central hall and, of course, her aunt, Helen Leigh, would have the room next to her. That meant Cappen would be in the other half of the place; at least, that was where Pursivant decided to begin his search, later on in the evening.

Then Jacqueline Leigh surprised him by appearing suddenly on the stairs; she had made her change as swiftly as an actress between scenes. He felt that he needed a bit more time to prepare himself for her coming, but there she was, coming swiftly down the steps in a dress of metal stuff with a sheen of half tarnished silver. She wore long sleeves that had a medieval puff above the elbow. She had red slippers; there were hints and long, disappearing lines of red as the dress stirred. The fabric was so thin and heavy that the folds of it flowed about her like water as she walked. There was not a jewel on her hands or at her throat. Jewels would be silly things except perhaps one big emerald like a green sun against the bronze of her. Her hair was knotted low and as Pursivant looked at her coming into the dimmer light of the hall, he found it impossible to imagine her as a child running about with a tousled, bright head; and for the future, time would be afraid to touch her.

She came up to him with a sort of brightening of recognition, but the smile was not on her lips. Small emotions would have but a small reflection in her face; yet suppose that one day her nature opened, what radiance would shine out then! And suddenly he thought of big Stan Wiley rushing out his soul into clumsy speech and the pitying quiet in which she must have heard, not understanding but forgiving him all the time.

Just as she reached him, she winced a little.

"Oh, isn't Mr. Verney here?" she asked.

"He had to get back to his guests. He asked me to bring you along. Across the lawn is the short cut but that would spoil your slippers; we'll follow the path," said Pursivant.

She came out through the door taking some of the light from the hall with her for a step or two; but a vague uneasiness had darkened the mind of Pursivant. For in the moment of pause when she came up to him in the hall and had looked for Verney, something had changed in her; a thing of spirit rather than of features, an obscure movement of the mind. And in that brief interval the thought of Pursivant had gone into the past and found the image of her in another place. He could not name it but there was a surety that the whole scene would come up clearly in his memory before long. He was only confident that it was not an American scene. With that other and very altered image of her he connected a sound of foreign tongues. But perhaps the whole matter was an illusion, the mind is such a deft necromancer.

He was wasting time. Every step took them closer to the big house where he would have to lose her in the sweep of lights and eyes and voices. She was holding up her train in one hand. When he first saw her, he had wanted to say, as one says of a horse: "She stands well." Certainly she walked well, without any high-heeled blundering. He wanted to say something to her but that infernal half-memory kept dinting its shadowy knuckles against his wits.

And she? Well, her face was raised a little and turned a

little as though she had quite sufficient companionship out of the smell of the grass and the garden earth and out of the soft-flowing clouds of the forest, and the stars.

"When men meet you," said Pursivant, "do they often think that they've seen you before?"

"I don't believe they do," said the girl. "But then, I haven't met many men. I'm just out of a convent, you see."

That explained why she was so untouched. In a convent, the days of the year might turn as casually as the pages of a book. That was why there was the freshness of anticipation in her eyes and no dark stain of foreknowledge or doubt.

"You were in the convent a long time?" he asked.

"Ever since I was a little thing. A dozen years," she answered.

He nodded. As for that other seeing of her, of course it was a mere trick of fancy. Besides, if ever he had seen her, even as a child or spindling girl, he would surely have remembered her like the flash of gold in the muddy wash of life. No, he never had laid eyes on her before. Yet in the back of his brain there was the murmuring of foreign speech which accompanied the old picture where his thought of her was set. At least, there must have been some likeness.

"An American convent?" he asked.

"No. In France."

He felt a foolishly great relief. It had been almost as though he suspected her of lying, before. Now the thing was explained. Probably he had seen some file of girls out of a convent in France, a little flock shepherded by the slow-moving nuns, and out of the long line perhaps one face had gleamed at him. French must have been the tongue that was muttering so vaguely in his recollection.

They were at the house before he had a chance to talk of any other thing.

He took her into the room where cocktails were still going about and watched the light receive her and observed the silence that ran over the crowd with a little hushing sound. He saw this from a distance, detached, as it were. He wondered if any other man in the world would ever walk with Jacqueline Leigh, as he had done, under the stars of a spring night and arrive at such calmness of mind. Even now, as he looked at her, heard the voices rising again, saw the subtle drifting of men towards the girl, a thought occupied him more than her beauty.

Mrs. Egbert Truman, big, blonde, and raw-boned, was saying nearby: "Why, she's a flower! That's what she is! She's a perfect flower, Charlie. Did you come in with her? Where did you find her? Look at the bees swarming, too. A regular flower, and the bees go to find her by night. Listen to me, Charlie. I'm getting poetic. What a rusty, dusty lot she makes all the other girls seem! *Where* did you find her?"

Just after that a quiet voice said: "Have you forgotten me, Pursivant?"

Of course, all evening he had been preparing himself for that voice and for that face. That was why the little shock of surprise with which he turned was all the more natural. There was Cappen, looking his fifty years. The bend of his shoulders and the forward thrust of his head always made Pursivant think of an all-night session at cards. And his small, steady eyes, as usual, were full of intent curiosity and no self-revelation. It was the supreme curse of chance that Franklin had called him in to work against this dangerous man. It seemed to Pursivant that he would more gladly have taken a commission against any other human in the whole world. But what a silly fellow Richard Franklin was to dream that the great Cappen would actually carry stolen rubies about with him in his vest pocket.

"I knew you were here," said Pursivant. "How are you, Cappen?"

Cappen nodded, answering: "Verney told me about Stanley Wiley and Jacqueline. You were there, Pursivant."

"I was there, when Wiley drove up. You don't know Wiley, do you? He's all right, but a little enthusiastic. He lost his head, this evening, but afterwards he went through his hell like a man. It's Wiley that I'm sorry for. No man can be sure of himself when he's around a girl like your ward, Cappen."

The steady eyes of Cappen moved a trifle on the face of Pursivant.

"No, *some* men could be sure of themselves," he said.

It was as though he had watched the two coming over from the cottage and had been able to rummage about in the mind of Pursivant all the way. A queer panic came over Pursivant. He told himself that he must not think of rubies or Cappen would read his thoughts. In spite of that, he began to stare at Cappen's vest pockets.

Afterwards, he knew that he had appeared ill at ease and he damned himself. However, he had to go on with the thing. To-morrow he would have to see Franklin and report. But it would be pleasanter to walk into a cage of tigers than into Cappen's room, this night.

Luckily, he sat next to Mrs. Egbert Truman and she rattled on about her horses all through dinner so that he could consult his thoughts and watch Jacqueline Leigh at leisure. Everybody else was watching her, too, but he wondered if any of the rest noticed what he observed, that she never smiled. Many times she seemed about to; there was always that brightening at the right moment to appreciate a joke or approve of a phrase, but no one could say that she had actually committed herself. When that dinner ended, every man at the table could feel that no one had been more favored than himself and perhaps most of them considered that if they had been her neighbors they could have done much more with her.

"Isn't she glorious?" said Mrs. Egbert Truman. "D'you see that she's perfectly aware of all the eyes that are fixed on her, and yet she's not embarrassed? She's been in a convent all her life and she's equipped with the true innocence. Usually it's either stupidity or self-consciousness. But see how she looks everything right in the face. Look at that horrible Sid Lawrence squinting and grinning but she can't see the evil; she can just see the man! I tell you what, Charlie—this is a great moment—to see a girl like that entering the world, I mean, and to have a look at the jewel before it's flawed. I suppose before even this night is over, she'll have a few glimpses around the corner at the dirty truth. That Stan Wiley already has made a jackass of himself. Now look at Chris Verney, all white and puffed with pleasure. He is a perfect host. See how his eyes dance. He can't waste time looking at the girl, he's so busy watching her effect on the others. Tell me, Charlie—what goes on inside you when you look at Jacqueline Leigh?"

He said, honestly: "I suppose a man could fall in love with her if he closed his eyes and simply listened to her voice. She's almost perfect."

But she seemed able to look behind his words and with a sharp side-glance she resented his coldness as though it were an insult to all femininity.

It was a big party. After dinner there were a couple of tables of bridge in one room; there was dancing in the hall which had been built on such a huge scale that even kings and queens on their thrones would have looked a bit foolish in it; and there was a good deal of strolling on the southern terrace.

Pursivant showed himself everywhere, and each time he joined a group he settled into it as though he intended to spend the rest of the evening there.

Young Perry Newcome, already very tight, got hold of him and wedged him into a corner where a group was chattering.

"I was out in your part of the country, the other day," said Perry. "I saw the old house. I wanted to go up and carve my initials on one of the columns of the portico, it all looked so damn historical, and that sort of thing. And all at once, while I was remembering that the Pursivants came over in sixteen what-not, I says to myself: 'Where was the great Charles William between college and New York? Where was Charles William between college and the end of the next six years, say?' And I made up my mind that I'd ask you, Charlie. And I'm asking you now. What were you doing then?"

Pursivant wanted to hit into the middle of the red, grinning face. He merely said: "I was out learning that two and two makes four. It's worth while learning that, Perry. You've no idea."

"Stop kidding me, and tell me something," said Perry Newcome. "It's only a question. It won't hurt you to tell us, unless you spent the time in jail!" He laughed. They all laughed.

"I was following the ponies," said Pursivant, "and I was a long way behind them."

But when he moved off, he was troubled. That portion of his life which, he sincerely hoped, no biographer would ever discover, was rarely out of his mind during an entire day, and it seemed only the proper fate that he should have it brought so forcibly before him on this evening when, for the sake of

Franklin, he had to go back across the border of the world of crime.

He heard Franklin's name mentioned, too, before long. It was grey-headed Chanley Peters who was saying: "Franklin is logical. That's why he lasts. He takes graft from nothing but the big corporations, and on the other hand, he gives the corporations their money's worth in opportunity. That's why Franklin is doing a good job. But one of these days, mind you, you'll see Franklin as he really is—the young Italian immigrant with the heart of a savage."

Pursivant went by.

"Hush," said someone. "There's Pursivant."

Another murmured, and he was barely audible: "If I knew what ties the pair of them together I'd know a very interesting story."

A very interesting story, indeed!

But now Pursivant spotted Cappen at a card table and knew that it was time for him to make his move. So he drifted out on the southern terrace with the Carriers and young Whitmarsh and managed to slip away from them into the darkness of a patch of shrubbery.

The night was warm. All the glass doors of the dancing room were open. And when he looked back at that brightness he found Jacqueline Leigh at once. She was dancing with a tall young tow-headed fellow whose name he did not know. She danced very well—too well. It seemed as though she could be moved here or there by a touch, and all through the sweep of the crowd her head and shoulders were as smoothly poised as though she were sitting at the dinner table again, listening to the talk.

He went off into the darkness shaking his head a little and he kept saying to himself that she danced too well. There was no sense in such a thought but it was nevertheless with him, until he came in view of the cottage where Cappen and the Leighs were lodged. When he saw its dark forehead with the three eyes gleaming out of it, he forgot all other things. Cappen, back in the main house, could hardly extricate himself from his rubber of contract for a few minutes, and this should give Pursivant a free hand for a little while.

But he did not go straight up to the cottage. It had become a thing of such dangerous importance that he circled around it like a cat around prey before springing. There was a run of hedge down one side. He followed that to the rear of the house, skirted the back of the place from bush to bush, and from the next corner peered towards the front. He had his reward then.

Just to the side of the entrance grew a tree with a big, divided trunk and the glimmer from the lights in front of the cottage was sufficiently strong to set the lower branches shimmering faintly and show Pursivant the vague outline of a man against the tree-trunk. A fellow placed like this could see anyone who approached the cottage and, by circling the trunk, easily keep out of view. It could not be a loiterer. For half a minute Pursivant waited, staring till his eyes hurt. After that, he was as certain as doom that Cappen had placed that watcher by the tree.

CHAPTER V

IF one guard were in front, common fear suggested that there might be another inside the place. If they were Cappen's men, they were armed, they knew how to use their weapons, and they would be restrained by no instincts. The legend was that Cappen never made mistakes in his choice of tools.

So Pursivant hesitated for a moment, convincing himself that it was futile to proceed and all the time aware of the imp of the perverse that commanded him forward. He was more afraid of that coldly irrational force in his heart than he was of dangers inside the cottage; and presently reason and logic had been conquered and he was at the back door of the place.

It was locked. He sighed with relief. Once he had tried the three rear windows, in turn, he could then report to Franklin that the thing had been impossible. So he tried the windows; but the last one gave readily, noiselessly upward under the pressure of his hand. When he leaned over the sill, the blackness moved slowly before his eyes. If there were, in fact, a watcher inside the house, the fellow might be sitting in darkness, might be in this very room appreciating the clear silhouette of Pursivant's head and shoulders against the stars. That would be it. To be killed among the stars. A poet's death. But damn the poets!

He climbed into the room and stood back against the wall. The pressure of it was like the flat of a comforting hand against his shoulderblades.

He pulled out a pocket torch conveniently shaped to the

flat of his hand and with a sensitive shutter to control the light. Then he drew the big automatic from beneath the pit of his arm. He could see himself in a perspective as the ideal figure of the midnight marauder, except that he lacked a mask. Well, the mask he wished for was one of steel.

With a delicate movement of the shutter, he loosed a ray that cut across the legs of several chairs, across the polished face of the dining table they clustered around, and finally made a brilliant eye of light in a mirror against the wall.

He closed the light and waited through a short count for his heart to quiet. After that, he found the door and opened it on the brightness of the main hall.

The thing was impossible. If he were a bird to fly in through an upper window, still the job would be dangerous, but with the only inside passages opening on the hall lights, only a ghost could move safely from the lower to the upper floor. But the perverse instinct would not be quiet in him. It urged as if to throw him from a height. He was dizzy as though he stood on the verge of a cliff. And again he was mastered.

He put away the gun and the light, stepped into the hall, closed the door, and walked with silent steps up the stairs. If he were caught, he would merely say that Miss Leigh had asked for a wrap. That might do, except that his face was sure to be as strained and hard as the grey of cold iron.

The upper hall was carpeted with a grey stuff whose thickness he blessed underfoot. On that side was the room where he had heard the quick steps of the girl moving about as she dressed. On this must be Cappen's chamber. He tried the door. It clicked softly open. Panic leaped on him from the rear and made him enter the darkness almost with a jump.

He closed the door with care. If there were indeed an inside guard, this was the most probable place for him. But there was an atmosphere of quiet and of assured peace that perhaps came from the faintly illumined images of the trees in front of the house; their heads rolled almost to the tops of the two open windows.

He used the ray from his pocket torch to slash the darkness this way and that, suddenly. No gun spat fire in answer. He could ease the grip of his teeth. First, there was the bathroom. He opened the door on the right. His ray of torchlight sparkled on the white of the tub and the tiling. A shaving kit spread on the glass shelf under the mirror assured him that this was Cappen's chamber, indeed. On the ivory handle of a shaving brush an "A.C." was inlaid in gold to give him the actual proof.

All the main fears were now behind him, except one; and this was the danger that Cappen might return at any moment.

That danger kept his nerves rigid and his eyes unsure as he began the search. He even found himself opening the drawers of the bureau and probing among Cappen's shirts and underwear; then through his socks, his neckties, his handkerchiefs.

If Cappen wanted to hide the rubies for the evening, he would choose a place more difficult to guess than the bureau drawers.

He loosed one ray into the dressing mirror above the chest of drawers. That showed him, in a dim glimmer, the whole top of the bureau, a round black leather collar case, a shallow porcelain tray for pins and what-nots into which Cappen had dropped a handful of small change that was too much of a burden for his pocket.

Pursivant opened the collar case. There was nothing inside. He found the fireplace and dropped to his knees and looked along the deep cracks between the bricks.

Two empty vases were on the mantelpiece. He glanced

inside them. On the writing desk in a corner of the room was a glass bowl, filled with red roses. When he saw them, his heart leaped. He took each rose from the bowl and shook it carefully, but no small rubies dropped out from the flowers. Then he thought he saw a sparkle of crimson in the bottom of the bowl, but it proved to be merely a random reflection of the rose-red.

Well, there was a thousand other places to hide things. The bed was a domain of vast possibilities. There were the tall curtains which were drawn back from the window recesses. There were the cushions of the window-seats, the lidded window-seats themselves.

But he kept trying to step back into the mind of Cappen to discover where a fellow of his wits would have been apt to hide the jewels if he had decided not to carry them with him this evening. Of course, the main possibility was that Cappen—if indeed he had the little rubies with him at all—actually kept them for the touch of his fingers in his vest pocket, just as Franklin supposed. But that supposition of Franklin's was, in the first place, no more than a gambler's gesture in the dark.

Pursivant turned up the edge of the big rug all around. The rubies were not there. He picked up a packet of papers on the writing desk and shook it, in vain. Then he returned to the bureau and was startled by the ghostly image of his own face. It looked like murder, even to him.

It was with an idle finger that he stirred the silver coins in the porcelain tray. Two or three of them slipped aside and let a little eye of dull red look out at him. He fastened the ray of the torch on it and the eye flamed with sudden fires. One—two—three of them, hidden safely under the coins. Of course that was the best place for them, and the very place where a servant, no matter how curious, would never peer.

Your chambermaid will rearrange everything except your change. As though her honesty could be damaged by a touch.

He put those rubies, and Arthur Cappen with them, into his own vest pocket; but what he was seeing was the vast, stony forehead of Richard Franklin; and the greatness of his admiration made Pursivant stand like a soldier.

He might have had time to get out, otherwise, but he was still standing there in the memory of Riccardo Francolini when he heard the footfalls coming rapidly down the hall.

He thought of the big, high-standing old bedstead, first, told himself that he was a fool, and then stepped into the second window recess behind the curtain. He should have put the rubies back in the tray under the silver coins; he would have left his hiding place to do that, but the door of the room opened, then, and the lights flared. The strength of them brought through the curtain a vague tracery of the pattern in which they were worked on the farther side. It came even through the lining of thin silk.

Then Cappen's voice spoke, and it spoke about him.

"You saw Pursivant where?"

"Everywhere. In the card room. Dancing. Out on the terrace. Walking in the garden," answered a second man.

"Walking in this direction?"

"No."

"When did you lose sight of him?"

"I don't know. Ten minutes ago. I couldn't shadow him. I had to do something about the serving of the drinks, and when—"

"Don't give me explanations. Everybody in hell has explanations. You lost sight of him ten minutes ago. He may have come to this place in the meantime."

"Johnny hasn't seen a soul."

"I should have had two men to watch the place," said

Cappen. "That's your job from now on through the rest of the night. Take the rear of the house and remember that every whisper in the air and every shadow that moves may be Pursivant."

"Is that bird out for you?"

"There was something in his face, to-night. I don't know what. However, he's hardly had a good chance to get here and—"

There was a slight jingling of coins. Pursivant held his breath with a pain behind his starting eyes. He looked down to his hand and saw the automatic quivering. The curtain had a fringe, but perhaps his feet were showing. He dared not move.

"What's up?" asked Cappen's man.

"Pursivant's been here," said Cappen's unchanged voice. "He has the stuff."

"What stuff?"

"Three small rubies, my son," said Cappen. "They mean life for me—the same as life, at least."

"If he's been here, he's still here," said the other. "He hasn't had time—we'll take a look—"

"If he had been here," said Cappen, quietly, "I would have run into the nose of a bullet when I opened that door. No, Pursivant is not here. And the point to decide is where he may be now."

Even an Arthur Cappen could be wrong. The springs of a chair creaked a little. A match scratched. The thick sweetness of Turkish tobacco reached Pursivant.

"But we've gotta jump, Mr. Cappen! We can't sit here."

"A man can't run as fast as he can think," said Cappen. "And the best way to think is sitting still. What would Pursivant do? Some fellows would rush right out of the house and go to the police. But Pursivant wouldn't do that because he knows that I might be gone before the police arrived. All clever men have an instinctive distrust of the efficiency of gangs like the police. Pursivant has three rubies because he wants to have me. He won't leave Verney's place till he's got me, I take it. Right now, he's probably up at the house on the search for me. If that's the case, we still have a chance. We know what he's found and he doesn't know that we know it. Go back to the house, Jerry. Find Pursivant. Tell him there's a telephone call. Get him away from the rest."

"Roll him, and go through him for the rubies. Is that it?"

"Of course."

"Who does the telephone call come from?"

"From Richard Franklin."

"Are they buddies?"

"You don't know that, eh? Franklin is behind all this. He's the only man who knows Charles William Pursivant well enough to call him 'Bill.' Pursivant wouldn't be at this job—he knows what sort of trouble it may make for him—except that Franklin called him in. Franklin's back is against the wall. And now that you know the story, my lad, suppose that you go to work."

There was a brief pause.

"I go it alone, eh? And he's a tough bird, this Pursivant."

"You go it alone."

"Well, all right," said the fellow at last. "I'm not going to give him a love pat, either. Suppose I hit him too hard?"

"You know your business, Jerry," said Cappen. "And you ought to know me."

"All right," said Jerry. "I'll go through. So long, Mr. Cappen."

"Good luck to you, my lad."

A footfall went off the rug onto the hardness of the tiles. The door shut with a gentle booming sound. Pursivant could hear the clicking of heels on the stairs, a light crunching on the gravel in front of the cottage. The two must have come most secretly because their approach had been inaudible.

He pushed the curtain back and stepped out behind his gun towards Cappen.

CHAPTER VI

IN the legend of Cappen there was a good deal of blood. Men like to remember such things and there was plenty to remember in the story of Cappen outside of all court testimony. That was why Pursivant walked so earnestly behind his gun, prepared for anything, but what happened was beyond his imaginings.

Cappen sat in a deep chair before the next window smoking a cigarette and squinting out at the night and at his thoughts. When he saw Pursivant, he gave him a sideglance, as though this man with a gun were a mere creature of his fancy.

Then he said: "I had to hurry Jerry out of the way so that we could have our talk, Pursivant. Sit down and we'll get to business."

There was something about the calm of Cappen that reminded Pursivant of Jacqueline Leigh. It was a little too perfect, like her dancing. Otherwise, the bluff was beyond criticism.

"The police will have to talk business to you," said Pursivant. "I'm not here for talking. Stand up and come along with me."

"It's no good," said Cappen. "My men are watching the house. You can't get me out of it. But if the rub came, you might do me some harm before you were wiped out. That's why I have to warn you."

"The back of the house isn't watched," said Pursivant. "We'll go that way."

Cappen nodded. He threw the cigarette butt out the window.

Was that a signal?

"Don't do anything like that again," said Pursivant.

"No? Well, certainly not. You're not going to blunder ahead and cut your own throat, though, are you? You're not foolish enough to think that you can hang me with three little rubies that have no history? Of course you cân make serious trouble for me but you couldn't beat me. It would only be trouble for *you,* in the long run. You're too intelligent to make big mistakes, though. That's why I trusted nearly everything to a talk with you."

The wise thing is to stop the ears when the Sirens sing, but such curiosity came over Pursivant as he looked into the steady brightness of those little eyes that he decided to waste a minute or two even at the cost of added dangers. Franklin had been able to persuade him into this business but the wits of Cappen were probably almost as good as the brain of Riccardo Francolini; perhaps Cappen would almost persuade him out of it again.

"You won't waste time," urged Pursivant. "So go ahead for a minute or so. I'm curious enough to listen. Only, don't try the obvious line. All three of these rubies can be identified by good jewelers. Franklin doesn't go in for things that are too obscure. I have the rubies, and that means I have you for the robbery of the armored truck that was robbed in the Weaver Trust removal. It was something more than robbery. Two men were killed and I have you for murder, Cappen."

Cappen joined his long, bony hands together and nodded above the tips of his fingers and all the while his eyes were getting a firmer hold on Pursivant.

He said: "What a word that is, eh? Murder! Something goes jump in my blood when I hear it. I've known murderers, too, but the word itself is what has the black magic. Well, Pursivant, I see you're going to be very open-eyed and cool-minded. Suppose that we talk as though you held every winning trick and only talk about the money in the pot?"

"Sorry to interrupt you for a moment," said Pursivant, "but if you'll stand up and turn your back to me, I'll see where you wear your gun."

"I don't weight myself down with hardware," answered Cappen. "There's no gun on me, but you're welcome to see for yourself."

"No, I'm going to believe you. It gives me quite a kick to believe you about something, Cappen. You were talking about money in the pot. The pot that you and Merrill have? Is that it?"

"Pursivant," said Cappen, "are you a money-maker or are you just a romantic damned fool?"

"Just enlarge that a little."

"Two million and a half can be cut in two parts. Also, it could be cut in three parts. Your slice would be more than eight hundred grand. You need money. You like the things that money gets. You like horses, You even begin to look at pictures. The result is that you're always scrambling for cash. Eight hundred grand will put you where you want to be—for ten years, at least."

Pursivant considered the thing for six booming heart-beats. Then he said: "I'm just a romantic damned fool."

Even then, there was no alteration in Cappen's expression. He gave up the bribery theme instantly and took a new trend.

"Suppose that Merrill were my partner," he said. "Suppose he should hear that I'm in the death house. He'd simply wait for me to take my trip up Salt Creek. Then he'd return and get the loot. Would that be any help to your friend, Franklin?"

"You won't go up Salt Creek," answered Pursivant. "Either you steer me to the cache or I steer you to a police station. That means, you'll steer me to the cache."

Cappen smiled. He said, quietly: "You don't know me, Pursivant. It seems that in the pinch I, also, am a romantic damned fool. Salt Creek can have me before I'll cut Merrill's throat."

"Then we'd better start for the police station."

"Certainly," said Cappen, and rose.

They went down the back way, arm in arm, like old friends. Pursivant unlocked the kitchen door. They passed out quietly to the rear of the cottage, then cut across the lawns towards the big house. Cappen said: "Let's walk slowly, Pursivant. I'm playing the game and making no trouble for you. So let's walk slowly."

Since Pursivant had last looked attentively at the sky, a new constellation was lowering into the west. From the house, the song of the music was a thin whisper but the beat of the drum followed them with an intimate step across the lawn. Cappen walked with his head up, in great leisure. Whatever his crimes, he was something more than a murderer and robber. But pity would have been an almost disrespectful name for the emotion that Pursivant was feeling.

"I daresay that you don't want me to see Miss Leigh?" said Cappen.

"That would be clumsy," admitted Pursivant.

"I don't want her to come to the jail," said Cappen. "I want to tell her that. This is going to be bad business, for her. I want to explain that even if you people hang the Weaver Trust robbery on me, she hasn't been living on that money.

I'm getting old and breaking up, perhaps, but I seem to be thinking more about her than anything else, just now."

"Suppose that I tell her anything you want to say?" suggested Pursivant. "Just now, I want to get you into safe hands. If I make any delay, now, Jerry and some of your other friends may begin to interfere."

"That's perfectly true," said Cappen. "I'm sorry about that. But you're right."

They came to the square parking place near the house. Behind its tall evergreen hedge there was a big array of machines, and Pursivant commandeered the first chauffeur to take them. The destination was enough to make the chauffeur active, when he learned that they wanted to get to the police station in White Forest. So they went out of Verney's place on the rush, the trees looming rapidly beside them and disappearing with soft rushing sounds towards the rear.

"I'm sorry to hurry you along," said Pursivant.

"It's all right," answered Cappen. "I'd like to have more time, but I can't ask for it. This shows that the brain crumbles as we grow older. We take things for granted more easily, as I took it for granted that you were out of the house when Jerry and I were talking together in my room. The main thing now is for me to be sure that you have my messages for Jacqueline and her aunt. I know I can trust you about them, Pursivant."

"Certainly," said Pursivant.

"Tell Mrs. Helen Leigh that I want her to carry right on as before. Tell her that I'll have enough to take care of my defense and to take care of her and Jacqueline. She'll understand and she'll believe, I hope. Tell Jacqueline that I'm thinking of her more than of lawyers. Tell her that I hope no soot that attaches to me will ever be smeared over her good name. Can you remember those things?"

"Yes. Every one of 'em."

"Tell her that I don't want her to visit me. No matter what happens, I'll be happier if I don't feel that I've dragged her into a jail to see me behind the bars."

"I'll remember everything."

They were out on the open road, the car rocking in long undulations of speed as it shot away for White Forest.

"I know I can trust you to do these things," said Cappen. "Now I have to talk of something else which I'm sure will interest you, also. The fact is, Pursivant, I'm already putting my teeth in some things that I remember about you, and I like the taste of them. You're what I detest most in the world—a crook keeping his face straight like an honest man—a rotten, sneaking, hypocritical, lying, pretending rat with a cat's fur pulled over you so that you can stay in the house with the family."

As his soft voice went on, he laid his arm confidingly on the arm of Pursivant, while he continued: "There's just enough of the element of fool in you to make you fail in your new rôle. You're trusting everything about the future to Richard Franklin. But Riccardo Francolini may be the very tool that I'll turn against you, before long. Not only that, but there are knives and guns, Pursivant. Every whisper of the wind, every creaking on your stairs, every step behind you is going to hold a gun at your head. You'll live on bread and milk and suspect the taste of even that sort of a diet. You'll look your old friends twice in the face. I may have bought your servants before you get back to your house. You see, Pursivant, I'm the beast with the hundred heads. Putting one head of me in jail doesn't kill the rest of the body. It simply tells the rest of my power how to find you and where to hurt you. My teeth will be in you from a hundred angles before you're a day older. The electric chair hasn't got me yet. I don't think it ever will have me. But I've got you, Pursivant, and I'm going to drag you down into the slime until it closes over your lips. You're going to snuff the filth up your nose and throttle with it."

Not once had his voice risen. There were small pauses, now and then, as Cappen considered words and phrases, and it seemed plain that he had not spoken in an excess of passion but calmly and logically in prophecy of what he actually expected to accomplish.

"This is kind of you, Cappen," said Pursivant. "Now that I know what to expect, I ought to be able to take care of myself better."

"Do that!" agreed Cappen. "I don't want you to go down at the first touch. I want to draw your blood a thousand times. I want to have you feinted out of position before the final blow falls. I want you to eat fear by day and drink it by night, 'till the marrow is rotten in your bones. That's why I've told you what's coming. You can start waving your hands, but the rats will be eating you before morning, I think."

The big light over the entrance to the police station loomed before them. The tires made a sound like rushing water over the smooth pavements of White Forest; but what filled the mind of Pursivant was that Cappen knew that the real name of Franklin was Francolini. There were not three men in the world who knew that, Pursivant had supposed. And therefore perhaps Cappen knew also about that night years ago when he and Alberto Francolini and Jack Smith had taken the boat load of Chinamen across the Rio Grande. Perhaps Cappen knew or could find out what had happened before the river was crossed. If so, it was the end of Charles William Pursivant. He kept telling himself that Jack Smith had disappeared out of the world and that therefore no one was apt to know, but at the same time the picture of the river crossing kept brightening in his mind like a ghost which he had always known would be fatal.

CHAPTER VII

AT the police station, he put the rubies like three little drops of bright blood on the counter; he saw Cappen disappear towards the cell-room, stepping slowly, looking more like a philosophical student than ever; he heard the desk sergeant shouting over the telephone to police headquarters in the city. Then his deposition was taken.

They treated him with a great deal of respect. And he said: "You can do two important things for me. The first is to keep police and reporters away from the Verney place tonight. The second is to show me a telephone booth."

They promised him both things and ushered him to a booth. Franklin's night man furnished him with three telephone numbers and at the third try the deep resonance of Franklin's voice came booming over the wire.

When he heard it, that insane imp of the perverse which worked in Pursivant made him want to cry out: "Listen to me, Dick. I want to tell you about the way your brother Alberto went under. I want to tell you the true story before you hear any lies—"

He had to click his teeth over the crazy impulse before he could say: "Dick, are you sure that any rubies that Cappen may have swiped out of the truck—are you sure that you can identify them?"

"Every one. And the jewellers can, too. Why?"

"Well, they're in the police station at White Forest. So is Cappen. You'd better get your men on the job and make Cappen safe for democracy."

After a pause, he heard Franklin saying: "This time I thought you'd be beaten. By God, Bill, it begins to dawn on me that you *can't* be beaten. When do I see you?"

"Oh, I don't know. Tomorrow, some time. I don't know."

On the way back to the Verney place he said to the chauffeur: "Who's the owner of the car?"

"Mr. Tom Kimball," said the driver.

"Unless Kimball asks questions," said Pursivant, "don't tell him about the trip to White Forest and that Cappen stayed at the police station. Don't tell the other chauffeurs, either. It's important."

The five dollar tip that he slipped into the driver's hand might help to prove the importance of being silent. Pursivant had to trust to that as he walked around the house and came in across the southern terrace, sauntering. He idled a moment at the open doors of the dance hall and looked back at the night. The trees and the shrubs rolled the blackness towards him. Cappen was behind it. He kept thinking of that. Cappen would be behind everything that threatened gloom from this time forward. The prison would not be able to contain him; the electric current in the death-chair would not end him.

"Mr. Pursivant?" said a voice beside him.

He saw a tall young butler, a blond-headed fellow with happy blue eyes, who was saying: "Mr. Richard Franklin is on the telephone, sir."

He looked at the servant again.

"You're Jerry, aren't you?" he asked.

The eyes pinched a little. So did the lips. That was the only answer.

Pursivant went on: "Cappen and three rubies are in the White Forest jail. If you were found, the blackjack or the sandbag you're carrying would make it black for you along with what I could say. But one at a time is enough for me. You'd better run along and take care of yourself."

"Thank you, sir," said Jerry.

He bowed as a butler should, stiffly from the hips, and then was gone without haste, an athletic and graceful figure that made Pursivant feel old, again.

Verney was the next on the list. He found his host in the dance hall, paler than ever and gleaming with sweat, and got him out on the terrace. Verney took the news in the true melodramatic fashion.

He said: "My God, have you done this to *me?"*

"It was murder, Chris," explained Pursivant, patiently. "Two men were shot when that truck was stuck up."

"Jacqueline Leigh!" groaned Verney. "You can't tell her!"

"I've got to tell her."

"You can't do it. Not yet. Wait an hour, Charles. Please wait an hour. She's made the party. She's so damned beautiful that the women aren't even jealous. They accept her like fate or measles, or something. The men don't pretend to look at anything else. See her now!"

Through the open doors, as the music began, Pursivant could see a big, solidly packed group of men dissolving in one corner of the room, and out of it came Jacqueline Leigh on the arm of Toby Fletcher. Toby was as carefree a young rounder as ever spent fortunes by night, but his insouciance was gone now. He held himself like a young soldier dancing with his empress. The greatness of the occasion stiffened his body and the muscles of his face. He danced slowly, reverently and never speaking, while the girl looked over his shoulder with dreamlike, happy eyes towards the others.

"Does it strike you that she dances too well? You saw Toby stumble then like a jointless booby, and she seemed to stumble with him—seemed to make a new little catchstep out of it? Does it strike you that she dances a little too well, Chris?"

"What the devil do you mean by that?" demanded Verney. "I see that she's perfect. That's what I see. I see that she's going to marry some handsome dumb-bell or some long-haired jackass of an artist. That's the way a girl like that is sure to marry. I'll tell you what, Charlie—I'd buy her! Not her. I wouldn't be fool enough to put a price on her, even. But I'd buy her—just to walk into my garden twice a week and take tea with me. I'd buy her, and I'd pay high as hell. I've got a necklace of big square-faced emeralds upstairs and every time I look at her red hair, I want to go and drop that necklace around her throat. She's so damned nice. She knows everything. She speaks all the languages there are. But she's just a child. And Cappen—she loves Cappen. You can't tell her what's happened!"

"Cappen asked me to, and I'm going to do it now. Will you let me go ahead?"

"Go and be damned, then. You'll wish you *were* damned when you see how you hurt her."

Pursivant got to the girl at the end of the dance, just as she was joining Mrs. Helen Leigh. The crowd that waited began to flow in around her and Toby Fletcher, looking as though he hoped for a kind word, but knew he hadn't earned it, allowed himself to be pushed aside. Pursivant said: "Cappen asked me to give you a message. Will you and Mrs. Leigh come outside and hear it?"

She was frightened, searching his face eagerly. She made him think, suddenly, of a child about to be punished and not knowing what its crime might have been.

"Is it something serious?" she whispered.

Mrs. Helen Leigh was at her side, instantly, saying: "Steady, Jacqueline! Steady, my dear."

"Yes—I know—" answered the girl. And she turned to ask Toby Fletcher to excuse her, because there was important news that she must hear. Toby Fletcher blushed like a silly fool. The eyes of all the men trailed angrily after Pursivant, as though asking him what the devil business he had to intrude himself like this.

He got out on the terrace and then into the garden to a place set apart by a great bower of rhododendrons. There was a small fountain in the center. The jet of it rose half black and half silver from the light that streamed out of the house; and the falling spray rattled softly on the pads of water lilies. The two women faced Pursivant as he halted.

"You may not know," said Pursivant, "that Cappen is suspected of certain irregularities in the past—"

"He's been perfectly frank about his—criminal past," said Mrs. Helen Leigh.

She put an arm around the girl but it seemed a futile gesture because Jacqueline Leigh was much the taller of the two and also Pursivant felt that there was in her the sort of strength that endures and makes no appeals for help. She said nothing but he could see the lustre of her wide eyes.

"Cappen has been taken up on a serious charge and put in jail. He asked me to tell you," said Pursivant.

Mrs. Helen Leigh cried out. The girl was as steady as a rock, and as silent.

Pursivant went on: "He asked me to tell you to carry on, Mrs. Leigh, as before. He wants Jacqueline Leigh to believe that he has not been using stolen money to assist her. He says that he has plenty of funds to defend himself against the present charge and also to take care of you both. He asks Miss Leigh not to visit him in the jail or the prison; he hopes that no soot which attaches to him will ever be smeared on her good name. I think that's about all of his message."

He wanted the girl to speak, because her silence kept loading his heart, but she did not stir or utter a sound.

Mrs. Leigh put both her hands together and struck them slowly against her forehead.

"What's the charge against him?" she asked.

Suddenly Pursivant was proud of the century in which he lived. If the women could be like this, what ought the men to be?

He answered: "The armored truck removing the funds of the Weaver Trust Company, a few days ago, was held up and robbed. Cappen is accused of that."

The girl spoke for the first time. There was no new strain in her voice, but the quality of it was always so full and rich that it seemed to Pursivant adequate for any words that must be uttered. She said: "I think I remember. There were two men killed when the truck was robbed."

"Ah, my God!" came the whispered scream of Mrs. Leigh.

The girl moved slowly, straight towards Pursivant. He found a meaning in that, too, as though she would always face the fire and march right forward. Something loosened and went to pieces inside him—his will power, his inner treasure of ice-cold suspicion and judgment, his self-control. Any or all of these powers were breaking up in him. He wanted to step out and meet her and tell her—

The flood that was rising like a tide in his throat reached his brain, too, with some of its unspoken words, and suddenly he was master of himself again.

She said: "Have they any proof?"

"They have three small rubies that were taken out of the truck and found in his possession. I think I ought to tell you that I found the rubies—and turned Cappen over to the police."

Mrs. Leigh cried out with that same frightful, whispered

scream: "You?" But the girl threw out her arms a little, not in appeal, but as though to hold back her aunt and the useless folly of any words she might speak.

"Are you going to kill him?" she asked. Her voice held right to the end. Only on the last word there was a pause, an accent, and then a break. But it seemed to Pursivant that she could not have said more if she had pleaded for hours, talking about the kindness, the gentleness, the goodness which Cappen had showed to her. Pursivant was willing enough to believe. A fellow who could hate up to the Cappen standard would have to be capable of love and selfless kindness, it seemed.

"Are you going to kill—*him?"*

That was all. But out of the quiet and out of that one break in the voice it seemed to Pursivant that she was saying: "If I can find a way to give my life for his, will you take it?"

"It's out of my hands," said Pursivant, with a strange ache in his throat. Why, he had to think back to his childhood to remember the last time that ache had been his. "It's in the power of the law, now. I don't want to defend myself. I went prying into Cappen's room and found the stuff. I came out here this evening on purpose to find it. But I'm sorry that I've hurt you so much, Miss Leigh. There are ways I can use my influence and if I can do anything for you—except to actually try to get him free—if I can do anything else, well—I don't suppose this sounds very sensible."

Mrs. Leigh suddenly went all to pieces, the way a woman does, with a high-whining sob starting at the top of a scale and running down it. She fell into a stone chair beside the fountain and dropped her head on her hands.

The girl went to her. She stood behind her aunt, and comforted her with the touch of her hands. She would be the burden-bearer. That was perfectly clear.

She was still facing him, but she was looking beyond him, so that he seemed to have been dismissed.

"Shall I take you back to the house?" he asked.

There was no answer except the sobbing of Mrs. Leigh, which she fought vainly against. Pursivant waited a moment; then he went slowly back towards the sound of the music.

CHAPTER VIII

THE newspapers had nearly everything, the next morning. Pursivant had motored in late during the night and he drove like mad, trying to leave behind him, it seemed, the memory of the girl beside the fountain. He was reasonably sure that he would never again be able to look at rhododendrons or lily pads, he would never again be able to see the delicate lifting of fountain spray in the air without a sick sense of defeat and of loss.

What surprised him was that sense of loss. Every man that left the girl after even a few moments seemed to feel the same thing. It was as though she had fitted into the lives of those around her, and then had been withdrawn, and hopelessly. So Pursivant had driven like a drunken boy, swaying and pitching through the traffic while Vasco moaned aloud on the rear seat.

He had not even spoken to Gregory when he came in. He did not speak this morning, but merely nodded and then accepted not the usual morning paper but a whole heap of them. Gregory had not needed to be told. The first look at the first headline had been enough to tell him what to do; and every publication in the city was now sprawled on the bed of Pursivant.

The more he read, the more his heart sank. They had pictures of him, of course. Now and then, pictures of him had been printed before this, but never over a story which was sure to go the rounds of the land. The infernal colored supplements, they would have him, now. He was national property for the making of headlines. And for a week or two they would continue, all of those hawk-eyed reporters, to call him a hero and a Sherlock Holmes, while at the same time they made sardonic remarks about the police. One of our favorite national pastimes is abusing the police and Pursivant had given good ammunition to the happy reporters. But the sight of his picture and his name in the large displays was what set his heart beating so hard that he could count its pulsations in the tinglings of his teeth.

He shoved the papers from the bed. They piled up with loud rattlings on the floor and he looked out the window at the little framed picture of the skyscrapers in the lower city. They gathered towards one summit, in spite of their incongruous styles. It was a grey day. The buildings were the color of the sky and the wind threatened to sweep them away with the rollings of the clouds. He glanced from this picture towards Gregory and it seemed to him that the man was a bearded brother of Cappen. There was the same droop of shoulders and head, the same down dropping of lines from the eyes and mouth.

"Gregory," he said, "you have a sermon on the tip of your tongue. Let's have it."

The deliberate voice of Gregory, husky as though with a great weariness, said: "Hands which touch pitch are soon defiled."

"That's enough," said Pursivant, brutally. "You ought to know!"

"Yes, sir, I ought to know," agreed Gregory.

"What started you on the loose, Gregory, in the old days?" asked Pursivant, all his body and mind relaxed as he considered the history of another man, and banished the memory of the threats of the great Cappen.

"A girl with a pink nose, sir," said Gregory. "She didn't

use face powder very much. And her skin was pink. She was a comfortable sort of a girl. She made me want to do things for her, as if she were a baby. But that was a baby that needed things like emeralds and diamonds done for her, sir."

"D'you know, Gregory," said Pursivant, "that sometimes I wonder why the devil I trust you so completely."

"Because you found me such a straight shot, sir, perhaps," said Gregory, without a smile.

"There's something in that," answered Pursivant. "Do you still go heeled?"

"Certainly, sir," said Gregory. "It's inconvenient but it's a habit."

He took from somewhere beneath his coat a blunt-nosed automatic, turned it in the light, and made the gun disappear again.

Pursivant closed his eyes. He began to remember out of the past the men and women who would be able to recognize in his newspaper picture a man who had been something other than a rising promoter, some ten years ago. Ten years is enough to season a wine or ripen a malice.

His telephone rang downstairs. He could barely make out the soft burring sound of it. But Gregory had left the bedroom and Pursivant listened with evil expectation for the muffled bell beside his bed. Gregory had orders to let no call come through to him, but grim foreknowledge assured Pursivant that the hand of the world would begin reaching for him and catching him, now.

Because he was prepared for it, as for the start of a race, the suppressed little whirring sound beside him was the greater shock. He grabbed the instrument and heard the voice of Franklin booming melodiously: "Come on down, Bill."

"I'll be damned if I come down!" cried Pursivant. "I'm out

of that business. I'm through with it. They've plastered my name and my face all over the country."

"That's a good thing for a rising young promoter," said Richard Franklin. "Hurry down, Bill. Nobody but you can finish the business you've begun."

Pursivant started to dress slowly, as a gloomy protest, but as he began to rehearse the savage words with which he would denounce the whole affair to Franklin, he found himself hastening. He was all rigid with purposefulness as he left the house.

Gregory, standing beside the front door, said: "Haven't you forgotten something, sir?" And he looked at the left shoulder of his master.

"I haven't forgotten it, but I don't want it," said Pursivant. "I'm through with it. I don't want to see it again."

"Exactly, sir," said Gregory. "Only—is that wise?"

It was not wise. He was so often wrong and Gregory was so often right that it was easy to capitulate. So Gregory went upstairs and came down carrying the big automatic and the shoulder harness by which it was slung under the pit of his arm.

"A gun," he told Gregory, as the thing was being arranged in place, "is what anchors a man in the crime world."

"Well, sir," said Gregory, "it's better to have some sort of an anchor in a storm."

"You waste your time," said Pursivant, ironically. "You ought to run a column of domestic advice in a daily paper."

"I'm sorry, sir," said Gregory.

By saying that, he seemed to maintain the upper hand, while Pursivant went out to his car and the sour, yellow face of Vasco. Twenty-four hours before he had gone down the steps in the same way to face some sort of trouble for Franklin. In the meantime he had added to unforgettable life, three little pigeon's-blood rubies, Cappen, young Jerry, the White Forest jail, the battered face of Mrs. Helen Leigh, and the girl.

As if he had known her for years, he could see her in so many attitudes and hear her voice sound so many notes that it was surprising to have to imagine her always in the same dress of silvery metal. But it seemed to him that the dress had been perfect. The wise old Greeks had worked glorious statues in ivory and gold, and the girl was in silver and gold —red gold for the hair and the paler gold of the sun on her face and throat. He remembered that he had suspected her— because she danced too well, because in his unawakened memory a sound of foreign tongues attended his first sight of her. But all things that are very beautiful are sure to go deeply into the mind and to arouse false echoes. However his train of thought picked her up, now, it ended on the picture of Jacqueline Leigh standing behind her aunt, cherishing her with gentle hands and looking steadily beyond Pursivant at the sorrows of this world.

He felt, inevitably, that he would have to see her again. Moreover, he had a strange surety that he need not lift his hand but that fate would bring them together again.

He reached Franklin's office building, rose in the elevator, spoke to the girl in the waiting room, all in this same dreamy darkness of the mind. The voice of his friend brought him suddenly back to the moment with the many bright windows looking in like eyes upon his thoughts. He spent five crowded minutes narrating just what had happened at the Verney place.

When he finished, Franklin said: "You ought to be with me, Bill. We two could break the back of the world. When we lean our shoulders on the same wheel, have we ever failed to roll it up the hills?"

"Are you up to your neck in something hard, again?" asked Pursivant.

"The infernal Times-Record got the whole information about my deal with the Consolidated Gas and Electric. A photograph of the check and all that. I've had to buy them off. I was broke, and it meant borrowing. I've just finished burning the evidence now, but it was a narrow squeak. If I had you with me, Bill, you could handle things like that. You'd throw the fear of God into the crooks. I need you, Bill. I'm not thanking you for what you did about Cappen. I can't thank a man for my blood and my life. But I'm wishing that you were with me all the time!"

"You remember," said Pursivant, "that in the old days you advised me to go straight? It was a good sermon. You see that I've never forgotten it."

"Going straight? Nonsense! I meant that you were a fool to waste your time with strong-arm men and thugs. A man has to do his job, even if it takes him dodging into a dark alley, now and then."

Pursivant said merely: "I'm keeping the gun you gave me yesterday."

"Cappen was only talking," said Franklin. "His teeth are blunt, now. But you ought to be with me, Bill. You ought to have that next office. We need an hour every day to talk things over and plan."

Pursivant was silent. Franklin went on: "You won't come in because you think that graft is a dirty business. But remember that it *is* a business, and that all business is dirty. I think I earn my salt in this city. I keep things going. I give money quick chances for investment and I give the city the benefit of the spending. The proof of the pudding is the eating. The tax rate is lower under my regime than it ever has been before. Bill, you've got to come with me."

Pursivant was silent still for such a long moment that Franklin flushed. "All right," he said. "All right, all right. You were bad enough once to scare you for the rest of your life. What? Running Chinamen across the Rio Grande? Bah! That's not a crime. Chinamen make good citizens. They're honest and they work like devils. Besides, you were a youngster and that was only a lark."

The imp of the perverse parted the lips of Pursivant and made him say: "It wasn't a lark for Alberto."

Franklin sat suddenly back in his chair.

"I'm sorry, Dick," muttered Pursivant.

"I cornered you. You had to say something," answered Franklin.

He jerked open a small top-drawer of his desk and reached into it.

"I've still got the bullet that murdered him, Bill," said he. "And one day I'll get the murderer."

Pursivant stood up and walked over to the window. He could not endure the eyes of Franklin for another moment. When he looked out on the grey city what he saw was the old image of the flowing Rio Grande and the hunched figures of the Chinamen in the boat, and the handsome, reckless face of Bert Francolini.

"Don't be upset," said Franklin. "I know you're sorry that you mentioned Bert. But come back here and let me tell you the next step you've got to take for me."

"I can hear you over here," said Pursivant.

"We've got Cappen in the jail," went on Franklin. "The clues are put together and there's enough of a case to break it either way."

"What do you mean by that?" asked Pursivant.

"Three small rubies," said Franklin, "are not much to hang a man with. But we have some other stuff and in addition there's the criminal record of Cappen. That's what will send him up Salt Creek—that and the way people are feeling, just now, about brigandage in the public streets. Cappen knows what faces him. If he faces a jury, he's facing the electric chair. The sensible thing for him to do is to turn state's evidence. We know that Merrill must have been in on the job, though we haven't a scrap of proof. But if Cappen will talk, we can turn him loose, send Merrill to the chair, and get the loot. We can do all of that if Cappen will talk."

Pursivant remembered the bright, steady, expressionless eyes of Cappen. He thought of Jacqueline Leigh.

"There's more to Cappen than you think," he declared. "He won't talk."

"Not to most people because he's afraid of the double-cross. He's afraid that if he tells us where the money is cached, we'll get it and then let him go to hell. He won't trust most of us, but he'd trust you, I think."

"Trust me?" cried Pursivant.

"Yes, in spite of the way you got at him. People can hate you, Bill. They can want your scalp. But they all know that you're straight. If you give your word, they know you'll go through with your deal. The very fact that you slammed Cappen will make him all the more willing to talk business to you."

"I wonder," muttered Pursivant. "No, no, Dick. I'm through with this game. I told you yesterday that it was the last flurry I'd take for you along these lines. I meant it too. I'm not doing any more."

"Are you afraid of Cappen?"

"Yes. I'm afraid of him."

"You're not afraid of anything but your crazy self," declared Franklin.

"I'm afraid of Cappen," insisted Pursivant.

"Look at it this way," argued Franklin. "We only have skinny proofs against Cappen. All things considered, enough to send him to the chair, and we know that we'll be sending the right man. But what good is that to us, if the Weaver Trust goes smash and the money is never found except in the pockets of Merrill? You can see that."

"Yes, I can see that."

"Go ahead one step further and try to see that you're the only man that might make Cappen talk. He's big time. He knows that you're big time. You two could talk together and get somewhere."

Pursivant looked at the green tapestries on the walls and damned the very trees of them, but he damned them silently.

Franklin said: "Go over and see Cappen now. The sooner the better. I'll be on the telephone and arrange everything, and you'll be able to talk with Cappen as though you were his lawyer. Absolutely in private."

Pursivant put both hands on the head of his stick, and lifted himself with an effort to his feet.

"Are you hating me, Bill?" asked Franklin.

Pursivant shook his head. He felt there was no room in him for hatred. Fear filled him to the lips.

CHAPTER IX

EXCEPT for the bars on the windows, the city prison had a face that was half Greek temple and half office building. Soot of many years had fouled it as the shadows inside begrimed in a few minutes the souls of those who were held there. Under the columns of the gloomy entrance, Pursivant ran into Jacqueline Leigh. She came right up to him, not with a smile but with that brightening of recognition, and gave him her hand.

"He says that you only did what you had to do," she told him.

The shock of finding her there stopped his voice in his throat. It was his own gesture, he felt, that had flung her down there into the bottom of the world. He muttered something about being sorry. Before he had ended her glance was going past him towards the sadness of the future, but there was that slight brightening again, like a child's, as she said goodbye.

He watched her going down the steps. She looked much smaller than in evening clothes. She wore a tweed suit of a rusty brown with a green scarf about her throat, a perfectly commonplace outfit, but as she reached the street and turned, leaning against the wind, it seemed to Pursivant that unless men were blind they ought to be rushing out from every doorway and forming in silent crowds to stare.

Inside the jail, everything was prepared for him, because Franklin had, as he promised, been on the telephone. Even without Franklin's help, he would have been well-received, and grey-headed Lieutenant Michael Kelly looked upon him with a professional eye of approval as he said: "It was a good job. It started good and it finished good. It was good all the way through, Mr. Pursivant. Sure you can see Cappen. I guess you won't hand him any rope ladders or diamond drills!"

There had to be another man present during the interview, but the guard remained in the farthest corner, with his back turned, while Pursivant faced the man in the interview cell. There was no change in Cappen. He looked as though whatever happened to his body, the spirit that showed through his eyes would always be the same.

"Thank you for telling the Leighs everything I asked you to say," said Cappen. "It meant a good deal to me."

"She came anyway?"

The eyes of Cappen closed and with that, the face looked like that of one dead from long weariness. It was the only trace of emotion that Pursivant had ever seen in the gambler. It was the only one that he had ever heard of. But in an instant the eyes opened again and their steadiness banished the body and left only Cappen's mind.

"Of course she came down here, anyway," he said.

"I've come to make a proposal to you," said Pursivant. "Perhaps you'll trust me to do what I promise?"

Cappen looked at him for a quiet moment.

"Yes, you'll do what you promise," he agreed.

"Very well. Turn in Merrill and tell us where the loot is. You'll be covered till Merrill is handled. When he's safe, you'll be free to go where you please."

"Turn in Merrill?"

"You can see how it is, Cappen. They have you for Salt Creek. It's a thin case against you, but it's enough. Sometimes a thin knife cuts deeper than a thick one. It'll cut as far as your life, in this case, and I dare say you know it."

"Certainly," said Cappen, with his usual candor.

"In that case, what do you say?"

"If I tell where the loot is—well, the district attorney's office may forget about the immunity problem, afterwards."

"I'm asking you to take my word."

"And your word is Franklin's?"

"Yes."

Cappen considered facts.

"I've never cut the throat of a bunkie before," he said, at last. "But I suppose that there has to be an exception to prove the rule. I'm going to talk to you, Pursivant."

"I'm surprised," said Pursivant. "I didn't think that you'd do it."

Cappen shrugged his shoulders as he answered: "Well, I have to look at it in a new way. A man with a family has obligations, Pursivant."

He meant Jacqueline Leigh, of course. A poisonous chill of dread and suspicion ran through the heart of Pursivant as he wondered if Cappen might actually be her father; but when he thought of her and looked back into the face of Cappen, that horror was at once removed from his mind. Cappen loved the girl simply because he had befriended her. And as for her—well, she was one to forgive Satan himself because of the first kind gesture.

And Cappen was falling—because he considered himself a man with a family!

"I'll give you my hand on my part of the business," said Pursivant, offering it.

Cappen looked at the hand that had been passed through the small speaking wicket.

He said: "When I touch you, Pursivant, I hope it will be

with a knife. But about the present business—well, I'll put it all in your hands. I'll have to give you a note. Got anything for writing? They seem to consider a pencil a lethal weapon, in this prison."

Pursivant pushed a pencil and a leaf out of a notebook through the wicket and on the inner shelf of it, Cappen scribbled a few characters. He paused in the writing.

"This isn't to be a raid, Pursivant?" he asked, doubtfully. "You go quietly by yourself, get what you're after, and come away again, disturbing no one else who may be around?"

"Certainly not," said Pursivant.

"Well," mused Cappen, "I suppose you'll do as you say. But if you don't—"

For an instant his pale eyes cursed Pursivant with a fiery brightness. Then he shoved the paper and the pencil back.

"Go to a hundred and fifteen Allen Street," he directed. "Ask for Quillan. Mind you, they may try to pass off somebody else on you as Quillan. You'll know him because he's a fat man with a small stomach, and there aren't many of those. He looks greasy. He's about thirty years old. He pulls his chin in when he talks. He's about six feet four, I suppose."

Cappen smiled.

"Quillan is so big that he had to go straight," he remarked. "No crowd could ever hide Quillan! Give him this scribble. He'll doubt you and he may even damn you a little, but after a time he'll let you go up to my room. In the room you'll find a pair of suitcases. They're big and they're both heavy. In them is every convertible penny of the Weaver Trust Company. Wait a minute. Sign this. Initial it."

Pursivant initialled the slip: "C.W.P." and above and beneath Cappen scrawled: "O.K., A.C."

"Quillan will let you in when he sees this," said Cappen.

"What sort of a place is it?" asked Pursivant.

"You'll see when you get there. A good place for some men to keep a bed and a packed suitcase. You'll agree when you see it."

He added: "By the way, do you think I'm doing right?"

"That's your business, not mine," answered Pursivant.

"You, for instance," went on Cappen, those pale, expressionless eyes always working away with curious interest at the face of Pursivant. "You, for instance, would rather go up Salt Creek than double cross a friend, I suppose?"

"What I'd do is my own foolish affair," said Pursivant.

"You, for instance," continued Cappen, gently, "would never let down a fellow like Riccardo Francolini. No, there's a deathless devotion between the pair of you. A beautiful thing, in a way, Pursivant. A great many people talk about it. A great many people know that Charles William Pursivant is a pretty hard fellow, but he's willing to die for Richard Franklin."

"What are you leading towards?" asked Pursivant.

"I don't know," said Cappen, more gently than ever. "I won't know what will be in your mind, either, when Franklin has you jammed in a corner and cuts your throat. In a pinch like that, perhaps you'll stop thinking altogether, and even forget to curse him as you start for hell. Or for heaven, Pursivant. I beg your pardon. I forgot that a fellow like you can always be saved, even at the last moment."

He smiled again, slowly.

"I'll run along," said Pursivant, "if you're through."

"I wouldn't keep you," answered Cappen. "I wouldn't detain you for a single moment. I send my admiration after you, Pursivant, and I give you my heartiest good wishes."

Pursivant got quickly out of the building. The wind was blowing so hard that it walked the cuff of his trousers up his leg. He leaned sideways against the blast as he went over to his car. The force of the air unsteadied him as he looked into the sallow face of Vasco who waited by the open door, with the rug streaming away from his arm.

Down there in the slums, at a hundred and fifteen Allen Street, it might be that the Weaver Trust funds were locked up in a pair of fat suitcases. It might be that he could enter the place with his note from Cappen and come out again carrying the treasure. There was another strong probability that, if he entered the place, he never would come out again; and in that case, after waiting a while, Vasco would certainly go in to find him. Vasco would go like a hunting dog into a den of lions; and there was no point in that.

Pursivant said: "You drive home and wait for me there, Vasco. I won't need the car for a while."

CHAPTER X

ALLEN STREET was not far away. Pursivant leaned his back to the wind and walked slowly on. At the first corner a side-sweep of air staggered and stopped him. He glanced back towards the city prison and saw a patrol wagon pulling up at the entrance, and a brisk young fellow with a leather brief-case coming down the steps.

Pursivant turned the corner. The gust of wind died and let him walk in some comfort though with his right hand uneasily ready to grab his hat. As he came to the next street he heard the voice of the storm increasing. Three girls were making the crossing, their bodies aslant, their skirts ballooning. As Pursivant entered the sweep of the wind, he pulled his hat down and glanced back beside his shoulder. That was how he saw the brisk fellow with the leather brief case swinging cheerfully along half a block behind him.

Pursivant made his course a zig-zag for three blocks, and still the man of the brief case was always there in the rear.

Well, it might be that the shadow was acting under standing orders or it might be that even from the prison Cappen could signal his will instantly to his retainers. Stranger things than that had happened. But in any case, it seemed a little foolish to go on to Allen Street. Already he was near it, and he could see the monstrous back of the Allen Street Bridge lifting above the low brick tenement buildings.

It might be best to throw a cordon of police or plain clothes men around 115 Allen Street, but if that were done, the building would probably be emptied before any search could begin. And more and more Pursivant was convinced that Cappen had told the truth, and that the Weaver Trust funds were waiting yonder in two thick suitcases. He was convinced because of the simplicity of the idea and the daring of it, exactly what one would expect from the brain of Cappen.

He found a taxi rank parked in the middle of the street, got into the first cab and ordered the driver to go straight up Melville Avenue for a dozen blocks, turn over to Post, and come back to 115 Allen Street as fast as he could make it.

The driver looked at him.

"A hundred and fifteen Allen, did you say?" he asked.

"D'you know the place?" said Pursivant, suspiciously.

It would have taken a hammer to alter the expression of the broad, blunt face of the chauffeur.

"I guess I've seen it," he said, and he took Pursivant rapidly over the prescribed course.

Turning down Allen Street, at last, they ran down by the head of the great bridge towards the edge of the river. The boys playing in the street waited till the car was on them, scattered then like leaves away from it. Peanut and fruit stands stretched along the base of the bridge which began to soar over the tops of the apartment houses, carrying the thunder of traffic into the skies. On the opposite side of the street little shops crowded shoulder to shoulder behind unwashed windows.

Pursivant got out at Number 115. It was like its neighbors, some eight or ten stories of old red brick with bedding and rugs leaking down from the open windows and a white flutter of laundry here and there.

Pursivant gave his card and five dollars to the cab driver.

"Yeah. I seen you in the papers," said the fellow. "Right when I laid an eye on you, I knew who it was."

"Go back to the city prison," said Pursivant, "get hold of Lieutenant Michael Kelly, and tell him that I've come to Number 115 Allen Street. Then go on to my own address, there, and ask for Gregory. Tell him, also, where I am. He'll give you a tip that will be worth while. Have you got all that?"

"Yeah, I've got it all," said the chauffeur, and started off with neither thanks nor farewell. Pursivant turned to the entrance of Number 115. From the door a steep flight of stairs went rapidly up into darkness. A gas light burned at the first landing. The red stair carpet was worn to grey in the center of every step.

But the place had one obvious attraction: no one would suspect it of being a hideout for a fellow like Cappen. The ghost of the great criminal went up those stairs before Pursivant with the familiar studious shoulders stooped more than ever under the weight of the two heavy suitcases.

Before entering, Pursivant glanced down the street and saw his cab driver wave to a friend as he took the next corner. That worried Pursivant. For if his driver had acquaintances in this neighborhood, perhaps he even was a resident, and under the control of—

"If I have half a brain in my head," said Pursivant, "I'll back out of this before a door is locked on me."

But his finger, as though of its own volition, was already pressed on the janitor's bell. He could hear the jangle of it in empty space. After a time a man with a cropped grey head came down the hall. He was dressed in overalls and a soiled undershirt. He wheezed with his fat and his fifty years. He had risen from the table, still munching, and about his mouth there was a sheen of grease.

"I'm looking for Quillan," said Pursivant.

The janitor nodded, turned his back, and waddled out of

sight down the hall. Pursivant lingered in the doorway. He ought to go on, quickly. He ought to hurry straight to Lieutenant Michael Kelly and show him Cappen's note.

Then, just across the street, he saw his brisk young man of the leather briefcase buying some fruit at a stand, or pricing it, at least.

Pursivant was glad to see him, for that ought to be enough to blast him out of his rooted place and start him down the street away from trouble. A train rolled thundering down the arch of the bridge above him, filling his mind with confusion, and as the noise diminished he found himself still in the doorway of Number 115 Allen Street. The imp of the perverse had him in its cold grip and he knew that he could not escape.

Down the stairs came the tapping of rapid feet. He saw a young fellow in a very much tailored grey suit running down the steps. He was dapper enough to be in place on a musical comedy stage. He had a big head and a rather small neck that allowed the head to jog back and back as he ran down the stairs. When he reached the bottom, he came right up to Pursivant. He had rather an ugly face that was redeemed by a very pleasant expression. He had a confidential way of leaning his glance on Pursivant as though they were old friends, or ought to be.

"You were asking for me?" he said.

"Are you Quillan?" asked Pursivant.

"Yes," said the dapper fellow, smiling and nodding as he held out his hand. "And you?"

"You don't know me?" asked Pursivant.

"Something tells me that I ought to," said the other, with concern.

"I'm John D. Rockerfeller," said Pursivant.

"Delighted to meet you," said the man in grey, quite eagerly. "How could I have failed to recognize you?"

"I don't know," said Pursivant, shaking the extended hand cordially. "You're Morgan, aren't you? But I've got to see Quillan. Will you tell him that I'd like to see him, at once?"

"I'm afraid that he's out," said the stranger.

Pursivant frowned.

"Find Quillan at once," he said. "Tell him that Cappen sent me, and that I'm down here losing my temper."

The other thoughtfully tapped his fingers against his chin while he looked Pursivant over.

"You're Charles William Pursivant," he announced, finally. "Well, if Cappen sent you anywhere, he must have a pretty good reason. Wait a minute, will you?"

He went up the stairs with a light flurry of his feet. A long strip of his pale hair became unplastered and flopped up and down on the back of his head. In the gloom of the upper hall he disappeared and presently another man came down, walking slowly. He was, as Cappen had described him, a fat man with a small stomach. He was built like a top, his whole body swelling from very small feet to a vastness of shoulders in the middle of which was a head that was another pyramid. It began with very wide jowls, and it ended with a forehead that rapidly narrowed away to nothing. Mr. Quillan was a man who bore himself with dignity. He had gold rimmed spectacles on his flat nose and his lips, which were very long, were compressed as though he were about to deliver a drastic judgment.

Mr. Quillan had been caught in a moment of repose, to judge by the moist tangle of the hair at the back of his head. His shirt was unbuttoned at the throat, and he was in the act of rolling down the sleeve of a blue shirt over a red flannel undershirt. He only finished the unrolling of one sleeve as he reached the bottom of the stairs and confronted Pursivant, but the dignity of Quillan was capable of rising, immense, above all mere details of clothes.

"You're Quillan?" said Pursivant.

"I am Adolph Quillan," said the big man, and closed his lips firmly and disapprovingly over a number of golden teeth. It was plain that in a country where all are born free and equal, Adolph Quillan was one of the freest and the most equal.

"I've come here from Cappen," said Pursivant.

"I never heard of him," answered Adolph Quillan.

The temper of Pursivant was exceedingly short. It was shorter than the temper of an Irish terrier and he looked at the small stomach of Mr. Quillan and wanted to punch him there.

"You never heard of Arthur Cappen?" said Pursivant.

"I never heard of Arthur Cappen," stated Adolph Quillan.

"You wouldn't know his writing, then?" asked Pursivant.

"I'll know when I see it," replied Quillan.

Pursivant gave him the slip of paper. On it was a row of numbers and capital letters with the initials of signature appearing beneath.

Quillan took off the glasses from the flat of his nose and squinted at Pursivant through puckering eyelids.

"You're C.W.P.?" he asked.

"Yes."

"Lemme see you sign," said Quillan.

Pursivant took out a pencil and signed his initials on the flat top of the pillar at the bottom of the balustrade, spreading out the slip of paper carefully. Then he passed it to Quillan who examined the signature without his glasses and then with them. His dignity grew every moment until his big chin was withdrawn to such a degree that it flowed down in easy folds into the huge bulk of his throat.

He made a gesture at the stairs.

"I'll show you the room," said Quillan. "Go ahead."

"After you," answered Pursivant.

Adolph Quillan fixed him with a glance of withering disapproval, turned his back, and went up the stairs with a measured step. With each stride, his thigh muscles filled his trousers tightly.

At the landing of the upper hall, Pursivant could see the well of the hall rising, diminishing through darker shadows illumined by paler flares of light. Below him, the brightness of the day was able to come only a stride or two into the hall, but directions seemed to be reversed, and he had the sense of being underground without sufficient air for breathing. Perhaps that was because the gas fixture that gave light on this landing was leaking a little. The smell was something like stale onions. He had forgotten that gas was still used for illumination.

Down the hall he continued behind the immense shoulders of Quillan. A door opened on his right. In it stood a woman who looked like Quillan's twin sister. She wore a tightly fitted, very tailored street outfit. An incredibly small hat perched on the top of her head. She was chewing gum, her mouth opening and shutting in a generously leisurely champing. And her eyes were rendered blank by the greatness of her content. The act of chewing occupied all her mind except one corner that was capable of showing a dim interest in Pursivant. So she stared blankly at him as he went by, slowly turning her head.

At the end of the hall, Adolph Quillan pushed open the door of a little room that had a narrow brass bedstead in it. On top of the bed lay one large suitcase. On the floor beside the bed stood another, its mate in bulk which the outer straps could hardly press into shape. The sudden surety of success made Pursivant feel something like affection for Adolph Quillan.

"I'll get the keys to them cases," said Quillan, and withdrawing, he closed the door with a decent deliberation and softness behind him.

Pursivant lighted a cigarette and walked back and forth, relaxing with every step. He thought of Franklin, when he should walk into the office and put down the treasure on the office floor.

After this, even if Franklin knew what had really happened to Alberto Francolini those many years ago, he would hardly hate Charles Pursivant.

Quillan was away so long that he had time to notice the details of the bed room which Cappen had used as a hideout, from the worn rubber mat in front of the washstand to the print of the "Angelus" on the wall. There were stains of blue and red ink on the naked little unpainted table. And the room was filled not with furniture but with noise that rushed in through the window from whistles on the river, the traffic thunder on the great bridge, and the coughing and brazen rattling of steam shovels not far away. At the highest pitch of all, like a thing in the mind rather than in fact, was the machine-gunning of riveters on a steel building; and also like a product of thought were the sounds from the streets, far and near.

By the time Pursivant had run this gamut of noise through his attention, he roused suddenly to the knowledge that a good deal of time had gone by him. He stepped to the door and pulled at it, but it was fast locked, and the hardness of his wrench merely made his fingers slip off the greasy brass of the knob.

The blankness of terror forced him to try the door again, shaking it heavily, till he heard a man say quietly, in the hall: "Listen to the poor mug, will you?"

Pursivant turned slowly from the door, and all the sounds that stormed through the open window grew louder and louder as though they were approaching him, shouting: "Charles W. Pursivant! Charles W. Pursivant! Charles W. Pursi*vant!*"

CHAPTER XI

HE leaned out the window. Below him, the wall without a break fell away to the edge of the water. Mold and river slime turned the bricks green for a little distance above. Two docks jutted out. A barge was loading barrels at one. That was the point where the donkey engine was coughing. The arm of the crane made a thin screaming sound every time it swung over the barge. On the other dock, men were piling lumber. They carried long boards over their shoulders to the piles. They walked with measured steps, the ends of the boards swaying regularly up and down. When the load was off, the men kept turning, one after another, and walked away at the same pace to the unseen receiving part of the endless chain. They were so close that he could almost see their facial expressions, and the next time there was a pause in the eerie gunfire of the riveters, he would try to reach the ears of those laborers with his loudest yell.

The glass crackled over his head. Something thumped the wall inside his room, and at the window of a building just beside this apartment house, he saw the shadowy head of a man and the bright gleam of a gun.

He ducked back inside his prison.

The air of it was suddenly hot and close as he stared at the bullet hole in the glass and the other hole that had bitten into the plaster of the wall. The powdered mortar was still running out of the hole and making a tiny heap on the floor.

They had him, safely enough. There was no way in which he could communicate with the outside world. Unless, perhaps, he turned on the water tap in the corner and let the water flood the room. If it would rise to the window height and then trickle down over the outside wall, that might catch the eyes of some of those workers who were crawling back and forth under their burdens.

He turned on the faucet. It gasped, gurgled, spat out a few drops, and then was still.

They had even thought of this; perhaps starvation by thirst was their idea, and a very good idea at that. He suddenly wanted water as he never had dreamed of wanting it before. And yet his vigil was only commencing.

He had to be careful, in crossing to the bed, that he did not come into the line of fire from that window where the gunman was posted. But he got to the bed, and stretched out on it with his head propped up on a pillow so that he could watch the door. He had his gun on the pit of his stomach.

The handling of it gave him another idea, and the imp of the perverse took hold of that idea and magnified it, and made it convincing. They had him and they would wipe him out. Men who possess any dignity and courage are always willing to end their lives when there is no hope left. Logic could tell him that there was no hope.

He pushed the gun to the side, out of his sight, but his eyes were dragged over to it again and again. There would be no pain. That was the great thing about it. It was just a gesture that would beckon the long darkness over him.

Footfalls went down the hall, paused at his door, went on again. Somehow, the passage of them called his thought away from himself into the outer world.

He was a fool to give up hope, of course! For there was the taxi driver who by this time was reporting to Lieutenant Michael Kelly. If Kelly was very deeply in the know, he might attach a good deal of importance to Number 115, Allen

Street. If Kelly knew nothing whatever, he was at least the sort of a fellow to take precautions. It would be very strange if, five minutes after the report, he did not send down a pair of plainclothes men to look the premises over from head to foot. And there they would find Charles Pursivant sitting locked into a small room with the Weaver Trust loot. If the newspapers had praised him this morning, they would have to shout themselves hoarse the next day.

Fear, that had been weakening him like a fever, ran out from his body in one great ebbing. Instead, he felt almost triumphant, but first he wanted to make sure about the contents of the suitcases.

They were strongly locked, but he forced them open, one after the other. What he found inside was not a mass of currency and high class convertible bonds but two complete outfits of clothes from dinner jackets to topcoats and tweeds.

His mouth kept twitching.

He shook out one of the coats and examined it with care. The tailor had obviously allowed for a stoop in the shoulders and the collar was set up high and forward. To make sure, he tried on the coat and certified himself that it was almost undoubtedly the apparel of Arthur Cappen.

If they met again, he thought as he took the coat off, perhaps Cappen would smile.

He put on his own coat, once more. The need of something to do forced him to refit into the cases what he had taken from them. He closed and strapped them as tightly as they had been bound before.

He lay down on the bed again, but the moment he was prostrate weak fear flowed over him. He had to sit up, or begin pacing the floor. That was how time went by him, dragging its feet like those laborers down on the docks. They had the better of it, perhaps. They got their three squares and their beer. After a while they didn't care. But the fellows who try to fly high are always getting themselves ready for a fall. Pursivant had flown high; now he was dropping and when he hit the bottom he would probably be counted in Cappen's bag.

After a time, he was aware that the riveting had stopped. He went close enough to the window to look across the river at the tumbling clouds which were beginning to burn with westering light. The wind had fallen with the day. The laborers had gone home, unless there were a night shift on the docks. It would be dark, before very long. The room was already so dim that he had to strain his eyes to make out the features of the "Angelus."

Then a hand tapped at his door.

"Charles Pursivant?" said a woman's voice.

He swallowed once and again. When he spoke he wanted his voice to be level.

"Charles Pursivant?" said the voice, more loudly.

"Yes?" he answered.

"Are you the real Charles William Pursivant, and everything?"

"I'm the one."

"You poor devil, I'm sorry for you," she said.

"Back out of this," said a man.

"Aw, shut your face, you dirty piker," she answered. "I seen Logician run, once. That's what I seen, and Pursivant leading him back to the stand."

The rap came at the door and her voice again.

"I'm sorry. There ain't anything that I can do, but I'm sorry. I just wanted you to know."

"Thanks," said Pursivant. "It's a help, too."

He tried to see her face by the huskiness and whine of

her voice. He smiled at the earnestness with which he tried to make the image clear.

The voice of another woman cut in. "Pursivant! Pursivant! That you, C. W. Pursivant, Esquire?"

"Aw, quit it, Dolly," said the other woman. "Leave him be, will you?"

"I'm Pursivant," he answered.

"Then I hope you rot. In hellfire is what I hope you rot in. You're the friend of Richard Franklin. He slammed the tenderloin. He smashed my place. He busted me. Oh, damn him and all his friends. I hope you rot in hell, is all I hope. You'll clean up the tenderloin, will you? You dirty grafter, you'll make the city safe for the young, will you? I'll—"

"Shut up, Lou!" commanded her companion. "It's Franklin that did all that stuff. It wasn't Pursivant."

"Get out of here the both of you," snarled a man's voice, "or I'll tell you what I'm gunna do; I'm gunna sock you, the pair of you! Move on!"

They left, their voices wrangling, snarling together.

It was true that Franklin had struck with a heavy hand at every vice that he considered foul and unclean. If some of the ways of Richard Franklin were criminal, it was because he did not know of any other means of pursuing his objects. Those objects were the good of the city. And as for money profit, Franklin would have lived on bread and water, so long as power were in his hands.

After that, the darkness settled. Across the river, he saw lights. The room began to die out. There was the gleaming arc of the wash basin, the faint sheen of the brass knobs at the foot and head of the bed. The chair, the table were obscure skeletons, lost in the darkness like objects drowned in dusky water.

It was time, in fact, for the hall door to fly open so that a machine gun could hose out the room.

It was because he was straining his eyes in this fashion that he saw something swing across the open window. He thought, at first, that it was the dim gesture of a hand, appearing above the windowsill. That was why he stole up to the window and looked cautiously over the edge. Something very light and crackling tapped smartly against his ear. It was a little fold of paper that hung from a thread running up beyond the reach of his eye. He pulled, the thread snapped, and then by the feeble flicker of his cigarette lighter he unfolded the paper and found writing inside.

That penciled scrawl said: "They want to rub you out with gas. I told them gas would make a terrible stink that wouldn't wash. I offered to do the job with a gun because there was a grudge. I'm going to come up and walk right in through your door with a gun and a flashlight. If you got a gat, open right up—but for God's sake shoot careful. I'll put a coupla slugs through the window. You holler some, and then do a flop. If you can smear some blood around your head it may look like the real thing, unless they look close. After you flop, lie still no matter what happens. I'll get the job of passing you into the river, and if you come up alive, maybe it's not my fault.

"You were white to me out to Verney's.

Jerry.

"P.S. There oughta be plenty of blood like you were shot through the bean."

CHAPTER XII

PURSIVANT touched the flame of the lighter to the lower edge of the paper and watched the yellow flame rise while the black carbon curled up beneath it. The last bit that fluttered down from his fingertips consumed to an ash before it reached the floor.

Well, that covered the guilty trail of Jerry. But, in fact, it might be a rather elaborate little device to persuade the prisoner to be harmless while an armed man stepped through the door and blew him into Kingdom Come.

Pursivant, in the end, could merely remember the happy blue eyes of Jerry and trust to luck that all was well. He got out his pocket knife, and with the point of the sharpest blade he cut a small cross through the hair above his ears. A steady trickle ran out. His hair began to be sopping with it. It trickled down his neck on each side and ran onto the shoulders of his coat. But the pain from the small cuts was the amazing thing, to Pursivant.

Then he heard a faint noise of metal against metal at the door and all sense of pain left him. He gripped the automatic, slipped the safety catch, and waited. He saw nothing. That the door was open, he knew by a soft, sighing noise and he had a frantic impulse to charge straight through the hall with his gun and to try his way down the stairs.

A white hand of light struck him in the eyes. He dodged the blow. Fire jetted from a gun in the doorway but the bullet had not found him. He knew with a great surety that Jerry was trying to live up to his part of the contract, and lifting his own automatic high, he pulled on the trigger. It thundered, jerking crazily in his hand. A woman was yelling somewhere down the hall. The light slapped him again. The little snake tongue of fire leaped twice again. Pursivant threw up his arms. His automatic whacked against the ceiling and crashed on the floor as he dropped. Face-down, he banged on the floor beside it. His chin struck heavily, bouncing his head back, throwing a wave of darkness across his brain. He was glad of the shock. It would teach him to lie still. Every muscle in his body had to relax. His eyes must remain a trifle open. Even if a light shone into them, they must not flicker.

And yet, as he lay there, he half expected an outburst of derisive laughter, and a voice telling him to stand up and take it like a man. The light of the electric torch found him, steadied on him. He saw blood on the floor; blood was running down across his eyes, too.

Footfalls came near. A match scratched.

"Leave the gas off," said the voice of Jerry, panting. "What you want? The whole town in to see what's up?"

"Well?" said the voice of Quillan.

"I guess I got him through the bean," said Jerry. "Lemme have a look."

A hand gripped the hair of Pursivant and jerked his head back suddenly. A sound flew up in his throat and he could not be sure that he had stifled it. He knew that his eyes had blinked.

The hand released its clutch. His face banged down against the floor.

"Yeah. Right through the bean," said Jerry. "He won't collect bets no more."

"I gotta say you're full of nerve," remarked Quillan. "Walkin' in on him like that, I mean, with a light and a gun. Turn him over on his back and I'll make sure."

"What you mean make sure? Can't you see for yourself, dummy? It drilled him over the ear, right through from side to side. Here's where it come out."

"Keep outa here, Belle," said Quillan.

The woman's voice that had spoken to Pursivant through the door now entered the room.

"I wanta see," she declared. "I never seen one before, like this. My God, he don't look dead, does he? You wouldn't think a little bit of blood like that, would you? Do something quick with him, Adolph. That racket could be heard a mile."

"That's what you think, Belle," corrected Quillan. "Matter of fact, it couldn't even be heard on the docks, not to notice nothing. Women, they kind of go off half cocked."

"Is that where it went in?" asked Belle.

"That's where," said Jerry.

"I'd like to see his face," said Belle.

"Gimme a hand. We'll flop him over on his back," said Quillan.

"Leave him be," commanded Jerry. "I don't want to see his mug any more."

"God, you had a nerve to walk right in on him like that, Jerry," said Belle. "I just wanta have a peek at his face. I saw him at a race track, once. I saw Logician run, too."

"Here, Jerry," said Quillan, "just because you put a slug through him, you don't own him. Gimme a hand to flop him over."

"There ain't any use, but here goes," said Jerry.

Hands fell on Pursivant and he was roughly turned over. He kept his rioting nerves quiet. He forbade life to enter his muscles. He forced his eyes to remain open a slit.

He saw the high-heeled shoes of a woman and the sleek of silk stockings over her ankles. He saw the green embroidery on the edge of the dress, also. He allowed his fixed eyes to see no more. Already they began to sting as though dust were being blown into them, but the lids must not so much as quiver.

"Look at him!" whispered Belle. "Look at his eyes, Adolph. Like dead fish, ain't they? Look at the way the drool is runnin' out of his mouth. Why would it run like that if he's dead."

"Listen to her," said Quillan, calmly. "You'd think that she knew something, wouldn't you? All right, you put your ear down on his breast and *see* if he's dead or not."

"I wouldn't touch him for a million dollars," declared Belle.

"Go on and be useful," said Quillan.

With a soft rustling, Belle dropped to her knees. A heavy breath of perfume reached Pursivant. He saw a gleam of pale hair, and then her head pressed against his breast.

He waited for her to cry out. Then, as she leaped to her feet, he would swing over on hands and knees. Yonder lay the automatic on the floor. He would get that, and aim for Quillan, first.

Her head lifted.

"Dead as a stone," said Belle. "There ain't a flutter. But look at the drool. Look at the sag of his mouth. God, don't he look awful, Adolph?"

"It's not looks that makes the man," said Adolph, heavily. "You been and left a clue on him, Belle. There's your powder all over his coat. Maybe they'll hang this job on you."

She screamed out a thin noise of protest.

"Get it off him, Jerry. Adolph, help me brush it off."

"Aw, don't be a fool," said Quillan. "The river'll wash it all off, all right. I'll go get the boat. Jerry, you lower him away from the window. Call Steve, Belle. Call Steve, Belle, to help Jerry. When I back the boat up, lower him away, Jerry. Understand? Wrap him up in some of that burlap and put the rope around him, and lower him away. Then come down and get in with me, and we'll slip Charles William Pursivant into the river. Here's Steve, now. Belle, look what you went and done. You got blood on your hands. Go fetch that burlap and the rope."

CHAPTER XIII

STEVE was that dapper youth in the grey suit. As Quillan went out, Steve came in.

"Give Jerry a hand. He just opened the door and walked in and slapped a chunk of lead into C. W. Pursivant," remarked Quillan. "Hurry along and get the stuff for 'em, Belle."

Belle's high heels went tapping out of the room, as Jerry pulled the spread off the bed and dropped it over the whole body of Pursivant, and his head.

The relief of closing his eyes was immense. But greatest relief of all was the chance to breathe half deeply for the first time since he had fallen.

"Charles William Pursivant, all over the papers this morning and in the river to-night," said Steve. "It makes one think, Jerry, eh?"

"Oh, I dunno," said Jerry. "Yeah. Maybe. Give me a cigarette, Steve. Thanks."

The smell of the smoke soaked through the thin cloth that covered the face of Pursivant.

"You take a big shot like this," said Steve, "and think of him going out like a light. That's what makes you think."

"That's what they get when they try to slam Cappen," commented Jerry.

"That's what they get. You'd think they'd be tired of trying. They'd begin to know, you'd think."

He added: "There's Franklin. He'll raise hell when Pursivant doesn't come back."

"He'd better raise the river than raise hell," answered Jerry.

"Here you are, boys," said Belle.

"Get some soap and hot water and a brush and scrub up the floor," directed Steve. "Look—there's blood all over. He did plenty of bleeding after you socked him, Jerry."

"That's what a woman always gets. The dirty work to do," cried Belle.

"Yeah. We get all the fun," said Jerry, dryly.

The heels tapped away out of hearing.

The bed-spread was snatched away from Pursivant, and a great rough layer of burlap thrown over him. The dust from it went up his nose at the first breath. He lay strangling, unable to breathe without sneezing. Hands flopped him over. The breath came out of him with a gasp.

"Hey!" cried Steve. "What's that?"

"Nothing, you poor fool," said Jerry. "There was some air inside his lungs, that was all, and when we bumped him on the floor, the air came out. That's all."

"It sounded like—" began Steve. But he went on: "All right. Gave me a jump for a minute, though. Pass me that end. Funny how warm he is. You can feel the warmth clear through the burlap."

"There's a lot of funny things about stiffs," answered Jerry.

They rolled the loose body of Pursivant in the burlap.

"Noose him around the feet. That's the easiest way," said Steve. "Wait a minute. Is there anybody on the docks?"

His footfall went away and presently returned.

"They're empty. The river's black. And Quillan has the boat right under us, already. This is a cinch."

"Yeah, it's a cinch *now!*" said Jerry.

A rope was thrown in half-hitches and drawn tightly about the ankles of Pursivant. They picked him up. And he kept himself loose as water, his head hanging down. His shoulders were dropped on the straight edge of the windowsill. He was pushed across it. He hung head down while the blood rushed heavily into his temples. He heard the squeak of the rope as he was lowered; a slight oscillation swung him from side to side, pendulously. Worst of all was again a stifling sensation. When he breathed he seemed to be drawing nothing but dust into his lungs.

His head struck sharply on something.

"Here we are," muttered the voice of Quillan. Then powerful hands lowered him and extended him. He smelled the river water, heard the light purring of the motor. The vibration of it came up through his body.

"Charles W. Pursivant in a roll of old burlap," said Quillan, and chuckled.

"All right," he called, after a moment. "Jump, Jerry. Don't turn the boat over."

A weight thumped into the bottom of the boat, which rocked far to the side.

"Sit down before you fall down," said Quillan. "We'll take him out past the Fort and slide him into the river. Cappen's gunna be pleased, when he hears about this. Who the devil is that?"

"Wait a minute! Back in there!" called the voice of Steve.

"That's Harmody with Steve," said Quillan. "That's Les Harmody, I think. Here's where you get a medal pinned on you, Jerry."

The boat moved, then stopped with a sudden jarring.

"Quillan, here's Les Harmody," said Steve. "Something's gone wrong."

"Quillan," said another voice that had a snarl in its huskiness, "is it straight that you bumped off Pursivant?"

"He's got a bullet through his head. Jerry did it for me.

Walked right into the room and threw a slug of lead into Pursivant. As game a job, Harmody, as I ever—"

"You fat-faced son of a Jew-fish!"groaned Harmody. "You got the order to hold him, not to croak him."

"Hold him?" said Quillan, breathlessly. "Hold him? Hold Pursivant? My God, I thought—"

"You got the order. You know how to read, don't you? It was written right down in black and white. *Hold* Pursivant—that's the only way he's worth anything to Cappen. Hold him! If he's dead, it's a blacker case against Cappen. But if he's alive, we can use him to pull out the back teeth of Franklin's influence for the chief. And you've killed him? My God, I always thought you were a fool; I've always known it and I've always said it; but I didn't know that you were a *damned* fool. I know it now. I hope to Christ I see you fed into a sausage machine one of these days. You and the rest of the dog meat. You rotten punk! You killed Charlie Pursivant, did you? Well, go and get yourself the hell out of here. Chuck him in the river; and then come back and face the music."

There was no answer except the whirring of the motor. The boat was under way. Small waves began to slap at the prows, sending shivers back through a frail hull.

"I looked at the paper good and straight," declared Quillan. "I didn't think that they'd ever try to hide out anybody as important as Pursivant. My God, they'll go and kidnap the president, some day."

The coolness of the river air soaked through the burlap and gave life to the breathing of Pursivant.

"They're going to kick me out," said Quillan, mournfully.

"They can't kick you out. You're in too deep to be kicked out," said Jerry.

"Maybe I am. Then they'll *cut* me out. They know how

to do that. Cut me out and cut me down. They know all about that. They know—"

Pursivant heard the sound of the blow that cut short the voice of Quillan, and it sounded almost like a gong struck against a stone. A weight pitched loosely over the legs of Pursivant.

"That's that," said Jerry.

CHAPTER XIV

WHEN Pursivant was free of hand and arm and foot, they were beyond the Fort. The central pile of the city was behind him to the left, heaped up in strokes of light and of darkness, and the river fled past them with streaks and oily whirls on its face. A river boat came at them, crowded with noise and music and brightness. After its passage, their way seemed securely shadowed again.

Jerry was at the wheel of the motorboat; big Quillan had begun to struggle vaguely as Pursivant tied his hands and feet together with the rope.

"Lie still," he commanded, as the voice and the wits of the giant returned. "Lie still and keep your mouth shut."

"Rap him again," suggested Jerry, "and we'll pass him into the river. There's a couple of chunks of pipe, here, to weight him down."

"I can't do it," said Pursivant.

"You can't? I'll do it, then. He wanted to feed *you* to the fish, Mr. Pursivant."

"The fish are going hungry to-night," answered Pursivant.

"Look," argued Jerry, cutting down the speed to half, so that the motor made hardly a sound. "Look, Mr. Pursivant; if this bird gets loose and yaps, I'm done."

"He won't yap. He won't open his head. The last thing he wants is to face the Cappen boys and your friend Les Harmody after I put in an appearance again. How much money is on you, Quillan?"

"It was a frame between the two of you, was it?" murmured Quillan. "But—I *seen* the blood!"

"That's all right," said Pursivant. "Tell me how much money you have on you?"

"A couple of hundred, maybe."

"That's enough to fade you out of the picture. Go far enough to make a new start, Quillan. Turn in here, Jerry, and beach the boat."

Jerry obeyed. With the motor shut off, they glided in and the little craft sank its nose in the mud. Pursivant freed Quillan and stepped ashore with Jerry.

"Your best out," said Pursivant from the shore, "is to stay with the boat, Quillan. That will take you down the shore as far as you want to go. You can cut inland and get a train. Ride the rods and ride them west. That's my advice."

Quillan said nothing. He sat bowed over the wheel.

"Tell me one thing," went on Pursivant. "How did you keep the taxi driver from going to the police?"

"Him?" muttered Quillan. "Why, Peg is one of the boys. He wouldn't turn in Number 115 Allen Street."

The brain of Quillan was stunned. He lifted his blank face towards Pursivant, saying: "It's gunna be funny, what I mean, outside. It's gunna be like being dead. Jesus, things is gunna be empty for Quillan."

The current, taking hold on the lightened boat, began to drift it from the shore.

"So long, Quillan," said Pursivant.

There was no answer. The river took the little boat more rapidly into the night and commenced to turn it in slow circles. It faded from the watching eyes.

"He's takin' it hard," said Jerry. "Well, who wouldn't? Who'd want to leave the old town for jay dives somewhere else? Where you wouldn't know the streets, even. Where you wouldn't know nothing. No wonder that bozo takes it hard."

"He won't endure the pain very long," answered Pursivant. "They'll get him. He'll be in a trance, away from his home town, and one of Cappen's agents will pick him off as a traitor, somewhere. Hard luck for Quillan. I'm almost sorry for him."

"He wasn't such a bad bird," said Jerry. "You know how it is. A fellow does what the chief tells him to do."

"And what about you, Jerry? Don't you want a ticket out of town? You can stop working. As long as I have hard cash, you can have what you need of it."

"Listen," said Jerry. "This is all straight and even between us. Up there at the place in the country—what did you know about me? I was nothing but a yegg ready to bat you over the head. That was all you knew. But you took a look and you said: 'Give the kid a chance.' Otherwise, I'd be up there standing the same rap with Cappen. That would be good, wouldn't it? No, Mr. Pursivant. You let me tail along with you till the wind blows over a little. If you don't mind, I'd like to be close to you for a while. But why not go straight to the police?"

"The moment the police nose into this affair, they find you, Jerry. Do you want to talk to them?"

He turned and led the way up the bank.

Jerry had lost his voice.

They got onto an empty, curving street as Pursivant went on: "You and Quillan pulled away from 115 Allen Street with a chill up the spine, after the way Les Harmody had talked to you. You passed the body of your dead man into the river. Then the pair of you decided that it would be better to cut loose and travel rather than face Harmody. You took the boat down the shore. You disappeared inland."

"What does all that buy?" asked Jerry.

"It buys my life," answered Pursivant. "In a few days, Cappen will be sitting in the electric chair for his last ride. If I were above ground, in the meantime, Cappen's men would find me and do me in. But I'm a dead man, so they won't begin hunting. What all of this buys you doesn't appear at once. But it buys me for you and whatever I have so long as I live."

"Quit it," urged Jerry. "Turn and turn about. That was all this was."

Pursivant laid his hand on the shoulder of Jerry and laughed and his whole soul began to sing.

They turned a corner.

"See if that car has a key in it," said Pursivant, pointing across the street. "If it has, we're going to borrow it for a little ride downtown. There's one man I have to talk to before we fade out of view."

That "borrowed" car was what slid the two of them downtown, Jerry curled up on the floor of the machine and Pursivant wearing Jerry's hat pulled down over the stains of his face. He avoided bright lights all the way to the dimness of a cross street where he pulled up, near the mouth of an alley. With Jerry he went down that alley, saying: "That little white house there, ahead of us, between the two big apartment houses, is where Franklin lives. We're going in to see him."

Jerry stopped short.

"You're going in. Not me," said Jerry. "Franklin was a bull, once. He knows all the crooks and he hates them."

"You're going in with me," said Pursivant, and tapped the arm of his companion. So Jerry went on, but he kept drawing himself up taller, preparing for an ordeal. They came to a twelve foot stone wall with a little postern door let into it. Pursivant pulled from his pocket a key that unlocked this door and let them into a bit of garden. They could not see the flowers but the fragrance of them lived in the air along with the damp smell of garden earth that has just been drinking. At the farther end a two-story miniature of a house came up through the darkness with a shimmer of white paint. One window was open and let out a wedge of light that showed a rocking chair on the back veranda, then scattered itself softly over a wet, green square of lawn.

Jerry halted again.

"Look at!" he whispered in the ear of Pursivant. "Everything else don't seem real, does it?"

The wide waving of his hand enlarged his idea to all sides. He banished from before them the lofty, straight-flanked apartment houses and the city glow over which the clouds were rolling like smoke above a red fire. All that remained was the white cottage, the veranda, the garden, and whatever imaginary prospect might please the mind.

Pursivant remained staring at his companion for a long moment. That gesture had banished the whole field of his labors and the labors along with the field of them except for a few green acres down there in Kentucky where the three old mares and the two long-legged yearlings were grazing, or sleeping. Their dreams could be nothing but content.

"Come out of this," muttered Pursivant, angrily. "We've got Franklin to talk to."

But as they went on towards the house he was walking through a region of profound wonder concerning this young fellow with the happy blue eyes.

CHAPTER XV

SMOKE was curling out of that open window into the light. Song began to burst out through it, also, a rolling and ringing Neapolitan boatsong. Jerry shook with the pleasure of silent laughter. They stepped silently onto the porch and leaning, looked into an old-fashioned kitchen all wreathed about with blue and white curlings and circles of smoke. Richard Franklin in person, swathed like a surgeon in a vast white apron, was grilling a steak over a charcoal fire which he fanned from beneath. The smoke streamed up rapidly; the breath of his singing knocked holes in it.

"You'd be easy getting now," said Pursivant.

"Come in, Bill," called Franklin. "There's enough steak for two or three, here. The back door's open."

He had not turned his head. Neither did he move it when Pursivant came in and looked at the place set out on the white oil cloth that covered the kitchen table. A large platter of spaghetti had just been finished; it was smeared with the red of a tomato sauce and a few strips of the *pasta.* There was a wicker-girdled fiasco of red wine, a purplish wine stain on the white of the oil cloth, and the torn and ragged heel of a loaf of French bread. Sudden hunger made Pursivant draw in a breath.

He went over to the sink, pulling off his coat, and began to run warm water over his wounded, blood-matted head.

"This is Jerry Somebody," he said.

He glanced back from under the run of the water and saw Jerry in rigid expectation, his smile freezing.

"Macklin," said Jerry.

"Hello, Jerry Macklin," said the boss, turning his head for an instant. "Glad to see you, but I've got both hands full. Get some plates and glasses and knives and forks out of that cupboard. I've got a porterhouse here, Jerry, with veins of fat and all shot through it. And damned little you fellows are going to let me have of it."

The frost went out of Jerry's face and let the eyes shine blue again. Franklin turned, suddenly, and walked over towards the sink carrying the grill in which the scorching meat was spluttering and hissing and dropping unregarded juices on the linoleum while Franklin watched the water run with a red stain from the head of Pursivant into the sink.

Then he turned without a word and went back to his cookery. Pursivant got a pair of clean dishtowels and began to dry his hair.

"Sorry, Dick," he said. "I'll explain the mess and why I had to come here; there was no other place to go."

Franklin gave him one abstracted glance. His brow was puckered, his eyes like those of a hurt child. By the time Pursivant had finished drying his hair and combing it smooth, with only a dull pain from the shallow wounds in his scalp, with no trace of blood now remaining, except on the shoulders of his coat, Franklin had slid the steak onto a warmed platter, Jerry Macklin had set out two new places on the table. There was a green salad of lettuce and herbs mixed in a big cheap, gay bowl of Canti Galli crockery. Franklin cut up the steak while the red juices of it ran freely over the platter; then he served it onto the plates.

Pursivant went upstairs and took a grey coat out of Franklin's wardrobe; then he returned and sat down with the other two.

There was nothing impressive about the room. The ceiling

was as low as a ship's cabin, and the two dormer windows were hardly more than the size of portholes. The furniture was most modest. There was only a rag rug on the floor and the only real decoration consisted of two oil portraits and a brace of enlarged photographs which hung on the wall, as well as a trio of smaller snapshots on top of the bureau.

All of those pictures were of one face. When Franklin lost his brother, he surrounded himself in his bed room with as many images as possible of the dead Alberto. Two oil painters had tried their hands at presenting the lost man after studying photographs of him. One work was that of von Lossing, who had labored with the most consummate care. The second had been done in a free-handed, modernistic manner by Tycho Barthelmy. Both were good likenesses though both of them lacked some of the real fire that had been in Alberto as a distinguishing characteristic more than mere structure of the face.

The pictures on the bureau showed a five year old with round cheeks, a lean, lanky boy of fourteen, and then Alberto as Pursivant had known him to the last, handsome, careless, casual, and reckless.

That picture was the central one. Franklin had had it enlarged several times but never was satisfied with the results. So he had set it in a frame of solid gold, and wherever he travelled, that picture travelled with him.

He used to say: "Suppose I should forget him for one day? Well, the devil would come up through the floor and spit in my face. But if I keep remembering, one day I shall have my hands on the murderer, Bill. Sometimes I dream about it. Sometimes I can almost see the face that's turning black between my hands!"

Pursivant went slowly back and sat down with the other two.

He said: "I saw Cappen at the jail, to-day. He told me where to find the stuff. It was only a trap but among the trappers there was Jerry Macklin and he framed things for me to get away. It was a little matter of his running in to fill me with lead but shooting out the window instead. He'd warned me what to do, so I had plenty of blood to show and I flopped on the floor. Afterwards, I played dead, and finally they lowered me out the window, wrapped in burlap, and put me in a boat. Macklin came along. After a while, he tapped the boatman over the head, turned me loose, and here we are."

Franklin put down his knife and fork. Instead of looking at his friend, he stared at Jerry Macklin.

"Up there at the Verney place, when Mr. Pursivant caught Cappen," said Jerry, flushing, "he could have had me in the soup at the same time. But he let me go. This was turn and turn about."

Franklin filled his glass with a gush of wine that spilled over onto the table. The red drops trailed down into his plate as he tossed off the drink. He dropped his forehead on the heel of his hand and studied the table.

Pursivant went on: "We swiped a car that we ran across and came down here from the river. I need this coat because there's blood on my old one. We'll take your Ford out of your garage and run out to your place on the beach. I'm dead and in the river, Dick. Jerry and the boatman were afraid to go back to the dive because at the last minute it appeared that the orders of Cappen had been misunderstood. What Cappen wanted was me, and I was to be held till you'd jimmied a pardon for Cappen out of the governor. So Jerry and the boatman, when they had passed me into the river, were afraid to go back and face Cappen's lieutenants. The boatman is travelling west. Jerry and I are going to disappear into your shack on the beach. We're going to stay there till the great Cappen is up Salt Creek. After that, we may be able to find more elbow-room."

"What have I done to you, Bill?" he muttered. "I've almost sold you. And you come back after death has been scratching your head for you, and you don't complain." He turned up an agonized face and lifted his spread hands slowly towards the ceiling. "When I try to understand big things—when I get religious ideas working in me—I think about you, Bill."

Jerry stared at them, delighted, half-frightened to hear such words.

"Three big things walked into my life," said Franklin. "Two of them are dead. Listen to me! The first was a big red-faced cop down on the waterfront. I was a poor Dago. I could speak six words of bad English. I walked up to him and asked him to tell me where to find a job. He found me a job on the street. I went to work. He got me into a night-school. He eased the way for me. I went on. He got older. Listen to me, Bill. Listen, Jerry. Kids are hard and mean. They forget. And I forgot. After a while, I remembered my partner, the cop. That was after years. and I went back to find him, but he wasn't on the beat. He wasn't at headquarters. Mind you, there I was with all the influence that a man needs to have. I could have made him anything. A lieutenant, a captain. But I was too late. He was gone. He was dead. All I had to remember him by was his red face behind a glass of beer, winking at me. He loaned me money. I loved him. And I forgot him; and he died. My God!"

"Stop it, Dick," said Pursivant. Jerry, tears in his eyes, stared like a child.

"The second man in my life—you know how he died, Bill. You're the only one who knows. And the third man is you

—and yet I've sent you out to face hell, to walk through hell for me. For *me!* I've sent you to Verney's and now down into worse trouble. I've put the gun at your head. Now, kind God forgive me."

He grew more excited in spite of the restraining gesture of Pursivant.

"Cappen trying murder?" he cried. "Cappen couldn't be such a fool!" he muttered. "Murder—"

He stopped, as Pursivant said: "You don't follow this. Murder wasn't what Cappen wanted for me, 'till later on. It was simply a little job of kidnapping to put pressure on you. You could get a pardon for Cappen out of the governor, couldn't you? It's a fairly thin case against Cappen. The governor could find reason for setting Cappen free if you talked on the right side. You see, Cappen is always right. He never wastes a motion, really. But this time his boys mixed things up a little."

"They could have killed you," answered Franklin. His voice went all to pieces, repeating: "They could have killed *you!*"

"Are you going to be a damned fool?" demanded Pursivant.

Franklin said: "No. I've got hold of myself."

He dropped the tips of his fingers against the forehead of Pursivant and pushed his face back. "God!" said Franklin.

"Don't be a woman," said Pursivant.

"I'm going to clean them up!" said Franklin, under his breath. "The murdering crooks, and the whole damned underworld—I'm going to blow it open and let the sun shine on it. Do you hear me, Bill? I'm going to—"

"Quit it!" snapped Pursivant.

Franklin was still. After a moment he asked: "Where was the place? Where did Cappen send you?"

"It doesn't matter," said Pursivant. "You keep your hands off. Only tell me how your finances are? Do you still think that the Weaver Trust business will sink you?"

"Sink me? I've opened all the faucets to see what I could raise and it seems that the tanks are full of gold. I thought I was cornered. That was because I was in a fool's panic. No, Bill, I've got a river of hard cash! But you're not going to dodge away to that beach shack. You're going to stay here. If you're afraid of Cappen, I'll show you that I can take care of my friends!"

"A bomb dropped off either of the apartment houses," answered Pursivant, "would blow hell out of this house and everyone in it. You know that. Besides, not even you could keep Cappen's men away because he has brains enough to know how to use his tools. And all his tools have a sharp edge. Give me the keys to the shack and the Ford. We're going out to hide our heads."

CHAPTER XVI

OYSTER POINT lay at the end of the world, where the forest stopped and the hills, turning into grey dunes, sloped away into the horizon and the sea. All winter the storms that had gathered speed across the ocean yelled and groaned among the little beach houses that were scattered down the shore; Oyster Point itself shrank to a population of half a thousand until the hot summer drove crowds out of the city to seek coolness. In the late spring, even, the shore was as deserted as in the winter. That was why Pursivant chose to come out to the place. There was no particular comfort in the shack. It had two rooms, an attic, and a shed that served as a garage. There was not a tree, not a shrub, not a vestige of a garden. But all during the days of Cappen's trial, Pursivant lived contentedly in the cottage.

It was a short trial, because the state wanted blood. Cappen's team of high-priced lawyers went down like nine-pins before the force of public opinion. Even Pursivant's absence as a witness was not a great handicap, because he had made his deposition at the White Forest jail; it was sufficiently proved that the rubies had been taken from Cappen, and the rubies in turn were identified by jewellers and by Richard Franklin as the very property which had been removed from the armored truck during the Weaver Trust removal. Moreover, the movements of Cappen on that day were traced and brought him to the scene of the crime. Finally, there was his criminal record. That was enough. The jury stayed out ten minutes; then the judge named an early date for the execution and sent Cappen to the death-house.

Every evening, Jerry Macklin walked over to Oyster Point and brought back a newspaper in which they could follow the details. In addition, there was the hue and cry which had been raised after the disappearance of Pursivant. The police, it was said, were working day and night on clues that always disappeared into nothingness. The disappearance of Pursivant, in fact, was one of the influences that charged the atmosphere most heavily against Cappen. No one doubted that Cappen's crew had put Pursivant out of the way to prevent his testimony at the trial!

But even with Cappen in the death-house, Pursivant refused to move. There were now three days to wait before the man sat in the electric chair. And that was when trouble began.

The day before, a small item on an inside page of the newspaper noted that in a railroad yard in Kansas had been found the body of a murdered man who was dressed like a ragged tramp. But more than a hundred dollars was found in his clothes, which removed the motive of robbery; and presently the dead man was identified as a character of the Eastern underworld, Adolph Quillan!

Jerry Macklin read that short article aloud to Pursivant and they stared at one another at the end of it.

"Cappen?" said Jerry.

Pursivant nodded. "Our point is," he said, "that Quillan may have talked before he died. If he talked, then Cappen's men know that you are probably with me; and they know that I'm not in the river. That may start some action."

But the optimism of Jerry Macklin was enormous.

He said: "Even if they know that you're not in the river, how will they ever find you? Who'd think of finding Charles

William Pursivant out here in the open? They'll search for you in your house or in Franklin's house, or somewhere else, or even down in Kentucky where you keep your horses. They'll never come out here to the beach. Why, this isn't a hideout at all. The beach is as open as the flat of your hand, and these shacks could be turned into kindling by a three pound bomb. They'll look for you three thousand miles away before they'll look for you here."

Pursivant answered: "If I had the brains to think of this place as a hideout, Cappen has plenty of brains to keep step with me."

The next evening, he set about cooking supper while Jerry Macklin said he would walk to the town for the paper. It was always Jerry's job to do that because, of course, the face of Pursivant was too likely to be recognized.

This time Pursivant protested. "If Cappen's gang is alive and working, then you may be seen and known. Don't forget that, Jerry. Sit down there and let the news go hang for one day."

Jerry shrugged his shoulders and leaned by the window, looking out.

"Reminds me of when I was a kid," he said. "I had the measles, and I had to stay inside, and the other kids were down in the street playing around, and big Al Copley was just back out of prison, from fifteen years. Al had gone up for second degree. He came back with the prison shakes, and the boys used to buy him beer because of what he'd done. He used to tell us about everything in the prison, and it was great to listen to him. He got the wobbles every time he talked about it. Kids are mean devils, I guess. Well, I think about that when you keep me in here and I want like the devil to get out and see what the news in the world may be."

He added, suddenly: "What was it like for you when you were a kid, Mr. Pursivant?"

"It was a hard life," said Pursivant. "A lot of languages to study and the whole day mapped out. A child's day ought to have enough leisure in it so that it seems long. You know how long an hour can be when you're a boy? Well, my days were all cut up into patterns, one like the other. Winter and summer just about the same. Always coaching for this and training for that."

"Yeah, but you got a swell education, I bet," said Jerry, shaking his head.

"It doesn't help a man to talk in three languages," said Pursivant.

"Yeah, maybe not," said Jerry. "But I wish—I'll tell you what I wish. I wish I could go and get that paper. Lemme go, Mr. Pursivant. It'll be all right."

Pursivant looked at him with that sudden smile which so often softened the habitual harshness of his face. "All right. Run along. And be a good boy, Jerry."

So Pursivant, left alone, sliced some potatoes for frying, worked up the fire in the little coal stove, and put on a tin of tomatoes and another of corn to heat. He sliced some bacon, also; but of course, that would wait to be cooked until Jerry Macklin came back. They would not enter a store to buy fresh provisions; it was more than sufficient risk, Pursivant felt, to allow Jerry to go to town for the paper once a day. So they lived like frontiersmen on canned stuff and bacon and potatoes.

Jerry was delayed, but that might mean that he had chosen to walk back to the shack by the inland way among the dunes. It was the only chance that Macklin had for exercise, this daily walk, and he liked to make the most of it. So

Pursivant pushed the cooking pans onto the back of the stove, put a chair in a corner of the room, and folded his hands.

Other men would have killed the time reading, but Pursivant was always most content when he could spend an hour or so with his own thoughts, letting them rise out of the darkness of the mind and come into view as they would, some dim and some bright. Many visions dawned and faded, now. But he thought most of a certain light-footed yearling filly on his Kentucky acres, beautiful as a deer and wild as a hunting cat. He thought of the filly and of Jacqueline Leigh. They seemed to pair together; they were made for one another, it appeared to him. He ran the tips of his fingers delicately over the hardness of his face, like a blind man seeing by the sense of touch.

A footfall came up to the kitchen door. The wind that had been blowing most of the day, thrusting the damp cold of the ocean air through the shack, had fallen away towards sunset. There was only the boom and mourning of the surf which did not quite cover a sound so much closer at hand.

The door opened.

"You're late, Jerry—" began Pursivant, and stopped.

It was not Jerry who stood on the threshold but a big middle-aged man with the eyes and the jowls of a fat pig. He bore a resemblance to the dead Quillan, with fewer distinctive features. The last time Pursivant had seen him was ten years before, on the night when Alberto Francolini died. He was called Jack Smith, in those days.

"Hello," said Smith, closing the door. "Can I come in?"

"Come in, Jack, and sit down," said Pursivant.

He held out his hand. Smith made an answering gesture which he checked, looking down as though surprised by the motion of his own arm.

"Listen, Pursivant," he said, "I'd like to shake with you.

But if I did, you'd want to cut my hand off at the wrist, later on. I'm on the other side of the fence."

"What fence?"

Smith jerked a thumb over his shoulder. "You know. Cappen," he answered.

Pursivant went to the window and drew down the shade. He worked by touch, never drifting his glance from Smith.

"Sit down anyway," he invited. "You're with Cappen, are you?"

"I didn't want to throw in against you," said Smith. He gripped the back of a chair and leaned some of his weight on it. "Just a question of needing some spot cash."

He trailed his eyes over Pursivant, adding: "I been seeing in the papers how you climbed. You got to the top of the heap, all right. I always figured you would. That Chink business out there on the river, that wasn't big enough to hold you."

"Where have you been, Jack?" asked Pursivant. "You dropped out of sight."

"The can for about eight years. I'm just out."

"How did they get you?"

"I knew a bird that knew a bird that had a cousin that was shoving the queer," answered Jack Smith. He began to grin. The smile threw wrinkles high up in his cheeks and over his eyes into the forehead. He looked like a great Buddha. "They said I was in a counterfeit ring and they framed me. You know how it is," explained Jack Smith.

"I know how it is," said Pursivant. "You didn't think of tapping me when you got out of jail, and were broke?"

"I figured you were down on me, after that night on the Rio Grande," answered Jack Smith. "You seemed to think that I could of jumped into the fight."

"You had a chance to grab young Francolini," declared

Pursivant. "You knew he was drunk. You knew he was always crazy when he was drunk, too. When he went crazy and tackled me, you could have nailed him from behind."

"Yeah, maybe," agreed Jack Smith, thoughtfully. "But it would of been like jumping a tiger. I didn't think that fast, anyway. But why didn't you let him go?"

"They already wanted him in town," said Pursivant. "If he went in, they would have grabbed him. Besides, he was half drunk already, and if he'd got into the town, he would have been using his knife in a saloon fight before morning. I had to keep him with us. Another thing, we had orders to bring the boat back across the river before morning. You don't remember?"

"Remember?" sighed Jack Smith. "Yeah, I remember everything from the cactus on the hill to the stars in the slack water. I could go and dip those stars out in the hollow of my hand right now, I remember them so doggone well. That wasn't the sort of a night that a gent would forget. When Alberto started shooting and you flopped, I thought you were dead. I thought he'd turn around and open up on me to make a clean job of it and wipe us both out. And then you nailed him while you were lying on the deck."

"I aimed low," said Pursivant, slowly. "I'll never know how it happened. I aimed for his legs—and—my God, you know what happened!"

"Yeah," agreed Jack Smith. "The slug hit him in the hip and glanced up into the soft of his belly. No gent has much of a chance when the lead tears into the soft of him. But he forgave you before he passed out. He understood it was all his own fault. He was kind of a white kid for a damn Dago wop, when you come to think of it."

"Let's stop talking about it," muttered Pursivant.

"Yeah," said Jack Smith, "but when he lay there banging

his fist on the ground and calling for 'Riccardo,' who would of thought that his Riccardo was the big boss, Richard Franklin?"

Pursivant, gradually, narrowed his eyes at his guest.

"Yes, who would have thought that?" he repeated. "Go on, Jack. What are you driving at?"

"Look," protested Jack Smith. "I don't want to do you any harm, Pursivant. I wouldn't for the world. But a bird has to make a living. You know that. I'll come clean with you, Pursivant. The idea is to get you to persaude Richard Franklin to put the pressure on the governor and get a pardon for Cappen."

"Or else?" said Pursivant.

"Or else—well, you see how it is. They know that Franklin has the bullet that was cut out of his brother's body. They know he's been spending money for ten years trying to spot the killer. And—well, Pursivant—I've got the gun you used that night. I guess a ballistic expert could prove—"

He broke off to yell: "Look out! Get back, Pursivant—damn you, if you try to—"

He had out a stub-nosed automatic, by this time, but Pursivant, with a cry that came only halfway past his teeth, had leaped the table and gone at him. The first blow knocked big Jack Smith up against the wall and made the gun slither out of his hand. He put up his fists as one that understood the art of using them but he might as well have tried to box with a panther.

When reason came back to Pursivant, he had Jack Smith by the hair of the head and was beating his face against the floor. He got up and went back to the table. He sat down and spread out his hands, looking at the blood on them and listening to the harsh rasping of his own breathing.

Smith pushed himself up to his knees, then regained his

feet. He took his fallen automatic from the floor but merely slipped it back inside his coat. Then he got hold of a dish-towel and began to sop up the blood that ran from his nose and mouth. Words came slowly out of his battered lips.

"No use taking it out on me," said Jack Smith. "But—where'd you learn that left hook?"

He took his beating patiently, as though he had received it in the prize-ring, for money.

"No use taking it out on me, Pursivant," he repeated. "You know how it is. I've passed on the stuff to the big boys. They've got everything. All I came down here to do was to give you the tip. I'm to show you the layout; then you can make up your mind."

He got a fold of paper out of his pocket and laid it before Pursivant. It was a typewritten carbon copy of a letter that ran:

"Dear Mr. Franklin,

Thinking you will want to know the truth about the killing of your brother, Alberto Francolini, on the Rio Grande, ten years ago, I want to state that I was present at the time with Mr. Charles W. Pursivant, and that I know what happened.

"You've been told that an opposition crew of smugglers laid for the three of us after we'd brought some Chinamen across from Mexico, and that in the fight your brother was shot.

"I was right there, and I saw Pursivant shoot and kill Alberto. Pursivant was full of hooch. He did a good deal of drinking in those days. We were supposed to take the boat straight back to the Mexican side after the Chinese were landed but Pursivant wanted to go on into town and have a spree. Alberto was dead against that. He was afraid that Pursivant would get into trouble and he tried to force Pursivant back into the boat. Before you could say Jack Robinson, Pursivant outs with a gun and shoots him dead.

"I can prove what I say. You have the bullet that was taken from your brother's body. And I still have the gun that Pursivant used. I can prove that Pursivant owned the gun at that time and if the experts say that the bullet came out of that old Colt, I guess it makes a tight case.

Faithfully yours,"

Jack Smith stood back by the door, his hand on the knob of it, during the reading. The bloody towel still masked the lower part of his face, but his eyes and his nostrils could be seen working with his fear and his hard breathing.

He explained: "There wasn't anything to do but to twist things around. You know how it is, Pursivant. I didn't want to do you no harm, but I was busted flat. And Cappen's men showed me the chance to raise the wind. You know how things go."

CHAPTER XVII

PURSIVANT looked away from the letter to the blood on his hands and then across the table, and down to the feet of big Jack Smith, and so up and up his body until he was staring into the eyes of the man. The simplicity and the perfection of the device overwhelmed him. And as he sat there, dreading the wrath of Franklin, he realized by the coldness of the shadow the full light and warmth of his affection for the big Italian. He tried to conceive the convulsion of Franklin's nature when he saw such manifest proofs that his confidant, his dearest friend of all these years had been the cold-blooded murderer of his brother. But his imagination could not grasp the picture and the eye of the mind could not measure the possibilities. At the least there would be an eye for an eye and a tooth for a tooth. So Pursivant sat with a still mind and an aching heart, and when he spoke, his voice was quiet.

"Why didn't the gang run down here and mob me? Why not another little kidnapping?" asked Pursivant.

"After the last fracas," answered Jack Smith, with his usual amazing frankness, "they all figured that you'd be dead before they got you into the net. Plenty of them would be glad enough to see you dead, but you'd be no use to Cappen, then."

Pursivant nodded.

"A friend was staying with me here," he suggested after a moment.

"Jerry Macklin?" said Smith. "Don't worry about him. We

got him safe enough. Not a break on his skin, neither. That's a compliment to you, Pursivant. In Cappen's outfit, maybe you know what they do to a fellow that puts over the double cross? But this time they're treating Jerry Macklin like he was a handful of silk. They're not even rubbing him the wrong way. And after you've persuaded Franklin to start the wheels going, and after Cappen is free, we'll send you back Jerry Macklin safe and sound. You'll get the old gun, too. And after that, nothing can ever be hung on you about that job. You'll be sitting pretty. Franklin will still be in your pocket; and Cappen will be your friend. Look at that for a picture, will you? There's only one thing. Cappen don't sit in the chair for three days, but he's got to be pardoned out of prison before that. Two days from this, somebody gets back to this country, and Cappen has to be out of the pen before that. Forty-eight hours that gives you to work. But that's plenty of time. A word from you to Franklin; a word from Franklin to the governor; and there you are. Look at how easy it all is, Pursivant, will you? It's a nacheral!"

He kept his voice low while he was speaking, as a man will do when he hopes that what he speaks will glide like involuntary thought through the listener's mind.

Pursivant looked down at the red on his hands and answered: "Go back and tell them to go to hell, will you?"

Jack Smith opened his bleeding mouth to bawl a protest but something about the bent head and the intent face of Pursivant changed his mind. He put out a persuasive hand. "Lookat, Mr. Pursivant," he said. "Give yourself a break, will you?" The dull eyes of Pursivant looked at a future in which Jack Smith was a vanishing figure of no importance. "You don't know what you're up against. You're too white to know. You were always too white. Take out West. You didn't know the game. You were never no crook. It was sport, for you, not the hard cash that counted. Running Chinamen across the river, it was fun for you. If there was trouble came up and a fight, you wouldn't take no advantages; you wouldn't hit a man that was down; you acted like there was a referee in the ring and all the sporting writers sitting around taking notes. You were useful because you weren't afraid of anything, but the crooks kept kidding you along. They knew you wouldn't get your hands dirty. You never knew how they were kidding you; you never knew anything about 'em—and you don't know anything about Cappen and his crowd."

It seemed to Pursivant that the voice came from far out of his past. A wave of darkness was rising and threatening to swallow him. Something said, inside him, that what the boy is the man will be. And when he had been the rich man's son in the house on the hill he had preferred to break away, now and again, and go roving with the toughs of the town. That, it seemed to him had been prophetic of the days of crime to come. And now, again, the underworld was reaching up about him and preparing to drag him down. This fellow Smith was a blackmailer and a scoundrel, and yet he talked with a certain kindliness and frankness. He was saying, now: "Those birds out West were pretty tough hombres, but they were babies compared with the Cappen crowd. Out there they were tough enough to handle you. But Cappen will twist you right around his finger. I'm warning you like a friend. Give yourself a break and get on Cappen's side of the fence. Help him out now, and everything's forgotten. But if you stand up to him, he'll smash you!"

No doubt this was all perfectly true. If Pursivant helped Cappen from the deathhouse, the criminal would be a valuable ally thereafter, a clever helper, a protector, in a sense. The temptation rushed over the mind of Pursivant like the unnerving warmth of wine. It was easy to give way; there would be no harm to him afterwards. Cappen would be useful, frightfully useful, in times to come.

The voice of Jack Smith went on: "Take it easy. Think it over. There ain't more than one way to see it, chief. You're too right to go wrong on it."

What came to Pursivant, then? It was very strange, but before his dim eyes brightened the picture of the old house, not as in the days of his childhood but as it was now, neglected, the fountains dead, the garden paths green with mold. The old glory had left the house, and now it was leaving the last of the name of Pursivant.

He lifted his head, suddenly.

"Thanks, Jack," he said. "You're a good fellow. As good as you know how to be. But I can't take your advice. Go back and tell them that it's a fight to a finish."

Jack Smith started to argue, but the word on which his lips had parted would not be uttered. The rigid pain in the face of Pursivant was even dimly reflected in the eyes of Smith.

"By God," he whispered, "I'm sorry it's gotta be this way. But I kind of guessed it. I told 'em you were a clean-bred one. So long, Mr. Pursivant."

He backed out into the darkness, and closed the door softly, softly behind him.

A long silence began for Pursivant.

They would go through with it, of course. Even if they could not help Cappen, they would take infinite pleasure in harming Pursivant. It was a perfect device. Somehow, it seemed to Pursivant that he had known all during the years that the blow would fall. He had been struggling up a height; and he would have the more fatal drop.

Jerking up his head, suddenly, he looked around him and remembered that this was the house of Richard Franklin. Therefore, it had been as his own, an hour before; now he was an interloper.

The fire was out. The stove was cold. The stovepipe began to hum and tremble in a rising wind that knocked up thin puffs of ashes, like a false smoke, through the interstices around the plates.

Jerry was gone. The sliced bacon that waited in the frying pan would never be eaten.

Jerry was gone, poor devil. The merry light in his eyes would soon be effectively darkened.

After all, what right had he to decide on his course since not his life, only, but that of Jerry Macklin depended upon his decision? But he knew that he would not do the thing over again, in a different way. The underworld might rise like waves of pitch and cover him, but he would keep fighting to the last.

He felt chilly, and weak, and surrounded.

He pulled the cork out of a bottle of whiskey, poured three big fingers, and tossed it off. Then he gripped the edge of the table, head down, and waited for the stuff to knock at his brain and send the familiar clouds across the sharpness of his wits.

But no effect followed. Colored water would have done as much to him except that he became aware of a slight thrumming in his temples that grew into a voice of the mind, saying: "Do something! Do something! Do something!"

But what was there to do?

For one thing, he had to get out of that place. Otherwise

the ghost in it would stifle him by day and freeze his heart by night.

After that, he must find the trail of Jerry Macklin. Whatever his position was now, it was better than to be back there in the rear room of the apartment house, with Quillan and the others outside in the hall, chuckling.

Then he had to do something to block the Cappen men from getting to Franklin.

He walked out of the kitchen, through the bedroom, and flung open the front door. There was still light in the horizon, a bright gap between the clouded sky and the leaden-colored sea through which a spirit could fly out of him and find hope of some sort. And the smell of the sea which adventurers have always loved blew freshly about him. But all the time the fear was growing in him. He could have endured anything if it were dawn that he was watching, but night was lifting like waves over the land. He dreaded turning back into the darkening house. Off shore a trim schooner heeled in the wind. The waves puffed into pale smoke about her bows. And that would be a place for him, he felt, in the dark cramped forecastle of that little ship, outward bound.

An automobile's motor whirred in the distance—like a humming wasp it seemed to Pursivant. Now he saw it sreaking down the road behind the beach houses and there was light enough to see the wake of dust spreading and rising behind the long-nosed runabout. Its headlights were on, but dimmed so that they looked like a great pair of eyes and as the machine twisted swiftly down the crooked way, it reminded Pursivant of a huge beast that was hunting down a trail. Perhaps it was—for that matter. Perhaps it was launched on the trail of C. W. Pursivant with a sub-machine-gun or two inside it and a few of Cappen's resolutes.

The brakes got hold. The car slewed a bit to the side and

stopped right behind the shack of Richard Franklin, but the driver was the only person that he could see and that driver was a woman. She jumped out and came on the run until she saw Pursivant step out from the front of the little house. That stopped her for an instant. The sea-wind got hold of her big coat with a sweep and a pull, and he knew her.

"Mr. Pursivant? Mr. Pursivant?" said Jacqueline Leigh, as she came on, hesitantly.

"Yes," he said.

She came on up to him with her hand held out a little as though she wanted to touch him and make sure of his reality. The light had been failing rapidly so that now he saw her as one sees a rubbed and time-stained charcoal drawing.

"Then you're all right? You're safe? No one has been here?" she was saying. "I thought, when I heard—"

"What did you hear?" asked Pursivant.

Her head went back. "Murder!" she whispered. "And I came as fast as I could, but all the way I told myself it would be too late! There was a great brute of a man with a face like a pig! Don't stay here another instant! He must be coming now, he and the others."

"He's been here and he's gone again. He just wanted to do a little talking," said Pursivant.

She turned and looked back down the road. Her hand fumbled, found his arm.

"Come with me!" she urged. "They'll be on the way, now. All of them. They want to kill you. I know that."

"I'm ready to go," said Pursivant. "I'll go inside and get—"

"Don't go back into that horrible darkness," she gasped. "That's the way I've been imagining it—the house all dark and no answer—and my feet stumbling against something on the floor—"

She caught her breath. Her eyes were closed and he steadied her with both his hands. Her head was at his shoulder. She was not tall when she stood close, like this. Perhaps she had never been so close to any other man, trembling, with her eyes shut. She had come from the city, sweeping the road with her speed, to find him, and now she was weak and sick with relief. He thought of his own ugly face, then, of the few moments he had been with her on the Verney place, of the meaningless words that he had spoken to her. Nevertheless, something seemed to have happened in her as something had happened in him. There is never a logical explanation. The golden lightning blooms and strikes and no one can tell why. Now that he was touching her, he knew how strongly he had been fighting against a thought and shutting a picture out of his mind.

"I'm all right," she said. "I'm sorry, but now I'm all right. Only you won't stay out here?"

"I'm going back," said Pursivant.

"Thank God!" she whispered, so that he had to guess at the words. Then, aloud: "Will you come with me? Will you let me see you safe in your house?"

"We'll drive to the door of it," said Pursivant.

CHAPTER XVIII

AFTER all, there was nothing in the beach shack that was necessary to him, and even if it had been filled with perishable treasure he knew that he would have shrugged his shoulders and gone on with her.

"You drive—and go fast—go fast!" she said, looking down the road up which she had come. She was in the car, still with her head turned, watching for danger, as he settled himself behind the wheel. The big, shining arch of the instrument board showed him what he needed to see. He trundled the car out of a sandy rut. The motor hummed and sighed; it gave a world of smooth power into his hands; it put the wings of flight under his foot; but he went along without too much haste, found the blackness and sheen of the main highway, and blew soundlessly down it at fifty miles an hour. He would take the long way around and go over one of the lower bridges into the city.

Her head was against the back of the seat, turned a little towards him, but her look was towards the smoky rolling of the clouds and the gleaming of stars between. Out at the Verney place he had wondered what her smile would be like, once it really dawned. Well, she was smiling now but he kept himself sternly in hand and refused to glance directly at her, though all the time he was seeing everything—body and soul together, as it seemed.

"I'd like to know how you understood about the fellow with the face of a pig. His name is Jack Smith, in case you want to hear it. How did you spot this cottage? Why are you sure that they mean murder?"

"Must I talk about it?" she asked.

"Please," said Pursivant.

They slid on for perhaps a mile before she seemed able to draw her mind away from this moment and back to other things. He could see in the distance the arch of the first bridge lifting like the round back of a sea monster. Beyond that was the glow of the city where the fire burns night and day.

She said: "They knew I would do anything for Arthur Cappen. You hate him, so you can't understand. But he's been like a father, always. But the others are terrible men. There's one called Harmody."

She paused. He thought of Arthur Cappen and of what those merciless eyes would be like if they were made mild by a generous and selfless affection. But that was unthinkable.

"They came and talked to me. They even wanted me to go to you and pretend—"

She stopped again, but Pursivant could fill in the gap. Of course they would have thought of that, sending her like a goddess out of the sky to touch him and make him do her will. Why, a smile and a gesture would have been enough pretending. And she loved Cappen, too; she was willing to do anything for him, except to be dishonest. It made Pursivant feel removed to a chilly distance. Women *are* sacred. God help us if we can't see that.

"When they couldn't persuade me," she was saying, "they went on talking about other things. They talked about the way you got free from them, not long ago. They still couldn't believe that you had slipped through their hands. They hate you, it seems. If they couldn't make you help Arthur Cappen, then they would put an end to you—tonight! I started to say things. I don't remember what I said. They threatened me if I didn't stop screaming. They locked me up. I stopped screaming and tried to think. All I could do was to see that pale, fat face of Christopher Verney and remember the things he had said about you. There was a fire escape that ran down near the window of my room. I tied a blanket to a chair and slid down to the firescape. Then I wanted to find the police, but everyone says that the police take ages to do anything. They had described the cottage at Oyster Point. So I got a car out of the garage and just came this way. Is that all you want to know?"

All? No, he wanted to know a thousand other things but she had said enough to let him guess at the rest. Only, what fools they had been, those savages of Cappen, to talk right out in front of her. No doubt they thought that because she was devoted to Cappen nothing would be too much for her to know.

He said: "Will you tell me if you've been dependent on Cappen?"

"For money?" she asked. "I don't know. Aunt Helen would know about that. But for everything outside of money, for kindness and gentleness and patience and—"

Her voice stopped before it began to tremble. In three days Arthur Cappen would be dead and she was riding at the side of the man who had put him in danger of the law.

He could find nothing to say. He knew that he had no measuring rod with which to survey the soul of Arthur Cappen. There were in it regions, perhaps, that were simply above his ken. There must be such regions if the girl could feel about him as she did. Kindness, gentleness, patience she had found in Cappen!

They were passing through suburbs. The car hummed between high walls and whispered at the crossings. They sank deeper into the city. A traffic light stopped them. Pursivant turned and looked at the girl, but to his amazement all trouble was smoothed from her face, and she was looking up again at the clouds which the city glow fingered dimly.

"What do you want me to do?" he asked, suddenly.

She closed her eyes with pain. "Nothing," she said. "I don't want you to do anything. I don't want to think, but just go on, for a while—"

Like trailing fingers, his eyes passed over her face. She looked back at him and smiled. What does it mean when a woman glances down from the eyes of a man and then up into them again, steadily?

Well, three days hence they would be fitting the black cap over the face of Arthur Cappen. They would pull up his trouser legs and rub the skin with a wet cloth before tying the electrodes firmly in place. She knew all about that; she was no child. But she was keeping her mind fixed on one thing so firmly that even the thought of Arthur Cappen could not intrude for a little while.

But afterwards? Well, of course she would never be able to see Pursivant without finding the bloodstain on him.

The traffic light blinked, turned green, and let him drive on. He turned to the right towards a bridge-head. They began to lift on the arch of the bridge above the tops of the buildings. They swept out over the river, over the ugly blackness of the docks. A tug passed underneath with red light trembling in the swirl of its wake. They kept on rising. The city held up its high hands before them.

"Do you know," said Pursivant, "that Franklin might get the governor's pardon for Cappen, if I ask?"

She refused with a gesture of both hands.

"Why do you do that?" asked Pursivant.

"Whatever you think is right," said the girl, "whatever you

think is true and right—oh, never dream that I would try to change it in your mind."

A queer jumble of things shook out of his mind. Clay said: "I would rather be right than be president." That used to sound like a schoolbook legend—just nonsense. There had not been such nonsense in the like of Pursivant! And somewhere in the Bible, the angels came down and mixed with the race of men. And he was up there on the bridge, swinging across the sky towards a great idea, willing to put his own conclusions behind him, and let another person do his thinking for him. No, it was not thinking. Something more than thought moved in the spirit of this girl.

He reached his determination up there on the crest of the bridge; he held it as the big car sloped down into the lighted streets of the city and their noise and their odors. It seemed only a moment later that he eased the machine to a stop in front of his house. The face of it was blank and dark.

He got out and she slipped over under the wheel.

"I want to see the door open, and you safely inside," she said.

Then he remembered, as he took her hand, that he had not uttered a single word of thanks. It seemed too late for that, now. Back there in Oyster Point the gunmen were still hunting through the Franklin shack and all about it, probably.

He kept hold of her hand and leaned closer, until the sense of nearness struck through him to the heart, and by the night light he made sure that something was living and trembling behind her eyes.

He said: "You're all I want. I love you. I think I'd go through hell to make you smile, but not the kind of a hell that Cappen can be found in. Maybe I could save him—through Franklin. It may make you hate me when I tell you that I won't lift a hand for him, no matter what he means to you. I'll tell you why. I've been in the underworld that he belongs to, and I'm not going back into it again."

He stepped back, waiting, but she took it silently. One hand went to her breast and her face tilted up, then down. He heard the gears click as they engaged; she slid the car away without another word to him. Her head was still down. She seemed to be driving blindly. A hand got hold of the strings of his heart and wrenched them so that he leaned to run after her, but he mastered that impulse, for the time had come when he had to be iron, all iron. Other men could hope for happiness before they died, but he felt that he could only hope to die clean.

He went slowly up the steps of his house and put the key into the lock. He opened the door, shut it behind him, and felt that in so doing a thousand doors of steel were shutting between him and the girl.

Gregory came hurrying up the hall, his eyes wide and his face stunned.

Pursivant said: "Get Franklin's secretary on the phone. Get his night man and tell him that I have to talk to the chief at once."

"Yes, sir," said Gregory, and began to turn slowly away.

The back door in the hall jerked open. Vasco and the round-faced cook crowded into view. They had all been here, waiting for his return day and night. He saw Vasco's arms fly up into the air.

Pursivant went to them and shook their hands.

"There's been a little bit of hell," he told them. "And I'm glad to see all your faces! Gregory, give Vasco a drink. Then get me that telephone number."

He went up to his room. It laid a familiar blessing on his eyes. The ivory horseman waited, ready on the spur to dash off on the mission of his lord. Gregory had a big bowl of cornflowers in front of the window. The bed was open. The newspapers of all the lost days were piled on the bedside table together with a neat stack of mail.

Gregory came in to say that the night secretary would ring back in a few moments. Mr. Franklin was out, but would be gotten on the phone.

Pursivant dropped one hand on the rounded shoulder of his man and with the other hand he gestured at the room.

"Good old Gregory!" he said.

Gregory said nothing. For the first time in his life he failed to speak when he was spoken to and, instead, looked down suddenly towards the floor.

The telephone rang, fortunately, at that moment.

Over the wire boomed the deep resonance of the voice of Franklin.

"I'm back at my house," said Pursivant. "You recognize my voice, Dick?"

"Of course, I do! What's up?"

"Come to my house and I'll talk," said Pursivant.

"I can't come," said Franklin.

"Do what I tell you," said Pursivant, and hung up.

CHAPTER XIX

RICHARD FRANKLIN came in to find Pursivant lying in bed smoking cigarettes and going through his mail in a leisurely fashion, making notes on a scratch pad. Franklin filled the room with the aroma of his cigar.

"Throw that damned thing away—throw it out the window," said Pursivant.

Franklin tossed the cigar behind him. He stood with his hands in his pockets, swaying a little from side to side like a great bull moose and singing softly in the deep of his throat while he stared at Pursivant. There was a flush of liquor in his cheeks but his eyes were clear; alcohol, danger, confusion of the world, nothing could affect that brain of his until his heart was moved. And who but Pursivant could move it? He was as lonely as a bull moose in the northern woods. His thousand henchmen were nothing to him but natural features of the landscape. He had neither child nor woman; but once he had had a brother, and now he had one friend. It would be possible to pity him in spite of his strength.

"All right," said Franklin. "Tell me what's been happening. Loosen up. Don't try to be the iron man with me. I can see that you've had enough hammering to crack you."

"They're after me," said Pursivant.

"Cappen's lot?"

"Yes. They're after me. They got Jerry Macklin, and they almost got me. A girl pulled me out of the hole."

"What sort of a girl?"

"The one I wanted to marry."

"You put it in the past."

"Everything's in the past," said Pursivant. "Everything needs a new start, now. Pour me a drink of that brandy."

Franklin obeyed, and Pursivant threw the drink down his throat.

"Stand there where I can see you better," said Pursivant. "I told you, at the start of this Cappen business, that if I stepped down into the underworld, the underworld would never let me go again. It would get me. Well, I told you the straight of it. They're about to get me now."

"They can't get you," said Franklin. "They'd have to get me, first."

"They're going to try to get me through you," said Pursivant.

Franklin folded his arms and waited. "Don't talk like this," he urged, gently. "You're excited, Bill. You've been through something pretty bad. Tell me all about it."

"It's all in the past and it doesn't count. What I have you here for is to let you know that they're going to try to get me through you. Don't think I'm crazy. I know what they're going to show you."

"What is it, then?"

"You'll find out, soon enough. I'm just warning you beforehand. They've cooked up something that looks very real. They're going to try to turn you against me."

"Are they?" murmured Franklin. He smiled down at Pursivant. "Old son!" he said, gently

"That's the way you take it now, but you'll take it differently before long They're going to hit you with what seems like true news. You'll have to hold yourself hard to keep from believing it."

"There's no news that could swing me around against

you," said Franklin. He went on: "You're strung pretty close to the breaking point, Bill. Or perhaps I've never told you everything that I feel inside me. I've never told you what you mean—"

"Ah, don't be a damned fool, Dick," broke in Pursivant. "I know what you mean. But I'm telling you that they're going to fire some bad news into you. I want you to be prepared."

"I'll be prepared for anything," said Franklin, calmly. "You know the news—why don't you tell me what it is?"

"Because my telling would do no good. You have to work it out for yourself."

"I'll work it out. Now talk about something else. Tell me where you—"

"I don't want to talk. I simply wanted to tell you that. Go home, Dick. There's a lot for me to do. I'm behind. Good night, Dick."

"Good night, old man," said Franklin, and went out of the room.

But Richard Franklin gave the matter only a little attention. He never wasted time on absurdities, and for Pursivant to think that he might be attacked *through* Franklin was manifestly absurd. The city boss was more inclined to be amused for it was not the first time that he had had to smile at vagaries of his friend. In fact, he looked on Pursivant as a thoroughbred too highly strung, too sensitive, capable of great accomplishment but needing a calming influence and a restraining hand from time to time. He found it typical of Pursivant that, after achieving the miracle of jailing Cappen, after slipping through the hands of Cappen's armed friends, he now should be startled by a mere shadow.

As Franklin drove home across the Park, he looked south

towards the enormous fronts of the lighted buildings and felt again, as always, that fierce and glorious sense of possession which had been his since the beginning of his regime as political boss of the city. He loved the great town with the passion of a foreign convert and in his heart he wished only to do it good. If his hands were not clean, if he dealt daily in graft and corruption, nevertheless he told himself that because of him the children went to better schools and that opportunity knocked more often at the door of every man. The wealth of power was the only treasure that Richard Franklin had heaped up, and his hands were full of his desire; but it seemed to him that he could poise an equal weight against all the rest in his possession of one friend.

That was why he still smiled and shook his head, remembering Pursivant, when he went to bed that night. He was still smiling when he rose in the morning. Then the telephone began to ring and the work of the day reached for him and engulfed him.

He was hardly in his office when a card was brought to him, the card of one J. Walford Smith and three words scribbled under it: "See him, Richard."

Those words angered Franklin. But he pushed aside other conferences and allowed J. Walford Smith to come in. He found himself looking at a fellow who might have been an ex-prizefighter, a vast bulk of a man with a pyramidal face built up from a wide-spreading pair of muscular jaws to a narrow forehead. Mr. Smith had been in trouble, recently. His faee was deformed by bruises and swellings, and strips of narrow plaster covered cuts here and there.

Franklin said: "I told Jim Craven that I didn't want any more go-betweens. I want him. Go back and tell Craven that unless I hear from him before three o'clock, I'm going to close down on him—and smash him flat!"

He gripped the air with his powerful hand, as he finished that speech, and then waved Smith towards the door.

"Chief," said the big man, "I ain't here from any Jim Craven. My name's Jack Smith. Maybe Mr. Pursivant's talked to you about me?"

"Pursivant?" said Franklin, his tone suddenly altering. "No. He's never talked to me about a Jack Smith."

"He never has?" echoed Jack Smith, in hearty surprise. "Well, I'll be—well, I've come here to talk big business with you, Mr. Franklin."

"Maybe you have," said Franklin, "but you didn't come from Craven—and I'm a busy man! Did you send yourself?"

"No, Cappen sent me."

Franklin sat back in his chair; his eye flashed towards the bell that was set into the near edge of his desk, and he casually put his thumb over it.

"Don't ring in the reserves," said Jack Smith, with that grin of his which moved thick wrinkles into his narrow forehead. "I ain't here for a strong arm play. I'm sent by Cappen because he wants a pardon out of the can, and he knows that you can get it for him."

"All right," said Franklin, calmly. "What will he pay?"

"He knows you won't do it for pay," answered Smith. "But he's going to offer you something else—the name of the man that killed Alberto Francolini yonder on the Rio Grande!"

Franklin said nothing. He looked down at his hands, breathing hard.

"We name the man, prove he did the job, and tell you where to find him," said Jack Smith. "Is that worth enough to get a pardon for Cappen?"

"Yes," said Franklin, suddenly looking up. "That's worth

Cappen's pardon. That's worth all the blood out of my body, to me. I'll take the roof, first."

Jack Smith slipped the open sheet of a letter onto the desk before Franklin. He could not see the face of the boss, at that angle, but he could mark the sudden swelling of a big blue vein at the top of Franklin's forehead. When he looked up, he was grey, with his nostrils spreading to get more air, straining it in, audibly.

Something went back and forth in front of the eyes of Franklin, like the gesture of a quick hand. He felt as though he would faint, and getting a hold on the edge of his desk, he gripped it till the pain in his fingers restored him a little.

Not that he believed what he had read in the letter. It was, of course, a lie, and he would prove it to be a lie. It was simply the last desperate effort of Cappen for life. And yet a fatal premonition worked in the back of Franklin's brain, for if the letter were true then the villainy of Pursivant was perfect. It was because of Pursivant's acquaintance with dead Alberto Francolini that Franklin, in the first place, had befriended him, saved him from the law, given him the second chance. What could be more damnably apt than to conceive Pursivant rising in the world from his knowledge of a man he had murdered!

It could not be true, and yet the shadow was there, quivering in the eyes of Franklin. The temptation to believe worked on him like the perverse desire to throw oneself from a fatal height. The wit of Pursivant was keen enough to enable him to stand on just such a narrow ledge. Danger he always courted and chance he loved. He was the very man to use such a perilous influence as that of the brother of his murdered man.

So worked the thoughts of Franklin, though still all the vast loyalty that was in him rallied to the defense of Pursivant. He felt, suddenly, that if Pursivant were stolen out of his life, he had lost more than half the relish of existence, more than half of his accomplishment had been snatched from him. And yet the deadly temptation to believe was working in him.

"I thought I was gunna just mail the letter, but the big chiefs figgered it was better to just come here and hand it to you."

"You have the gun," said Franklin.

"Sure. Here it is. You get your ballistic experts going and they'll tell you that this is the gun that fired the bullet, all right."

"Let me see it."

Jack Smith drew from his pocket an old Colt, the butt of which he turned up and revealed, carved into the handle, the initials: "C.W.P."

"All right," said Franklin. "You're no doubt right when you say that this is the gun that fired the bullet. But the only way you identify the gun is with a set of carved initials!"

"Hey, but look! That's the way that Pursivant makes his letters."

"It couldn't be forged?" asked Franklin.

"Well, sure it could," said Jack Smith. "And the chiefs have thought it all out. They *have* fixed up another gun that's a ringer for the real one. I've got that one with me, too. They're gunna use that to prove that Pursivant is the man you want."

"How will they go about their proof?" asked Franklin.

"Sure, they got it worked all out. They go to Pursivant and they tell him that the gun and the letter have been sent to you through the mail—that you'll have the two waiting for you when you get home in the evening. They tell Pursivant that if he'll come over to their side—to persuade you to get a pardon for Cappen—they'll break into your house and steal the letter and the gun. You see?"

"So far. What does it lead to?" asked Franklin.

"It leads to this. Pursivant has all the nerve in the world. If he's the guilty hombre and thinks you've got the gun and the letter waiting for you, he won't surrender to Cappen, but he'll make a try at stealing the gun himself. Ain't that correct?"

"Ah?" said Franklin. And his heart felt a great stroke of pain and of cold fear. "If Pursivant tries to steal the gun —yes, yes, that would be the proof, I suppose."

"God, God," whispered Franklin under his breath, "I'll have to know before the night of this day is over!"

He wanted to put off the trial of his friend. He himself wanted more time to prepare for the shock.

"Smith," he said, "I know you were there. There was a Jack Smith with them. Tell me what happened, will you? Can you remember anything?"

"Sure. I can remember everything pretty straight. You know how it is. When a thing like that happens, it sort of gives you a sock in the eyes. You hang onto it. The thing gets blue-printed in your head. I've seen gunplays, too. But it was the way Pursivant done it that beat me. He seemed a straight sort of a guy. You know. Kind of wild and all that, but nothing mean. It kind of beat me. You know, because Alberto was a good kid. He was strong-headed, but he was a right kid. There was something about him that was kind of right."

"Yes!" whispered Alberto's brother.

"I can see him easy," went on Jack Smith, wrinkling his brow with the effort of mental vision. "He was mighty handsome. He always had his head up and singing a lot."

"That's enough," said Franklin through his teeth. But then he rallied his strength. "No. Go on!" he directed.

"Well," lied Jack Smith, thrilling to his rôle as he saw the effect of his acting, "this bird Pursivant didn't have any reason for hating Alberto. Not much reason. There was a girl—"

"A girl?" cried Franklin, suddenly.

"There was a girl," said Jack Smith. "You know how it is. We were all young, and some of those Mexican girls are pretty, and Pursivant got fond of one of them across the river. But all she could see was Alberto. Because Alberto had a way with the women, you know how it is."

"Yes," said Franklin, faintly.

"They got into a couple of arguments. One day they were boxing a round, just fooling, and all at once Pursivant started a real fight—and you know Alberto was pretty strong—well, he hung one on the button, and Pursivant went out like a light. Alberto was terrible sorry. He gave Pursivant a drink, and he wouldn't stop fussing around till Pursivant shook hands and said they were friends again. But I guess that Pursivant always carried a grudge around with him."

Franklin thought of that swarthy face, those bright, keen eyes. It was the very image of one who would not easily forget an injury.

"Then Pursivant was pretty well plastered, that night. I mean, he wasn't dead drunk. His feet were under him, all right. But he was sour. The booze was sour in him. And when we got the Chinks across the river, Pursivant, he wanted to go on into town, and that was crazy, because the police would of liked to get their hands on him, anyway. He'd raised too much hell in that town before. You know how it is. He was young. So Alberto started persuading him, and then took hold and held him back. And all at once—

bang! Pursivant had his gun out, and I saw Alberto go down. Pursivant seen me, then, and realized what he'd done, and he took a crack at me, but I wasn't having any of that. I dived into the water and got off. After a while, Pursivant's head cleared up and he called to me to come back. I got out of the water and sat down dripping beside Alberto. He wasn't dead, but he was dying, and Pursivant was saying nothing, and Alberto kept saying: 'Jack, never let my brother find out. Charlie didn't mean it.' He called Pursivant Charlie. He kept saying: 'Charlie didn't mean it. Charlie didn't—' "

"Get out!" commanded Franklin, rising suddenly.

For he felt the hard, cold, solid weight of conviction in his heart. He was seeing the truth, those many years and thousands of miles away—and he wanted to have the voice of the informer out of his ears until he could rally himself, and try to rebuild his faith in his friend.

"Sure I'll get out," said Jack Smith, backing towards the door. "You know how it is. I was just remembering the way things happened. Sorry you got all cut up. I know how it is. Anyway, you'll know by to-night."

"I'll know by to-night," agreed Franklin.

He saw the door close softly behind Jack Smith. Then he lowered himself into his chair once more. There was a heavy pounding in his ears that continued until, vaguely and small-voiced, the roar of the city began to rise into his consciousness once more and he felt the needs and the claims of the day coming back upon him like a soothing influence.

CHAPTER XX

TWO things hounded Pursivant all through that same day. The first was of course the dread that Franklin might be turned against him; not mere grief for the loss of his best friend but actual physical dread if Franklin's headlong anger were turned against him.

But aside from the thought of Richard Franklin there remained a dull and empty pain in the mind of Pursivant, and that was the thought of Jerry Macklin. That constant melancholy crystallized in bright flashes of memory, and however he saw Jerry Macklin a torment took hold on Pursivant.

Now that the blow had fallen and that Macklin was lost, it seemed to Pursivant that he could have foretold the thing from the start, for Macklin was the sort of a fellow who had to go down. There was too much good natured, reckless, careless boy in him. For the sake of an evening newspaper he had run his neck into danger.

Well, he might be in the bottom of the river, by this time. Or perhaps Cappen's lieutenants were keeping the traitor on a longer and more hideous trail to death. But Cappen had to die. There was only a short time remaining before the searing electric current would leap through his body and after that would come peace and, somehow, a chance to see Jacqueline Leigh again.

So Pursivant got through that day in his office like a man walking through a mist. Things began to happen soon after he had started up town.

A limousine drew up beside his car and he saw Verney waving through the side-glass. Vasco pulled over to the curb and took Verney in. The fat face of Verney was all white about the lips and red every other place.

"Take me up to your place and give me a drink," he said. "I won't ask any questions about where you've been. You may have been on the moon with the queen of Sheba, for all I care. I won't talk about your kidnapping, or whatever it was. Just make me a cocktail and let me talk about myself."

He took Verney to his place and made him a cocktail of rum and lemon juice, sweetened with apricot brandy and cointreau. Gregory shook them up till the silver was white with thick frost. Over the tops of the glasses he squeezed the pungent oil from lemon peel and served them with little anchovies on toothpicks. Verney put down three drinks in a row, hoisting his fat arm with each while he said: "Here's to crime!"

After that, the white disappeared from around his mouth. His lips loosened a significant bit and his eyes got a trifle out of focus. The late afternoon was warm, with a wind ruffling through a great bowl of yellow calliopsis.

"A fellow can talk with you, Charlie," said Verney. "You've got a mouth and you know how to keep it shut. Nobody can say anything half as good as his not saying it, and you know that. I need somebody to talk to. I'm all shot."

"Booze, money, or a girl?" asked Pursivant, brutally.

"The girl is the trick," said Verney. "A girl that won't say yes and can't say no."

"Disappear for a few days," suggested Pursivant. "That may help her to make up her mind."

He smiled a little, as he said this, but without mirth, for

the thought of Jacqueline Leigh went through him like a bullet.

"Disappearing would do me no good, when there are a hundred other men hunting her."

"There aren't a hundred other men hunting her."

"There aren't a hundred with Verney millions," said Pursivant.

"Some of 'em have a lot more money than I have. Not that she's mercenary. No, she's not that. But there's young Chet Furness out of his head about her, and he could buy me and sell me ten times over. There's that rich Englishman, Overton, ready to sail all the ships in his lines to any old port she'll name. Loftus will bury her in gold mines and railroad stocks. There are plenty others, too. Why she will keep half an eye open for me, I can't tell, but she does. I asked her the other day to be frank. She looked at me in a sad sort of way. 'I want to be frank,' she said, 'but I don't know what to say.' She's not mercenary, Charlie. Don't smile at me. I tell you, she isn't!"

"All right," said Pursivant.

"She just doesn't know. She's unawakened. That's what she is. What she said to me, she said to Stan Wiley, too. Almost the same words. Look at all the Wiley money—all the money he'll have some day. If she were mercenary—well, wouldn't Wiley be the man for her?"

The name of Stan Wiley struck a nerve center in Pursivant.

"Who's the girl?" he asked.

"Why, you know her. You met her out at my place. Jacqueline Leigh is her name. You've been out of town while she's driven me crazy. She had a birthday, a while ago. Raeburn sent her his emeralds. You know the Raeburn emeralds? He sent them over for a birthday gift. But there's nothing mercenary about her. She sent 'em back. Listen to that, Charlie, and call her mercenary if you can!"

Pursivant heard only part of the words and followed their meaning only half a step. Whatever she said to other men, he could have sworn that he had been deep in her mind that other night when they were driving from Oyster Point.

"Do you know where she lives?" asked Pursivant.

"Sure. Twelve Culver Square. What I want to know from you is how to wake her up? How can a fellow shake a girl like that out of the trance?"

And Verney was thick-lipped and cheerful when Pursivant at last took him to the front door and saw him walk past the immobile face of Gregory and down the steps to his limousine, which had trailed him uptown. Still in the open doorway, Pursivant watched the car drive off and then told Gregory to bring him his hat.

Gregory brought it.

"If you are going out, sir," said Gregory, "possibly you'll be better off if I go along?"

"Why do you say that?" asked Pursivant. "Do you think that I'm hunting trouble every hour of every day?"

"No, sir," answered Gregory, "but I thought that trouble might be hunting you. The house is being watched, for one thing."

"By whom?" asked Pursivant.

"Now and then an automobile goes by, very slowly. Not the same machine but usually with the same man in it. Handsome, sleek-looking young man in a grey suit, sir. And there's always someone in one of the windows that look down on the back yard of the house."

"I suppose they're watching. Of course they'll watch till Cappen goes up Salt Creek. Let them watch and be damned. Cappen is going to burn and then—" He finished off with a gesture. "Don't worry about me, Gregory. I'm going across town, and I think I'll find some happiness at the end of my walk."

At the foot of the steps he looked back and saw Gregory closing the door slowly, reluctantly. "There," thought Pursivant, "is one piece of the true steel. They can never buy him away from me!"

And he struck off across town towards Culver Square, with a nervous, tiptoe anticipation increasing in him every step of the way. His heart lightened like a bubble and floated higher and higher in his throat. Then he turned out of the great rushing and humming of a main avenue of traffic into the quiet of Culver Square.

Culver Square was a still inlet between two large rivers of sound. It was always empty. One never saw an automobile turn into it. One never saw a child playing behind the iron fence of the park, though every householder around the square had a key to the gate. The people of Culver Square seemed entirely respectable but not entirely alive. Once all the houses had been of red brick faced with white stone, an endless chain of primness, but now there were half a dozen apartment houses lifting high shoulders above the crowd. Number Twelve was one of the taller buildings.

In the calmness of Culver Square, the doubts of Pursivant flickered out of his mind. If Jacqueline Leigh had told both fat-faced Christopher Verney and Stan Wiley that she could not make up her mind about either of them, it simply meant, probably, that she did not know how to tell them the truth without hurting their feelings.

He turned in under the brown awning of Number Twelve and asked the Negro doorman to announce Mr. Pursivant to Miss Jacqueline Leigh. The doorman stepped to a pretty little fuzzy-headed mulatto who sat in a uniform in front of her switch-board.

"Mr. Charles W. Pursivant," said the doorman, with unnecessary loudness, "to see Miss Leigh."

The girl flashed one glance at the big negro and then gave her down-headed smile to the switchboard.

At the end of the entrance hall with its sheen of granite and of marble pilasters, an elevator door clanked open and young Archie Dexter came out in a dinner jacket and an opera hat, crunching a pair of yellow chamois gloves in his left hand and swinging a walking stick until it flashed like a sword. His hat sat back at a happy angle. His face was flushed. He was so filled with content that he seemed about to break out into laughter. And he walked straight by his clubfellow, Pursivant, blind to his existence.

As Pursivant started for the elevator, he knew that the doorman was exchanging looks with the switchboard girl again. "Take Mr. Pursivant up to Number Seven," said the doorman.

The elevator boy did not quite smile. He avoided that by tucking in the corners of his mouth. But Pursivant's brain was once more in a whirl. Somehow he did not need to be told that Archie Dexter, who lived far up the avenue, had just descended from a visit at Number Seven; it was not liquor that had intoxicated Archie. Had he been hearing that Jacqueline Leigh could not quite make up her mind?

The great thing was not to be a blind fool. A man in love is always blind and to him devils appear to be angels. Pursivant kept on arming himself in calmness. The elevator stopped; the door of Number Seven was opened by Mrs. Helen Leigh, in a black lace dress, with her grey hair knotted in a chignon. He was relieved by the sight of her broad, ugly face, colored only by a healthy tan; her homeliness seemed to be equal parts respectability and good sense.

He apologized for calling so late. He would only trouble them for five minutes.

She closed the door behind him, looking right up into his face.

"Of course you're welcome," she said. "Jacqueline is so happy that you've come."

She took him into a room that was all French grey, rugs, walls, and curtains, with a big pot of pink azaleas filling the fireplace, and the quiet, the comfort, the order soothed him; the radiant face of Archie Dexter began to grow dim and fade out of his memory.

The maid was dressing Jacqueline, Mrs. Leigh said. They were hurrying as fast as they could.

"Are you sure she holds no grudge because I wouldn't help Cappen?" he asked her, bluntly.

"Don't you see that we understand?" said Mrs. Leigh. "We're the only people in the world, perhaps, who know the good in Arthur Cappen. We can't expect other people to see anything except the evil in him. We're sick at heart, but —may I make a cocktail for you?"

He thanked her and watched the hand that she pressed against the bell. It was a hand twenty years younger than Mrs. Leigh's face. Her soul was young, too, he felt, and strong and living. When a servant came, she ordered a tray to make dry martinis; she asked for curaçao.

"That takes the edge and the horror out of the gin," she said.

Pursivant was amused. If only the room could be freed of ghosts! If only the images of Archie Dexter and fat-faced Chris Verney, and big Stan Wiley would vanish utterly!

"I was looking at my Jacqueline book," said Mrs. Leigh.

"Do you want to see it? I know most photographs are a frightful bore, but Jacqueline—"

He sat down beside her on the davenport while she held the small black album and turned the pages. Every woman has to have her vanity. Mrs. Leigh had set off the smallness of her feet in black satin slippers that had bright buckles of paste; and as she turned the pages of the album, the polish of her nails kept flashing red across the eyes of Pursivant. The album was not such a bore as most. All the pictures were clear and they were all enlargements, one to a page. Above all, they were of Jacqueline. There was Jacqueline smiling out of furs, Jacqueline wind-blown at the wheel of a sloop, bracing herself on the slant of the deck. There was Jacqueline lounging in the summer ease of a rose arbor, and even a glimpse of her in a bathing suit. Mrs. Leigh turned that page hastily and glanced up in embarrassment at Pursivant, but he smiled at her.

"Why not?" he said. "Statues are never immodest—not if they come from a good period."

"Oh," said Mrs. Leigh, and seemed to consider that remark for a moment. She even tried to smile in turn, but made a bad job of it. After all, a woman ought to be modest. The damned flappers and their flippers—Pursivant was sick of them.

She had the book open at a picture of the girl jumping a big hunter over a stiff gate. She rode side-saddle—of course, thought Pursivant—and she was a horsewoman. She was in perfect balance, though she had just let out the head of the horse at the top of the jump; she would have him in a steadying pull the moment he landed. Pursivant held down that page with the tip of his finger so that he could have a good look.

"Yes," said Mrs. Leigh, when he took his finger away. "I like that one, too."

Then there was one of Jacqueline in a Spanish costume with a thin shadow of lace over her head. Mrs. Leigh would have turned that quickly, too, but Pursivant stopped the page again. For Jacqueline was no statue, here. She was not merely brightening towards a smile; the smile itself was there, a bit askance. And suddenly Pursivant jerked up his head as the memory began to grow up out of the twilight of his past.

Back there at the Verney place it had been a ghostly touch, a fleeting gesture of thought, but now he knew that the clue was almost in his grasp. That faint babble of a foreign tongue that surrounded the old picture was identified, now. It was Spanish that he had heard, and the moment he was sure of that he knew with absolute certainty that he *had* seen Jacqueline Leigh before—but all changed from what she seemed to-day.

She came in at that moment. He stood up and looked at the airy flowing of her dress of sea-green chiffon. The pearls were very white against the bronze of her throat and she wore her hair in a great carefully woven braid about her head, a coronet heavy as metal. But only a dim portion of his senses was aware of this new picture; all the rest of him was striving so hard with the past that the effort turned him to stone. The girl paused and looked wonderingly towards Mrs. Leigh who seemed—or was that a trick of his fancy?—to make a warning gesture.

Fancy or not, that gesture scattered the mists and he saw again the café beside the Rio Grande, the big old trees, the lantern that hung from the lower branches and made the foliage half luminous green, half deeper shadow. He saw the men at the little round tables. It was all so clear that he could see again the thin green-white of the tequila in the glasses; the taste of the stuff came back with a tingle on his palate; he heard the quiver of the mandolins and above all the quick clashing of the castanets as the dancer whirled and swayed among the tables, laughing, her eyes busier with the men than with her song.

"Mary Carthy!" said Pursivant.

He stepped back out of the distance and into the little room in discreet French grey. All the dream was gone and there remained before him the face of Mrs. Helen Leigh, now puckered and withering with malice.

The servant came in with glasses shivering together on the tray. He put down his burden on the table and went hurriedly out from the silence.

Mary Carthy had been relaxing all this while; a few inches of dignity seemed to have melted out of her.

"Oh, all right," she said. "If you hold that expression another minute more, Helen, your face will break. After all, I told you and Cappen that this hombre would see around the corner, before long. Charlie, shake up a drink. You look as though you need one. What I win out of all this is a chance to have a smoke, thank God!"

"Jacqueline, be silent! Where are your—what do you mean by this?—Jacqueline, go to your room!"

"Oh, quit it," said Mary Carthy. She slid into a chair and crossed her legs. She leaned back at ease and picked a cigarette case off the table. Pursivant walked out of his trance and lighted the smoke for her. "Quit it, Helen," repeated Mary Carthy. "He's on the inside. I knew he couldn't be so dumb all his life. I told you that. I told Cappen, too."

"You fool!" gasped Mrs. Helen Leigh. "You red-headed—you fool! You damned, red-headed little rat! What are you doing to me?"

Mary Carthy inhaled her cigarette smoke and, as she blew it out again, through the pale drift smiled up towards Pursivant.

"She'll quiet down in a little while," she said. "Then we can be comfortable. Helen, ring up Buddy Lancaster and tell him that I've got a frightful headache. Tell him I'm so sorry. I'm sick about it, but I can't go to-night. Shake up a drink, Charlie. Don't look so stony. Here, I'll mix them myself. Helen, pull yourself out of the uglies and try to be human. Nothing is lost except honor."

She went to the tray of drinks. Mrs. Leigh gripped her head with both hands and then ran to the door.

"Wait a minute!" called the voice of the girl. "Stop there a minute. I told you to ring up Buddy Lancaster. That's the only one you'll ring up. Get that straight. Don't telephone twice! You've ruined your chignon. Fix it before you come back. Charlie hates a brawl."

Mrs. Leigh waited to the end of this speech, her face shuddering with beginnings of words that never were uttered. Then she slammed the door.

"She'll be all right," said Mary Carthy. "She thinks that you've undone several years' work for her, all in a moment. She doesn't understand."

She was busily at work with her slender brown hands all this while. Now she shook the drink up until the silver shaker was white with frost. She filled a glass and brought it to Pursivant.

"I'll wait for the second one," he said.

"Don't be silly," said the girl. "Polish it off. I know how you feel. You've been wasting serious thought on a dancing girl, and you need a drink. Here's to you, old son!"

She made a slight gesture with the shaker, and he swallowed the drink. The dry curaçao had in fact taken the horror out of the gin. He found himself thinking of neither Richard Franklin nor Arthur Cappen, but only of the curious smoothness of the cocktail.

She filled the glass again, and he drank it off once more.

"Sit down," said Mary Carthy.

He sat down in the big easy chair beside the pink cloud of azaleas. She brought him a cigarette, lighted it, put an ash tray on the arm of the chair.

"Where shall I sit?" she asked. "Do you like me in a bright light or more in shadow. How would this be, say?" She pulled up a fire bench before him and slipped down on it. "Of course I'm a rat," she explained, "but I want you to think that I'm a pretty rat. Are you going to talk to me at all? Do you want to strangle me, or just curse me? It's your right. Only don't walk out on me. I'm fighting for my life."

"I won't walk out on you," said Pursivant.

"Thanks," said Mary Carthy. "How much rope are you going to give me?"

He tried to think. His brain moved very slowly, but the pain was not a thing of the mind only. It filled his entire body.

"I'm still seeing double," he said. "There's still a vision in the back of my mind of a Jacqueline Leigh who is breaking her heart because Arthur Cappen is getting closer and closer to the electric chair. And here's another one who—"

He paused.

"It's exciting, isn't it?" said Jacqueline Leigh. "I don't know which horse to bet on—Arthur or the electric chair. If he burns, you've done it to him; but why should I break my heart because he invested an idea and some hard cash in my future. Let's forget about him for a minute. You know about me now, Charles. I'm a gold-digger, a diamond expert, anything you want to call me, and you can blow me to bits by letting the world know that I'm Mary Carthy. Go on, Charles. Tell me how much rope you're going to give me; or are you going to smash me right now, flat?"

"I ought to ask you one thing," he said. "Some people I know—like poor Verney and Stan Wiley and some others—they're rather serious about you, Mary."

"Ah, I see what you mean," said the girl. "I won't marry any of them. Will you believe that? On my honor! But I shouldn't use that word, of course. I won't rob your friends. List them down and they're safe."

"I think—yes, I think I can believe you," said Pursivant. "I've always wanted to believe you, you know."

She jumped up from the bench, crying softly: "Ah, Charlie, what a good fellow you are! What a kind, straight-shooting fellow you are! Let me—well, you have another drink?"

"There's some whiskey, yonder. May I have a whack at that?"

She put the whiskey bottle on a smoking stand beside his chair, with a fresh glass.

"Straight, I suppose?" she said. "That's the old Western style."

He drank it straight, lifting the glass silently to her, and she through the wisps of the blue cigarette smoke studied him. The light struck the metal sheen of her hair and glanced across the brown of her shoulder.

"Will you tell me something?" she asked.

"Yes," he said. "That's the best way. I want to keep on talking."

"Then, the other night, it wasn't shamming? You did care about me a bit?"

He smiled at her. Even the smiling was painful. He hoped the liquor would get some color up into his face.

"No, you weren't shamming. I know, because I can still feel your voice in me. I wasn't shamming, either."

"No?" said Pursivant.

"Not altogether," said Mary Carthy. "I knew there was no one like you because you were the man who had beaten Cappen; but I didn't need reasons—"

"Wait just a moment, Mary," he said.

"I'm sorry," she said, gently. "You're tearing me out of your mind, and it hurts a little."

"A good bit," said Pursivant. "The whiskey helps, though."

He filled the glass again.

"Talk it right out at me," said Mary. "I wish you could say it all out at me, no matter what the words have to be. Will you tell me what you're thinking of?"

"I'm thinking about other men," said Pursivant.

Her eyes closed and her face tipped back until the light streamed over it. That was acting, no doubt.

After a moment she drew a breath.

"You *do* like me a good bit," she said. "And I like you—so much that the other night when you told me things I had to hold hard to keep from letting you have the truth. If it does any good, I can tell you one thing that's straight—when you think of all the other men—I mean, not one of them has ever touched me. Will you believe that?"

Pursivant said nothing.

"Ah God, ah God!" said the girl. "Helen was right when she said that I'm just a red-headed rat, and I know it, but I've told you true. Will you believe me?"

"Yes," said Pursivant.

She caught her breath on a sob.

"Steady," said Pursivant.

"All right," said Mary Carthy. "It's self pity that makes a

girl cry. I'm through with it. Talk of something else. Make me talk of something else."

He could not help saying: "Jack Smith, for instance." And she winced, but took up the thread which he had offered.

"He said you turned into a tiger when he mentioned Richard Franklin, that night at Oyster Point," she declared. "Franklin—you really love him, don't you, Charlie?"

He could feel the whiskey all through him; it was fingering his brain, numbing it a little.

"He's my friend," said Pursivant, carefully, "but I'm not big enough in the soul to love him as he ought to be loved."

"You mean that?" said the girl. "You think he's a bigger fellow than you are?"

Pursivant smiled.

"Well," she said, "no matter what happens, I'm going to tell you. They're trying harder than ever to get between you and Franklin."

"I know that," he answered, "but thank you."

"Will you turn me in," she said, "or give me a chance to get out of town?"

He hesitated. "I haven't kept any of the stuff they've sent me," she broke in. "When I started gold digging I wanted to do it in a big way. I've sent everything back to them, except flowers."

"I don't think I need to turn you in," said Pursivant. "As long as there's no marriage in the air—well, men have to learn about the other things, and pay for the knowledge, I suppose."

"All my cards are on the table. You name the ones you want to see," she said.

That was when the door flung open and Mrs. Helen Leigh came in, banging it behind her. She had been drinking. The ruined chignon had not been repaired. She walked with the step of one prepared to encounter trouble.

"The band is going to play 'Home, Sweet Home,'" said the girl. "You'd better go."

CHAPTER XXI

ONE glance was enough to throw at Mrs. Helen Leigh; then Pursivant studied the girl and saw that she was merely curious and a little disgusted as she watched the older woman.

That was why Pursivant said to Helen Leigh: "I know the sort of trouble that I could make but I don't think I'll make it; if that interests you."

It interested Mrs. Leigh so much that it staggered her to a halt and left her rather agape. She went over to the cocktail tray and poured herself a glass of pure gin which she tossed off and stood for a moment to regard the emptiness of the glass afterwards.

"Jacqueline," said Mrs. Leigh, "am I hearing right or am I cock-eyed?"

Mary Carthy said nothing at all; she just kept on looking at Mrs. Leigh with the air of one who understands without being pleased.

"Pursivant," said Mrs. Leigh, "you've broken the ice. You've smashed it all to pieces. Are you going to let it freeze again?"

"If that's a favor," answered Pursivant, "will you tell me how this game started?"

Mrs. Leigh lighted a cigarette and inhaled the smoke so eagerly that a long bright coal was glowing immediately. Little flakes of ash fell down towards the floor and some of them rested unobserved on the bosom of the black lace dress.

"The cards are faces up, Helen," said Mary Carthy.

"Does that mean that he gives us a break?" asked Mrs. Leigh, in a great voice.

"It does," said the girl.

"From the minute I laid eyes on you," declared Mrs. Leigh to Pursivant, "I knew you were the whitest damned man that I ever saw. You want to know what's what, do you? Well, I'll tell you! Casa del Ray was the start of it, right there on the old Rio Grande. You saw her, there. So did I, but I had the eye. I'd only been getting about ten weeks a season on the small time. There's nothing like that to sharpen the eye, and when I saw that red hair and those blue eyes and watched the dance steps for a few minutes—and when I saw her giving the eye to a lot of vaqueros and cheap cow-punchers and sourdoughs—I knew that something ought to be done about it. I got hold of her and we had a talk. Then I discovered that she had a brain, too. She was holding down her job by making all the boys happy and keeping away from the whole gang of them. She was a good girl. G—O—O—D, is the way you spell that word. Another way of spelling it is B—R—A—I—N—S. She had looks and brains. I had brains and an idea. Put the two together and all we needed was time and capital. Do you follow that?"

Pursivant looked at the girl and nodded; the girl looked at the floor and said nothing. Mrs. Helen Leigh took the center of the stage and poured herself another drink.

"That poor kid talked like a cow-hand," she said. "And she had the manners of a long-horn steer. She needed polishing before she'd be the key to the big bank accounts. Not just a little. A long, hard job. If she couldn't be the real thing, she had to be plated so deep that nobody would know; acid wouldn't burn through to the brass. It meant money; it meant work. I got Arthur Cappen to put up the hard cash and I put in the hard work. She was fifteen when I first saw her. She's twenty-four today. And she and I have worked like a devil in between. That's the story. Are you bored?"

"I've probably heard all I need to know," said Pursivant, rising.

Mary Carthy lifted her hand. "Helen wants to talk; you want to listen. Stay and hear it out," she said. "Helen is proud of herself."

"One hundred per cent," said Mrs. Leigh. "I saw the job from beginning to end, and I went after it. Look here—you saw her back there on the Rio Grande. Pretty, that was all she was. Now see what I've made of her!"

She caught up the album of photographs and opened it to the picture that had been taken beside the sea.

"Look at the way that neck comes out of the shoulders," she directed. "Look at the way the head sits on the neck. God, you say. Well, partly God and partly Helen Leigh. Look at those arms—no fat and no muscle bulges, either. Look at those legs. What percentage of a girl's charm is tied up in her legs, I ask you? And if you think God made those legs, you're a half-wit. Nine years of Helen Leigh did that. But don't pin yourself down to points. See the whole picture. Long and slender. That's the modern taste. But everything rounded. No corners. God? Rot! It's hard work that does it. Nine years of hard work. It only took ten to capture Troy!"

She began to laugh. The gin was already in her voice.

"I have to go along," said Pursivant.

"Stay and hear the whole story," said the girl quietly. "There's a lot more of it."

"The body's only one thing. The brain's the big bet," said Helen Leigh. "Where would she get off with some bright young millionaire who's been educated in France, Italy, Germany and what not? She had to know how to talk about

Burgundies with the *sommelier* in his own language. She had to learn how to make a black sauce and when to order it. Books, too. These modern brats are full of books. They throw the classics at you one minute and talk Proust at you the next. God help me from going through the Dante days again! But I held the book on her till she got the famous passages pat. Poets aren't the whole thing, either. You meet your logical billionaire, now and then. Some dithering blighter talks Plato from the Charmides to the Laws. So that had to be sketched through; and history. And travel with a guide book and a guide, a camera and a notebook. She knows the faces of the cathedrals as well as she knows the faces of men. She can tell you how Old Norman branches off from Late What-not. She did ancient China as deep as porcelain and paint, and God didn't help me while she was going through it.

"Nine years!

"Deportment, too. Do you think a girl is born with a knowledge of how to stand up and sit down, how to walk, how to talk? She had brains. Had to have brains for the smart boys. But never show knowledge till you have to, or it scares the dummies away. And the fools are always the ninety per cent.

"She had to learn the world, too. That was where I helped most. Do your murder in the dark. Don't steal because it's better to take it as a gift. Don't covet anything that's not convertible. Sleep six days and collect for seven nights. Forget your home town before it has a chance to remember you. She had to get things like that, and remember that a man in the hand is worth ten in the heart.

"It cost nine years of my work, and how much cash it cost Arthur Cappen for travel, schools, tutors, clothes, and all the rest, he can tell you. It was plenty. But Cappen was willing to spend and I was willing to hold out my salary and wait. When we collect, it's going to be sweet. She's going to skim the cream and let the milk stand to get sour. She's twenty-four, and she's been saved all this while. She's still good. G-O-O-D! Don't you laugh when you hear that, Pursivant? She's been trained for the minute, and now the minute has come. It's millions, my lad. The moment we say the word, she begins to take the ready cash. And after a while, if we find a man old enough not to last and with enough millions, we may even let her marry! Millions, Pursivant. And since you've come in with us, you get your split. We know a good man when we see one."

"Thank you," said Pursivant. "But suppose that the whole thing went up in smoke—suppose that she fell in love with some poor bank clerk on twenty dollars a week?"

"Love?" said Helen Leigh. "Love?"

She began to laugh so heartily that she had to grip the back of a chair and as she rocked back and forth her hair loosened more and more and fluffed wildly out about her face and hung in strings around her neck.

"Love?" she cried. "Man alive, do you think that she's learned how to diet on whole wheat bread and fruit so that she can fall in love? Do you think she's starved her body and worked it like a Spartan for the sake of marrying some dummy? Love? Has she worked herself groggy on swimming, dancing, tennis, golf, riding, boating for the sake of love? Has she got a gymnasium in the next room from a rowing machine to parallel bars for the sake of love? Jacqueline, help me laugh! I'm all out of breath!"

Pursivant stood up. He needed a drink, but he shuddered at the thought of taking another in that room. The walls were closing in on him; the ceiling dropped lower; the air was old and stale. For the girl was laughing more loudly than Helen Leigh.

She stepped to the table and offered the glass and the bottle.

"Have a shot, Charlie!" she called to him.

"No thanks!" said Pursivant.

"A stirrup cup!" said Mary Carthy. "Well, I'll have a dash myself. And here's to you, Charlie!"

She began to sing in the true Highland brogue:

" 'Twas on a Monday morning,
Richt early in the year,
That Charlie cam' to our toun,
The young Chevalier.

And Charlie he's my darling,
My darling, my darling;
Charlie he's my darling,
The young Chevalier."

"I've got to go," said Pursivant. "All been very interesting. Goodbye, Mrs. Leigh. I won't be talking in the street. Goodbye, Mary."

But the voice of Mary Carthy still was swinging easily through the difficult rhythm of the old song, the high notes coming as carelessly as the smiles on her lips:

"As he was walkin' up the street
The city for to view,
Oh, there he spied a bonny lass
The window lookin' through."

She broke the strain for an instant to cry: "Don't go, Charlie! Stay a while. One last drink with Mary to show that we're all friends!"

Mrs. Leigh was laughing more hoarsely and heavily than before. "Oh, stay and have a shot, Pursivant!" she urged.

But Pursivant was already bowing himself through the door, with Mrs. Leigh making only a half-hearted effort to show him out, while it seemed from the back-tilted head of the girl that the song was sweeping her away, and leaving the rest of the world an oblivion before her.

"Sae licht's he jumped up the stair,
An' tirled at the pin;
And wha sae ready as hersel'
To let the laddie in?

He set his Jenny on his knee,
All in his Hieland dress;
For brawly weel he kenned the way
To please a bonny lass."

Pursivant, at the elevator door, pressing the bell, remembered the walking stick he had left behind him, and since the latch of the apartment door had not clicked, he turned back as the elevator commenced to rise and heard the last stanza of the song faint behind the wall, but as full of the jolly rhythm as ever.

"It's up yon heathery mountain,
And down yon scroggy glen,
We daurna gang a-milkin'
For Charlie and his men."

He pushed the door open, gently, and heard the chorus come rollicking:

"And Charlie he's my darling,
My darling, my darling,
Charlie he's my darling,
The young Chevalier!"

But as the song ended, another and very unexpected sound reached the ear of Pursivant, and as the draught blew in from the outer hall it swayed open a little the door of the front room. That showed him Mary Carthy flinging herself on the davenport, and as she lay there sobbing, Mrs. Leigh stood over her, looking down with a face from which the jollity had not yet gone, the astonishment had not yet fully entered.

Pursivant got his stick from the rack and drew hastily back into the hall. He pressed the front door firmly shut, taking care that the latch should engage without a sound. The swift shadow of the elevator brushed up, slowed, and paused behind the glass doors. Presently he was again stepping into Culver Square. The city smoke had turned into rain clouds. He took off his hat and let the drops fall on his face, but still the world that housed him seemed to be as small and stifling a box as the little room in French grey.

CHAPTER XXII

WHEN Pursivant turned the last corner towards his house, he saw a familiar silhouette come out into the light of the street lamp. It was Jack Smith, coming up cautiously, with small steps, like one ready to jump and flee.

Pursivant said: "All right, Jack. You're not a sandwich man yet, I see. When the salt burns Cappen, I hope you don't come on any bad days."

Something in this speech so stung Jack that he shouted, suddenly: "You gotta tongue in your head like a native Malay nigger. Can't you talk decent to a man?"

Pursivant said, laughing a little: "I'm sorry, Jack. I didn't want to hurt your feelings. I didn't know that you had any." For it was almost pleasant to leave his thoughts for the sake of even a Jack Smith.

"Yeah, you didn't know I had any, didn't you?" said Jack Smith. "I come here waiting to tell you that I was sorry that you put my back to the wall. But now I'm gunna go the whole hog and tell you the facts. The letter and the gun are in the evening mail for Franklin. They're waiting at his house for him right now, and as soon as he comes home, he'll have the dope. Put that in your pipe and choke on it, and be damned to you, you smart-cracker!"

He went off, hastily, jerking his head to look over his shoulder as though he were afraid that he might be pursued. But Pursivant did not move. It had been bad enough to know that the event was going forward, but the reality stunned him.

He saw the picture of the small white house, overhung by

the electric-lighted gloom of the big apartment houses on either side. He saw Franklin opening the heavy package with strong, swift hands, and looking at the C.W.P. which was carved into the butt of the gun. Things would start moving quickly, then. Very quickly, indeed.

He saw with perfect clarity, also, that there was only one thing for him to do, and that was to get across the town to the white house and try to steal the fatal package before Franklin put his hands upon it. Jack Smith had said a little too much. He had said "when" Franklin got home. Well, that meant that Franklin was out, and that there was still time.

A cruising taxi picked him up, let him down two blocks from the address, and hummed away, and Pursivant went up the street in a small rain that was clotting on the pavement in little irregular patches of brightness. He stepped into the thicker shadow behind which lay the face of the little white house.

The mail would be upstairs in Franklin's own room—where the pictures of Alberto stood! Pursivant took off his shoes, touched the comfortable weight of his gun, and then climbed a narrow porch pillar to the slant of the roof above. A step among the entangled ampelopsis stems brought him to the right window. One light, burning inside, showed him the afternoon mail heaped on the table beside the bed. Usually Franklin lay down, when he reached the house, and went through his letters with his body, at least, relaxed. Aside from the letters was one long and narrow package.

The window, luckily, made no noise. When it was raised, he slipped through into the close warmth of the room, with a thin, sweet smell of cookery tainting the air. The picture of Alberto looked at him out of its golden frame.

He turned his back on that faintly sneering smile. Downstairs there was a dim and purposeless stir of voices, but they would not disturb him during the few minutes he needed. The package went into his pocket. Rapidly he slipped the envelopes, one after another, until he found the big, familiar sprawl of Jack Smith. He ripped the paper open. A drop of sweat from his forehead spatted on another letter. He stepped back from the table and read the opening lines.

It was the right letter, so it went into his pocket and he was out the window, down the roof, and standing again on the ground in a moment. Then his shoes were on; he was standing on the little central path.

If he were seen, now, he could say that he had stepped by to speak to Franklin, but had changed his mind. But nobody saw him. He left the garden, closed the gate safely behind him, and got into a taxi half a block away. That cab he left when it had taken him close to the river.

A man had to work fast and on the spur of the moment. That was the point. But action could trouble even a gang like that of Arthur Cappen!

He walked across the city to the river. As he stepped out on the slow arch of the first bridge, lifting gradually above the water, he saw the night settling and the smoke of the town rising up to meet it. The future seemed to Pursivant a picture of equal confusion. Jacqueline might be gone in fact, but not in thought. The electric current had not yet shocked the life from Cappen. And then there was Merrill, who would have started back the moment he knew of Cappen's imprisonment. He never had seen Merrill but he had heard that the man was a partner quite equal to Cappen. If the fellow decided that he had an outstanding score to settle, Pursivant's days on earth were probably numbered even after Cappen's death.

The wisest thing for him to do, he knew, was to keep

away from Jacqueline Leigh; but he could not do that. His mind kept turning to her like a Mahommedan towards the East.

He was out on the crest of the bridge, now, and he leaned beside the guard rail for a moment. A tug went past, hurrying down the river with its smoke making a broad stroke of charcoal in the windless air. Pursivant let the gun in its box slip out of his hand. As it dropped, he could hardly believe that it was bound for oblivion. It had too much meaning. It seemed as though the very birds of the air should have sense enough to stoop at it, and snatch it away.

It struck; a small, dim leap of water marked the spot; then there was no token.

A large hand gripped the arm of Pursivant. He turned towards the towering shoulders of a big policeman.

"What was that you dropped, Johnny?" asked the man of the law.

He drew back and saluted, instantly. "Beg your pardon, Mr. Pursivant," he said. He waited for no answer, but turned sharply on his heel and strode away, making his shoulders higher and squarer than ever. It was plain that he did not wish to embarrass the great or the near-great; but nevertheless Pursivant felt that a bird *had* stooped at his mystery and snatched it out of the air.

Keen minds can decipher a great many things from their small beginnings. After all, what might a wrapped package of that size contain, other than a gun? Out of this, a story might be made intact for the ears of a judge and a jury.

He turned back towards the city, frowning. He was losing his touch, his wit, his adroitness, he felt. Ten years ago he had come to the town as lean as a wolf in winter and as wary and keen. Today, he stood like a blind fool and let a policeman walk up to him in the vital moment. He still felt the tingle that had passed along his nerves when he first saw the broad expanse of blue uniform. Only fools forget the power of the law, he felt, but wise men remember the dread or the comfort of it. He might have been kinder to Jack Smith. A couple of drinks and a bit of hard cash would have turned the edge of Jack's malice, perhaps. Crooks are the most human people in the world.

CHAPTER XXIII

WHEN Pursivant got home, the door was fairly jerked open in front of him by Gregory.

"There's a man in here waiting for you, sir," said Gregory. And his wandering eye, as it roved over Pursivant, plainly showed relief at having him back.

"Just a man?" said Pursivant.

"Not, sir, a gentleman," said Gregory, firmly. "Perhaps I should wait at the door?"

"Keep out of the way," said Pursivant, and going into the front room, he confronted that dapper young man in the same dapper grey suit, the youth with the large head and the small neck and the long, plastered hair who had come tapping down the stairs on a well-remembered day to say that he was Adolph Quillan.

"Hello," said Pursivant. "I might say that I'm a little surprised to see you."

"Are you, Mr. Pursivant?" answered the other. He leaned his glance on Pursivant in the confidential way that could be remembered. "Just a bit of business brought me up here, you see."

He stood beside his chair. Now and then, as he talked, he bowed a little, and his left hand kept gathering the open flaps of his coat, not in embarrassment, but in excess of surety. He was like an actor trying to fill out a small part and without the needed lines for doing it.

"I don't know your name," said Pursivant.

"Ah, well," said the stranger, with a graceful and forgiving gesture, "just call me Bert."

"Bert, what's your business. It has to be enough to keep me from sending for the police. Let's have it."

"It's good enough for that," said Bert. "The fact is that some of the fellows on the inside—some in the top flight—have begun to think that Cappen won't get out of the can, after all. In that case, why should we tap Jerry Macklin on the head? You can follow that?"

"Sit down," said Pursivant. "Sit down and have a drink."

"No, Mr. Pursivant, I won't drink. After business, but never during hours. You know—we have to have a few rules."

"What about Macklin?"

"Good fellow, isn't he?" remarked Bert. "Jerry's one of the best. That's why I don't want to see him put out like a light. I talked it over with some of the heads, and they agree. We might as well make a little quick profit and turn Jerry over to you."

The relief of Pursivant was so immense that he half closed his eyes, for a moment. He could see, suddenly, that this was to be one of his red-letter days. He had settled the matter of the gun; now he was to settle the fate of poor Jerry Macklin.

"What do you call a little quick profit?" asked Pursivant.

"Ten thousand," said Bert.

Pursivant laughed. "Jerry's a good lad, but he's nothing to me. I might pay you twenty-five hundred more for luck than for Jerry."

"Oh, I see," murmured Bert, gently. "We were wrong; that was all. We all make mistakes."

He started for the door.

"Or, for that matter," said Pursivant, "maybe I would make it five."

"Thanks a lot," murmured Bert. "I understand exactly how

it is, Mr. Pursivant. If it were just me, I'd take the money. But there are a lot of us gambling on the chance that Cappen will never walk out of that prison. That's the reason we're willing to make this little deal. But anything under ten thousand wouldn't be worth while to us. You can see that—a man of your brains! No? Well, then, good-night, sir!"

He half opened the door into the hall.

"Did you call, sir?" said the harsh voice of Gregory, just beyond.

Bert stopped short. His grey eyes flashed once from side to side. He stood still and looked straight before him.

"You see how it could be—a fellow of your brains?" said Pursivant, ironically.

"I see how it could be," answered Bert, gravely.

"But I won't do it," said Pursivant. "I'm writing you a check for five thousand dollars, instead."

"And why not?" said Bert, instantly at ease again. He closed the door, turning back into the room. "I call it a pity when a couple of fellows in the know can't do business with one another, even when they get a slow start."

Pursivant, at the center table, wrote out the check to cash. He put the check in his pocket. He took the automatic from beneath the pit of his left arm and put the gun into his coat pocket. He kept his finger on the weapon.

"You understand?" said Pursivant. "We're going to do this together."

"Of course I understand," said Bert, resting his eyes calmly on that bulging pocket. "We'll see it through shoulder to shoulder."

Under the silent, protesting eye of Gregory, Pursivant left the house with his companion. It was only six blocks, said Bert, and they might as well walk it. But those blocks were long ones, right across the town to a quiet side street near the river, with scores of old stone houses marching their identical steps down to the street.

When Bert halted, he said: "Here it is, Mr. Pursivant. I'll go up first and—"

"No, no, Bert," answered Pursivant. "I like your company so damned well that I think we'd better stay here together."

"Not go in?" answered Bert, with his invincible and quiet assurance. "Why have it exactly your own way, Mr. Pursivant. You'll help us bring poor Jerry down the steps though, won't you? You'll come up to the door? Jerry's a bit used up."

"I'll bet he is," agreed Pursivant. "But I'm not going any closer to that door. Just let them know that we're here."

He pushed the muzzle of the gun against the ribs of Bert. "You know," he added, "that I'm jumping at the first stump I see?"

"Oh, well, if you feel that way about it—" said Bert; and tilting back his head suddenly, he whistled.

It would not have surprised Pursivant if a burst of machine gun fire had answered that signal. He edged closer in behind his companion, and saw a shade of a first floor window raised. Behind it shadows stirred. Then, against the glass, appeared a blank, white, staring face.

It was Jerry Macklin, with the brain out of him!

His gaping visage disappeared. "Why the devil did they do that?" muttered Bert, aloud.

The front door opened. Three men came out, supporting the limp, sagging body of Macklin, walking him loosely forward.

"One is enough," said Pursivant. "Send the others back."

There was an instant of pause. Then Bert said through his teeth. "Go back, the rest of you. Bill, bring him down here."

The whole trio halted and stared, gloomily. But presently two of them went back, slowly.

"Inside the house," commanded Pursivant.

"Inside the house," repeated Bert. The two disappeared through the front door, as Pursivant waved at a speeding taxi and saw it deflect towards him.

Bill, a powerful brute of a man, got Macklin safely down to the pavement. It was a horrible thing to see the head of Macklin wavering from side to side, or to look into his dead, senseless eyes. It seemed possible to Pursivant that he had been fatally drugged. Morphine, perhaps, given in such a dose that the man would die after he reached the hands of his friend.

"Bill, you go back into the house," ordered Pursivant.

"Yeah? I'll just stay here to help him into the cab," said Bill.

"Go back into the house—you fool!" snarled Bert.

"Yeah? Oh, all right, all right," said Bill, and shambled cheerfully up the steps.

The taxi had halted.

"Ain't he plastered, eh?" said the driver, looking over Macklin. "Ain't he blotto, though?"

He laughed a little, and with both hands worked Macklin through the door and onto the back seat. Perhaps there was ten per cent of consciousness in Macklin.

"All right," said Bert, stepping back and dusting his hands as though *he* had been doing the work. "I guess that's about all, except your check, sir."

"Certainly," said Pursivant, and put the check into the quick hand of Bert. "But you'll come along to keep me company on the way home, eh?"

"Keep you company?" echoed Bert. "No, I stay here. Have my hands full of things to do, and—"

"Listen," said Pursivant. "Your pals in the house have had a chance to work on the telephone, before this. They've had a chance to go out the back way and take another car. Don't be foolish, Bert. You're escorting me home."

Bert looked at him fairly and fully in the eyes. His mouth pulled aside in an ugly twist before he could answer: "Well—all right—"

Pursivant took the middle place, with one shoulder bracing up Macklin, and the gun, still inside his pocket, nudged against the ribs of Bert. Then he gave the direction to the taxi driver, and they started.

Two blocks away, a big closed car came around a corner with a groan of tires against the macadam. In a breath it was beside them, and Pursivant saw dimly the silhouettes of half a dozen passengers. The driver sat low behind his wheel, slouching comfortably to one side. Thin curtains were draped here and there, helping to obscure all significant details of faces and forms. The man beside the driver turned the full blast of an auxiliary headlight into the taxi; the keen ray of it dazzled Pursivant.

It made Bert almost jump out of his skin. He started waving both hands and screaming: "Lay off, boys! For Christ's sake, lay off! Lay off!"

The big car hesitated, swayed like a living thing, and then swiftly shot away from sight down the next avenue.

Bert lay back in his place with a groan: "My God, I thought they were going to give it to us. I thought it was the finish."

"They like you too well to do that to you," said Pursivant. "I thought they'd like you too well."

When the cab reached Pursivant's door, he got out and took the limpness of Macklin between himself and the driver. Bert still lay back against the cushions with a sick face, while Pursivant manoeuvred Macklin up to the front door. The bell rang with a sweet, faint jingle far inside the house. And as the quick, soft footfalls of Gregory approached, the driver was saying: "That was a funny play, back there. Who's that mug you left in my car?"

"An old friend of mine who needs to do some thinking," said Pursivant. "Here's ten dollars worth of thought for you, too, my friend."

CHAPTER XXIV

THEY got Jerry Macklin straight into a hot tub, and then into a cold one, without denting his nervous reactions. They walked him up and down till the doctor came.

He said, quietly and quickly. "Opium. Morphine, I suppose. Don't let him sleep."

He gave two injections, and left. Vasco, the cook, Gregory were all at work when the telephone called Pursivant away and he heard the voice of Franklin telling him to come at once. It was something important. Pursivant would have to leave living or dead, and come.

Pursivant went back to see how the sick man progressed and found Jerry Macklin backed into a corner, supported on sagging legs, making vague efforts to defend himself while Gregory slapped him rapidly in the face with the flat of his hands.

There was no sense in the white face of Macklin. His eyes were the horrible feature. The pupils were pin points, as though he were facing a powerful light; his lips were grey lead.

Gregory sank wearily into a chair as Vasco and the fat cook walked their man rapidly up and down the room, shaking him violently.

The lips of Macklin were twisting. Finally they parted.

"Pursivant!" said the ghostly voice.

"It's all right," said Pursivant, loudly. "Walk up and down with me, Jerry. Try to swing yours legs. Keep your hands moving. That's better. You're coming out of it!"

He took Macklin under the armpits and walked him rapidly back and forth. The head of Jerry dropped over and joggled against Pursivant's shoulder.

"Get me away," said Macklin. "It's been hell, but I knew you'd show up. Pursivant—never lets down—a pal. Get me away, quick! Don't let Harmody—don't let Harmody—don't let Harmody—"

His voice went out. He began to groan with the drawing of each breath. So Pursivant had him put in bed and, listening to the breathing, and to the pulsation of the heart, he knew that his man was safely through the crisis. There was color in the lips of Jerry Macklin, now; color was seeping up into his face, also, before Pursivant left the place to seek Franklin.

And all the way the thought of Macklin in the bed, staring, with a small twist of a smile as though he were seeing something behind Pursivant—some image of Cappen, or Harmody, or of the faceless death itself.

"Come alone and come heeled," Franklin had said.

Pursivant went alone, and heeled. It was not so very far, so he walked all the way. Every now and then he ventured to lift his eyes from the traffic of the street and the sidewalks to the bright sky and he stepped out with a good long swing because exercise is the best way to put a distance between us and our thoughts.

He got to Franklin's little white house with the thick shadow pouring over it still from the apartment buildings at its side. Stepping into that shadow was like passing into a later hour. The wooden gate clanked softly behind him. The wooden walk made him step carefully.

When he rang the bell, Franklin's gorilla-faced Negro opened the door and showed his fangs in his best smile. He ushered Pursivant into the library.

Franklin sat with rumpled hair, in shirtsleeves at his desk, with his back turned. He had been pacing, scattering cigar ashes and trampling them into the roses of the carpet. There were chewed and half-smoked cigars lying in ash trays, here and there. One of them was on the edge of the little Chippendale table and the length of the ash showed how far it had burned into the polish of the wood. The air was thick and foul.

Something had happened. This was Franklin's sanctum. It represented his ideal of American culture of which he knew that he could never be a portion; but in this room he always felt that he was safely enclosed within the dignity and quiet of an eighteenth century which was closer to the source of all American ideals. Yet now he had chosen to defile this sacred place with one of his rowdy vigils.

He seemed to be reading with care, his head bowed. Pursivant crossed the room and saw on the desk before his friend a ghost-gun, a replica of that which he had dropped into the river. He understood with the first glance. Initials can be duplicated. And Jack Smith's letter, in another form, was under the eyes of Franklin. No doubt there had been a report from a ballistic expert by this time.

Well, now he knew the truth; rather, he knew Smith's cruel contorting of the truth. He had been thinking of that all night, and he had placed on the desk before him that picture of his dead brother in the golden frame. Everything ended, for Pursivant, like a road at the edge of a cliff.

Franklin's head swayed far back and he looked up into Pursivant's face. After that, he rose. He seemed to have been made up for a part, his eyes were painted so black with the purple, triangular stain descending from them. Pursivant drew back from him, saying: "Will you let me talk, Dick?"

"Are you heeled?" asked Franklin.

"No," said Pursivant.

"You lie," said Franklin. "But if you're not heeled, it doesn't matter. You take what's coming."

He picked up that old Colt and stood a little taller. A great brightness of joy began to shine out of him. And Pursivant pulled the automatic. He stood on the farther side of the little slender-legged Chippendale, looking through the stale blue of the cigar smoke towards Franklin. He was able to remember that the gun in his hand belonged to Franklin, just as Franklin's gun belonged to him.

"I count three!" said Franklin. "Like this."

He rapped with the knuckles of his left hand on the desk, beside him. He paused and rapped again. Pursivant had made up his mind. He stared at the sallow skin of Riccardo Francolini with the dark Italian stain in it; he tried to tell himself that the man was a brute, a crook, a political grafter and the world would be well rid of him; but all the while he knew that he could not shake, really, his first resolve.

Yet when the third rap came, an instinct made him jerk the automatic up to the firing position. That was how he stood, covering the breast of Franklin, when the old Colt exploded. The sound of the bullet flicked past the cheek of Pursivant like a thought across the mind.

The heavy boom of the explosion choked the room. A little after-dinner coffee cup tinkled softly against its saucer and its tiny silver spoon.

Franklin was lowering his gun, little by little, staring.

For all that worked in him, he could find only one word, and he uttered it in Italian. The door was snatched open by the big Negro. He saw the guns. He watched the two men for an instant. After that, he stood aside and let Pursivant go past him, and so out the front door.

An automobile posted across the street, suddenly started

up and jerked away down the street. Pursivant knew who had posted the spy at that place.

He walked on into the street, and into a gathering darkness. There would never again be real warmth or real brightness.

Everything had ended. The road had passed over the verge of the cliff, and he felt that he was moving through nothingness, among the ghosts of things.

CHAPTER XXV

RICHARD FRANKLIN, after Pursivant left the room, had continued to stare at the spot where his bullet smashed through the wall. That was how Jack Smith saw him, as he cautiously pushed wide a door which had remained open a crack throughout the interview.

"Jeez!" said Jack Smith. "Did he have a nerve? Yeah, he did have a nerve. Jeez! Standing there and taking it had him covered. I was gunna shoot when I seen you'd missed, but then I seen that he was just standing there and taking it, like he didn't want to live. Jeez! What a nerve."

"Get out of my sight!" said Franklin.

Jack Smith swiftly eased himself from the room and Franklin began to gather himself.

Pursivant had not fired because he knew that Franklin was totally out of practice, that he was sure to miss. It took nice calculation for a man to work out his action like that, but that was characteristic of Pursivant, the player of long odds. That was his distinguishing feature—the sort of a man who murders another and then goes to the brother of the dead and, like a ghoul, makes a claim on him for Auld Lang Syne!

Pursivant had to die. With his own hand he had failed to make the killing. The law could not do the job. But there was Cappen! He owed Cappen liberty for the sake of this priceless information, and Cappen should go free—on a blood trail.

An aeroplane jerked Franklin north in two hours. A little later he sat in the study of Governor Blane and knocked the sleep out of the dim eyes of that politician with his first remark.

"I want Cappen," he said. "I want him free."

"Cappen?" shouted the governor. "Cappen? God in heaven, Richard, you know that the electrocution of Cappen will be enough to re-elect me? The first great counter-stroke against the crime-wave—under my regime—"

"You won't be re-elected without my backing. You don't get my backing unless Cappen comes out," said Franklin.

The governor made a pause and tried to believe his ears. The strong hand of Franklin had lifted him to an eminence, he knew, and that hand could be as hard as iron, as all men knew. But it is not like this that a common citizen should speak to the head of a sovereign state!

Governor Blane took in a breath and expanded both his chest and his stomach.

"Richard," he said, "you're excited. You're disturbed. My dear fellow, I understand—"

"If you understand me," said Franklin, "you'll sit down and write out a pardon for Arthur Cappen."

The governor's breathing was very audible. "This is extraordinary," he said. "This is hard. I may go so far as to say that this is very hard, Richard! With no explanation!"

"Explanation?" said Franklin, thrusting out his chin. "I tell you that I need Cappen in order to cut the throat of such a damned scoundrel—of such a damned black villain, that Cappen himself is like a little child! You understand me, Blane? If it makes you hate me tomorrow for what you're doing tonight—write out that pardon."

"There are obligations of which I am aware—" said the governor.

"This cancels anything I've done for you," exclaimed

Franklin. "Give your patronage to the devil, after this. I want Cappen. And that's all I want. Is it clear?"

"A scoundrel, a fox, a murderer, a thief!" said the governor. "If I pardon him, public opinion will boil in the pot."

"Damn public opinion," said Franklin. "I want Cappen."

"You damn the public, but the public will not be damned!" said the governor. "The public will want reasons—"

"Blane," said Franklin, his lips moving stiffly over the words, as though there were frost in his flesh, "you've never been bright. Don't show yourself an absolute fool, now. You're going to pardon Cappen, not because you are perfectly sure that he's innocent, but because you're perfectly sure that the process of law under which he was brought to trial and convicted was a wrong process, a false process. You hear me, Blane: There is a loftier aspect of the law. It must not be made into a dangerous mockery—a mockery dangerous to the personal liberty of every citizen, dangerous as a fact and as a precedent. I am not pardoning Arthur Cappen because he is a good man but because he is a wronged man, not because he is a perfect citizen, but because he is an injured citizen . . . you follow that, Blane?"

The governor was not, in fact, a very bright man. His stomach, his face, and his smile, were all large and fat and his shashy handshake was the very symbol of a great democracy. He was a figurehead which was served with the brains of others, and now he walked up and down his study for a moment, looking down with pleasure on the long, flowing lines of his dressing gown and trying the words of Franklin almost inaudibly, with gestures.

He was pleased. He paused.

"As a matter of fact, Richard," he said, "we must build for the future, and in nothing so much as in our laws. There, if in any place, the rights of man must be considered sacred, and the—"

"Save it," said Franklin. "Say it to your looking glass. And now sit down and write that pardon!"

The governor glared, but only for a brief instant. He had one great power, and that was his ability to see the votes of a man through his skin. When his X-ray eye revealed to him the number of votes that resided inside the pocket of Richard Franklin, he swallowed his wrath and sat down obediently at his desk.

That was why, in the rainy dawn of the next day, Richard Franklin sat in a little bleak backroom of what had once been a saloon and would be a saloon again. Two pairs of eyes considered one another with curiosity and with respect.

"You've made a fight that I thought you never could win. I never dreamed that you'd be able to use me as a tool," said Franklin. "But you have to pay."

"A sensible man always pays, even when a price isn't named," said Cappen, gravely.

"The price is Pursivant," said Franklin.

"You want him untouched?" said Cappen, frowning.

"I want him dead," said Franklin. "I want him cut off. I want him murdered. I don't care how. You could make it perfect if you let me see him die."

He sprang up from his chair. "If not that, then he has to know before he dies that it's coming from me through other hands! Cappen, he has to die!"

Cappen nodded. He had the look, at that moment, of one who tastes a very strange but a very delicious wine.

"Everything is in my hands?" he asked.

"Everything from the start to the end, with every ounce of

support that I can give you," said Franklin, and beat the table with his hand.

"Well," said Cappen, "we'll wangle it. He's rather a tough bit, but he can be managed. Between you and me, Franklin, from the first moment I laid eyes on him I knew that he would die young, and that I would have something to do with the killing of him."

CHAPTER XXVI

THE news got to Pursivant in the morning paper; there were two items that struck him, heavily. The first was that Cappen was pardoned. It was not a big headline, though it made the front page. Governor Blane, in delivering his strange decision, had said in part: "There is a loftier aspect of the law. It must not be made into a dangerous mockery, a mockery dangerous to the personal liberty of every citizen. . . . I am not pardoning Arthur Cappen because he is a good man, but because he is a wronged man. . . ."

It was a very strange act, the editorial of the day declared, and particularly because in his last crime Cappen had injured so greatly the political helper and close personal friend of the governor—Richard Franklin. It was known that Franklin had taken an aeroplane in the middle of the night and gone to the capital city to interview the governor. Perhaps he had gone purposely to protest against the liberation of this dangerous criminal; but if so, he had protested in vain.

Franklin could not be reached. Exposure in the open plane during his return to the city had caused him to be attacked by influenza; he was now confined to his house, delirious, in charge of two nurses and doctors by day and night!

But Pursivant understood. When Franklin had failed to make Pursivant fight the thing out, he had determined to get rid of him by other means, and Cappen had come into his mind as a sure agent. Cappen was now loosed to take up the bloodtrail, and what a passion of delight must be surging in Cappen when he found himself given freedom if he would turn his hand against Pursivant, whom he loathed so utterly?

The picture of what was to happen now was not complicated.

Merrill, the police said, was either already in the country or about to get there. Merrill and Cappen might now join forces again or else they might decide to deny one another. In the latter case, each of them would be making an effort to get to the treasure cache before the other managed it.

That was one aspect of the affair that promised to Pursivant a little peace, at any rate, while Cappen was getting his hands on the money.

Another grimly cheering aspect was that Franklin lay delirious and therefore could not with a word swing the police heads against Pursivant. For a day or so, Pursivant's word at headquarters would be almost as influential as Franklin's own. Therefore he could use the police as he willed; he had only to point out possible points of attack to them until Franklin, recovering from his delirium, was able to set the officers of the law right.

He was beaten, now. There was only one thing for him to do, it seemed, and that was to get out of the country. But, if he could, he determined that he would take Mary Carthy with him. So he went straight over to Culver Square, under a sky that was covered with a patchwork of monstrous clouds, letting down curtains of rattling rain from time to time.

There was sun in Culver Square. It was so bright, hollow, and empty that it seemed life could never have stirred in it. The trees in the park were still. The sunlight was painted on the pavement. It seemed to Pursivant that he alone was living, or he alone was dead. At Number Seven, he found out that Miss Leigh was at home and that she would receive him. When he went up, Helen Leigh opened the door and looked him slowly up and down with a malignant withering of her face. He stepped past her into the room of French grey. A radio or a victrola was playing somewhere and there was a slight tremor in the floor.

"She'll be in," said Mrs. Leigh.

She paused at the door, holding it open for a moment while she continued to survey him. Her scorn and mirth forced her to laugh, at last, and she closed the door. Mary Carthy came almost immediately afterwards with a robe of towelling hanging loosely about her, the wooden grips of a skipping rope in her hand. Her hair was tousled, her face bright with sweat. In the flat gymnasium shoes she looked small and more boyish than feminine.

"Hello, Charlie," she said. "Open the window, will you? I have to keep on breathing deep. There was so much smoke in the air, the other night, that it's made me husky. And that won't do. I've got to keep my voice 'soft, gentle, and low.' The first thing some hombres notice are the vocal cords."

He opened the window. There was a blank wall opposite but the sun slanted out of an unseen sky and soaked his clothes with warmth.

She was walking up and down, swinging the rope.

"It's hard to sweat out champagne," she said. "And even if you sip the stuff like a bird, you blot up quite a bit in a four hour session. What's the matter with you, Charlie? You look as though somebody had hit you on a brittle place. Are you breaking up? I'll give you a shot of something, shall I?"

He waved his hand.

"Who was it last night?" he asked.

"Clarence Digby. Do you know him?"

He saw the debauched face of Digby as clearly as though a ghost had risen in the room with a little twist of moustache and lips as red as paint.

"I know Digby," he answered.

"Is the big shot on a cash basis?"

"He has plenty, plenty. He won't miss what you take."

"He'll miss what I take, all right," answered Mary Carthy. "My idea is a percentage. Like a first class doctor. Tell me the income before I tell you the price."

He frowned at a cigarette he was lighting. She sat down and crossed her legs. The edges of the robe were kicked away by the movement.

"A good pair of knees, Mary," said Pursivant.

She sat up and considered herself critically.

"In a way," she said, "it's a pity that I wasn't started on that basis, instead of all the dignity. A good pair of legs can walk a girl right into the bank account of many an empire builder. Maybe the impression isn't so lasting, but the turnover is awfully quick. Did you want to see me about something, Charlie?"

"I do," said Pursivant.

After he had considered her for a moment he went on: "For one thing, I'd like to know why you show me all the rough and none of the smooth."

"What rough?" she asked.

"The slang and the dirt," he answered. "You're not like that."

"No," said Mary Carthy. "I'm just a real good girl. Not so very big, but really awfully good."

He shook his head.

"You're not like this. You're only playing a game, Mary," he said. "You're not a little ratty-minded brat, as you're pretending."

"You said you had an idea to talk over. Is this the idea?" asked Mary Carthy, contemptuously.

"No," said Pursivant. But there was something imperfect in her sneering attitude, he was certain. At least, she was not showing her real self, and he wondered what she expected to gain by exhibiting a phase of her character which, she must know, was offensive to him. Perhaps, however, she was simply being natural, and rejoicing in her chance to throw off the artificial mannerisms which she had to maintain the rest of the time.

She was saying:

"Blaze away, then. The more I cool off now, the harder I'll have to work when I get back into that damned gymnasium. It's a strange thing, Charlie, how I'm beginning to hate the smell of sweat. When I make my roll, I'm going to spend the rest of my life getting fat and smelling perfumes. The wind that fans me has gotta be flavored with attar of roses to make up for what I've been through."

He rubbed his knuckles so hard across his upper lip that it remained white for a moment.

"You haven't picked out your man, then?" said Pursivant.

"The woods are so full of deer, Charlie, that I'm getting buck fever. The whole herd may drift past before I decide which one to aim at. Titus Lincoln ought to be a good bet, though, don't you think?"

Pursivant thought of that bloated and pop-eyed young man and drew in a deep breath.

"You've been working a long time and a hard time, Mary," he said. "What do you say to coming away with me, for a vacation?"

"Oh," said the girl, calmly.

She leaned back in the chair and rested her chin on her linked fingers.

"Are you propositioning me, Charlie?" she asked.

"You don't have to talk like that," said Pursivant. "I wish you wouldn't."

"Shall I throw away my baser part and be the lady?" asked Mary Carthy.

"Yes, I wish you would."

"I shouldn't be surprised," remarked Mary Carthy. "Samson was always fond of his girl. His head must have felt so much cooler; he must have liked the breeze on his neck. Well, I'd like to please you, Charlie, but I'm just too damn tired to be interested, this morning. It's hard to wear the new face by day. I'd bloom like a regular rose for you every evening, though."

"Stop it," said Pursivant. "I want you to listen to me."

"Shoot," said the girl.

He mastered another strong wave of distaste.

"I'm leaving town," he told her. "I'm going away and I'm staying away. I can clean up two or three hundred thousand dollars before I start. I'll take you wherever you want to go. South Seas or Paris. I don't care."

"Charles W. Pursivant, even!" breathed Mary Carthy. "This is quite a day for the little girl! Cappen won't believe it. Not when I swear on the Bible—he won't believe it! But what's the other side of the picture? What's the seamy side? There's an 'if,' somewhere; and I know you wouldn't deceive a poor child, would you?"

"The seamy side," said Pursivant, "is that I'm getting serious about you. If we lived together for a while, I'd want to marry you, I suppose."

"Your sacred honor, Charles; and the Pursivant good name. Great heaven, you haven't forgotten such things, have you?" sneered Mary Carthy.

"I'll take time out," said Pursivant. "You have a hard punch, Mary, and you keep hitting all the time."

He lighted another cigarette and walked up and down.

She was perfectly patient, sitting with her chin on one small brown fist, now, and following him up and down with her stare like a caged thing.

When he halted in front of her, she said: "Are you taking it big, Charlie? Is it going to be something in a big way?"

He looked steadily down into her blue eyes and felt the color staining his mind and his soul.

"Quite big," said Pursivant.

She shook her head, muttering: "If only Cappen could hear this! If only he could hear!"

"Well," said Pursivant, "perhaps he can."

She sat up.

"He may be laughing behind that door, for all I know," said Pursivant.

"Well," said the girl, relaxing again, "I'd like to know what the big idea is? You're just opening up the town. You're getting ready to get at the kernel. Richard Franklin can open the steel doors of the safe, for you. Why do you talk about moving? If you and I wanted to start housekeeping, why the South Seas or Paris? Why not some little duck of a house on top of a skyscraper?"

"Franklin's through with me," said Pursivant. "That's another thing you ought to know."

"Aren't you the boy that comes clean!" said Mary Carthy. "But why should the big, fat-faced Dago be giving you a run?"

"It doesn't matter why," said Pursivant. "Cappen could tell you. Or, for that matter, you could know yourself."

"Are you through with Franklin?" she demanded.

"Yes."

"For good?"

"Franklin had Cappen pardoned, so that Cappen can murder me."

"Franklin—" she murmured faintly, "why should he—"

"Why are you so curious about it?" said Pursivant. "Do you want to pass the news on to Cappen? He knows about it already. His men were waiting across the street to listen to the ruction. They heard the gun, when Franklin fired."

"Hey!" said Mary Carthy. "A regular duel, eh?"

"You would have enjoyed it. Cappen would, too."

"That's why you're so groggy," said the girl. "You still love that hombre after he's been gunning for you? My God, you're a queer mug, Charlie! When he missed you, was it because you already had planted some lead in him?"

"I didn't shoot," said Pursivant, slowly.

That brought her out of her chair.

"You stood there and let *him* shoot?" she cried.

She threw her arms up with a wild gesture. "Oh, bah!" she said, and stepped to the window and leaned out of it a bit into the sun. Pale gold or metal red, her hair burned.

"Well," said Pursivant, "you're not very enthusiastic about the offer, Mary."

Her head jerked back with a queer suddenness.

"Offer!" she said. "You think I'd play lady to your gentleman for twenty-four hours a day, six months at a stretch? I'd see you in hell, first. Anyway, I'm not a half-wit. I can add to a million, anyway. What a cheap fool I'd be to cut in on your lousy little couple of hundred thousand! Sock that into an annuity, and what does it mean, anyway? One maid and baked beans twice a week!"

She began to laugh. She was laughing as she spoke, mirth rippling through her words, or tearing them to pieces. He thought what a good thing it would be for the world and the men in it, if he pulled out his automatic and smashed in the back of that pretty head with a bullet.

But he was saying: "I'm not trying to get you forever. I'm trying to buy you like dope. I know I'm a fool. That doesn't matter. I want to wind up the first part of my life, and I want to wind it up with you."

"Well, I won't have you. Shall I tell you why?" she cried.

She wheeled suddenly around on him from the window. Laughter moved her body and kept her head swaying.

"I won't have you, and I'll tell you why. It's because I don't like you. I don't like your ugly mug. I don't like anything about you. And when I take a scalp, I want it to be off the head of a chief. Oh, get out of my sight and don't come back! I'm sick of you. I don't want your damned money. I don't want your damned soul. I'd—I'd spit it on the floor! Get out!"

CHAPTER XXVII

PURSIVANT got out. The laughter of the girl was still quaking in his nerves as he reached Culver Square. He headed out into the big avenue and walked with his hat in his hand, letting the sun burn against his face, against his eyes, trying to purify himself with fire. And still the vile ranting of the girl kept dinting into his ears. She had even followed him to the front door of the apartment, crying: "I'll tell you why I don't want you. It's because you're a fool. That's what I loathe. Fools—and blind fools! It makes me sick. You make me sick. Man? You're no man. You're a damned puling brat. You'd take me first and gas afterwards. You'd be a dirty dead corpse on my hands and a stinking scandal to start me in the world. Get out! I never want to see your face again!"

She'd kept on laughing, till the laughter turned into a snarl of hatred.

He stopped and put his hand against the pillar of a street lamp.

Something had been wrong with the whole thing.

One dash of the Mediterranean would be enough to dye the entire sky, and out of her eyes the blue of peace had soaked for a moment through his whole soul. After that had come the explosion. And something about it was wrong. It was too much. She had herself under better control than that.

If she had been to some degree acting, there had been one moment at which her art grew thin, and that was the moment after she had heard him say that Cappen was pardoned so that he could murder Pursivant. Something about that had shocked her to silence, for an instant, and through that silence, through the sudden widening of her eyes, he tried to tell himself that he had glimpsed another and a finer reality in her. But it was Cappen, Cappen who possessed her; it was the fear of Cappen which dominated her life.

But the words she had spoken kept dinting into his brain, sickening him with many blows.

The rain came on with a sudden roar, as he reached the end of the block. The spray blew like a thin dust along the pavement and as he leaned into the wind passing the entrance of the corner apartment house, he looked into the interior of a passing taxicab and saw a man with a pointed grey beard.

He had only a glance but sometimes it is in such a flash that the unshuttered mind sees most deeply. It was not the grey beard that struck him but something eager in the forward stoop of the head and shoulders.

"Cappen!" he thought to himself, and hurried out across the street to have the houses of the square in better perspective.

His heart gave one great hammer stroke as the cab drew up in front of Number Twelve. Pursivant turned and sauntered away but by sideglances across his shoulder he saw a tall figure climb from the door of the taxi, look carefully up and down the street, then hurry into the building.

If it was Cappen, the smallness of the valise he carried might have some significance. Certainly he could not have visited the cache of the Weaver Trust money and come away with such a small portion. But in any case, he would hardly have been mad enough to carry stolen goods into the city so openly. Considering the time, it was probable that he had come straight down to the city from the prison, only pausing to cover his too familiar features with that beard.

He would be perhaps an hour or so with Helen Leigh and the girl; they would have a great deal to tell him. After that, if he intended to disregard Merrill and go after the hidden money, he would probably start at once for the loot. There would never be a better chance of trailing him.

So Pursivant went straight back to his house in a taxi. The picture of the girl kept rising. He could not understand. All of that scene, except one moment of grave, staring concern, had been unreal. At last, grimly, he lifted the idea of her out of his mind and cast it away, but the pain remained all the closer to his heart.

Gregory, for once, was not waiting to open the door for him. Instead, the cook came into the hall and took off his high white cap.

"Where's Gregory?" he asked.

"He can't leave Jerry Macklin—at least, somebody has to be with him."

"Quite right," said Pursivant, and went up to Macklin's room. Gregory stood up from the book he had been reading aloud, and Pursivant stood by the bed.

"God," said Macklin, "but it's good to see you, chief. It puts everything right."

There was a blue shadow, a stain all around his mouth. Now that life was freshening in his eyes, Pursivant could see more clearly how close Jerry had been to death. "You lie here and take things easy," he directed. "Everything will be all right. Send Vasco to Jerry, Gregory, and come down to me in the front room."

A minute later he was with Gregory downstairs.

"After all," he said, "I'm going to use you outside the house. Are you willing?"

The grey head of Gregory began to nod as he said: "I've been expecting it, sir."

"You know how to change your face," went on Pursivant. "Go change it now. Spend ten minutes on that and then go to Culver Square and watch the front of Number Twelve. There's a middle aged man in there with a pointed grey beard and with stooping shoulders and an outthrust of his head. When he comes out of Number Twelve, he may not be wearing a beard."

"Is his name Cappen, sir?" asked Gregory.

"The wits still work in you," said Pursivant, smiling. "Gregory, when you were on the loose, did you ever hear of a man named Harmody? Les Harmody?"

"Yes, sir."

"What sort of a man is he?"

"He's been working for a long time, sir, and every step is up the ladder. He learned a few things in a reform school but he came out of that as a prize fighter and shifted up from the ring to second-story work. That led into safe-cracking. He served a term on a charge of that sort and then switched into brain work, pure and simple. When he uses his own hands it's sure to be on an important case."

"What's the look of him?"

"He looks," said Gregory, carefully, "like a gentleman of good family who has too much money to spend and is tired of the world. He has very heavy shoulders and a thin face, with a long jaw. He's about thirty-five years old. He has dark hair and a pale face. There's a small red-brown birthmark under his left cheekbone."

"You know him like a brother, Gregory," said Pursivant.

Gregory paused for a moment.

"He knows me equally well, sir," he answered at last.

"Well," said Pursivant, "Les Harmody is somewhere in

this game. We're sure to run into him before very long, I suppose. Get yourself ready. Mind you, if you see Cappen come out of Number Twelve, get around the block as fast as you can leg it and you'll find me in the next street, right behind Number Twelve. Have the number of the car, if Cappen has gone off in one. If he's walking, have the direction spotted. And take a gun with you. That is," he concluded, slowly, "if you really think it's wise for you to get into this game."

"I shall bring a gun," said Gregory, "with great pleasure. And if Harmody—"

He stopped himself there but Pursivant had heard enough to guess that no target could possibly agree so well with the wishes of Gregory as the broad shoulders of Les Harmody.

For his own part, Pursivant took a raincoat, a pair of sandwiches from the cook, and slipped downtown towards Culver Square in a taxi. He left the cab a block from his destination, and then walked on through the street north of the square until he saw the high shoulders of the apartment house lifting above the old houses. Under the steps that went up to a high front porch, Pursivant sat down to wait and to watch. The rain turned the day into a long evening. He stayed at his post until the actual night began.

CHAPTER XXVIII

ANOTHER rainstorm darkened over the city with thunderings close at hand and in the midst of the downpour, he remembered that he had forgotten to take one of the first precautions—he had not made sure of a taxi to be stationed, or to cruise slowly, at each end of the block. Therefore he left his spy-station and went east down the block at a good clip. He was almost at the next avenue before on the opposite side of the street, penciled in dimly behind the thick of the rain, he saw a figure that might be that of Cappen. It came out of obscurity into the bright globe of mist above a street lamp and he made certain of those stooping shoulders, that forward angle of the head. A savage little thrill of happiness and confidence was darted along his blood as though Fate had given Cappen into his hands. Certainly it was a sheer stroke of luck that brought him on the heels of his quarry.

But he remembered having read in a book: "Luck comes only to good generals."

As he rounded the corner, he saw Cappen step into a long, low automobile that began to move before the figure of the man had disappeared in it. It picked up speed rapidly; it was ducking with a red sweep of the tail light around the next corner to the west as Pursivant got into a taxi. His driver was a sodden lump of a man in a patched overcoat, one of those doughy, half collapsed forms such as one sees driving horse-cabs in Europe. His face was chiefly lost behind the bushing of eyebrows and the downward arch of long moustaches and Pursivant would have chosen him last out of a thousand. "Follow that tail light; keep after it!" he said. He got a grunt of an answer, but as he sat down gingerly, tense with anxiety, the car came to life and went away like a greyhound. The cushion whacked against the shoulders of Pursivant but his grunt was all approval.

A tall truck and a three horse dray were lumbering side by side at the desired corner, coming from the west. The taxi driver did a skid turn and flipped his car between the two monsters like a trout between a pair of salmon.

But the red tail light was out of sight. They went straight west for two blocks, Pursivant groaning in disappointment, when he saw a red glint around a corner a couple of blocks to the north. The driver saw it also and went after it with a last minute turn that took him half over the sidewalk on the wrong side of the street. He threw the spray from his tires at a pair of respectable gentlemen who left their yells of fear in the nerves of Pursivant as the taxi swerved back into the open street.

They dodged around a dozen blocks, north, south, and west, before the red light over the chosen license number straightened away on a steady northern course before them. They followed. Never was there better driving through traffic. Never did corner jams so melt away before the cunning of a chauffeur.

They passed through the darkness of the uptown streets among the skyscrapers; they jumped and twisted through the lighted theatre district as through a fire and then settled down again to easier driving as Cappen still held north.

Pursivant pulled back the sliding window behind the driver and let a fresh gust of rain-mist and wind strike his face.

"Can you make a quick change of cars out here?" he asked. "Those fellows may spot our front license plate."

"Yeah, with you aboard I can do a lot of quick changes, Pursivant," said the driver.

A block or two later they were in the rear of a traffic pack halted by the red light, their quarry dammed up with them a bit ahead, when Pursivant's driver slipped out, saying: "Come on, brother."

Pursivant stepped with him to the side of one of those big closed cars which are on hire by time and which would pass as private machines except that something adheres to the drivers like pitch to the hand.

"Tumble out, Johnny," said the man of the moustaches. "Take my cab. We've got a tailing job and we wanta change our faces."

"You need a new mug," said the uniformed chauffeur, contentedly. "But what makes you think you know me, Grandpa? Back up! There's the green light!"

"D'you know Charles W. Pursivant when you see him?" asked the cab driver. And Pursivant, pressing close, was almost glad of that flurry of publicity which had put his face in every paper in the land for a few days.

"Quick, my friend, quick!" he urged, thrusting a greenback into an automatically receptive hand. "The traffic's starting, and our fox is away!"

The chauffeur came out of his seat and stood with his cap lifted, grinning.

"You can fix me with the chief," he said. "Good luck!"

In the deeper seat of the big car, Pursivant settled back more completely at ease. He had only a moment's fear that his man would be less a master of a strange vehicle; in fact the skill of that stodgy lump made the heavy machine small and light. It grew sinuous to twist through traffic puzzles; at every opening it went away like a four-footed hunting beast, and there was need for every whit of his skill, for the tail light they followed was setting a murderous pace. They hardly needed to scrutinize the license plate or the familiar low set of the body; the speed of the moving light was enough to identify it.

That was how they came out of the town into the suburbs and so to a state highway, huge and black and gleaming as a river. For the rain still fell and the shining road poured swiftly back upon them.

They were led off the highway to a narrower road that aimed at the sea. The heart of Pursivant began to quicken. He had the most perfect sense that he was drawing closer and closer to the goal. If he gained nothing else, on this night, he now knew, he thought, in what direction one must travel in order to come towards the burial place of the Weaver Trust funds.

They took a sudden elbow-turn and shot past a filling station beside which was drawn up the long, blue car of Cappen. And there was Cappen himself beside the machine overseeing the filling of the tank. It was strange that he should trust that bit of grey beard to disguise him completely! But Pursivant groaned as they went by, for now everything was made ten-fold more difficult.

As they took the next turn his driver slowed and said over his shoulder: "Cappen spotted us plenty as we went by. He knows all about the face of this rig. What'll we do now?"

"Get wings and follow him that way," said Pursivant through his teeth. "Damn all my luck! Only one chance in ten thousand that that tank wasn't full when they left town."

"It was full enough for their job," answered the driver. "But they wanted to look over anything that was coming behind. What next?"

"Take that side road. Back into it," said Pursivant. "We'll have to see if they come by again."

It was a mere lane that gave back with a sharp twist from the main road, and fortunately it was bordered with trees. Into it the chauffeur backed the big machine with an uncanny dexterity. The trees gleamed for an instant, they went black and dim as the lights were turned out.

"Suppose they make the same turn, they'll give us a bloody nose," said the driver.

"What's your name?" asked Pursivant.

"McLellan."

"McLellan, if bloody noses are coming our way, we'll take 'em."

"Yeah, but a good sock on the nose is hell on the eyes, too," said McLellan.

"What's your real work?" asked Pursivant.

"Don't I handle the old bus good enough?" asked McLellan.

"Too well," answered Pursivant.

McLellan chuckled. "I had a milk route up around Detroit," he said. "But beer knocked hell out of that whiskey business for me."

"All right," said Pursivant, "if you remember me tomorrow, I'll remember you."

Cars had been going by the mouth of the alley at regular intervals and as one shot past, now, to Pursivant a mere sightless blur behind the rain, McLellan snapped on his lights and jerked the machine out onto the highway.

They hummed in first and whined sharp and high in second, then they slid away in the swift, easy flight of top speed. They picked up and passed half a dozen cars before a wavering red light before them enabled Pursivant to read Cappen's license plate again.

They were close to the sea, now. The salt of it was sour in the air; breathing grew deeper and easier. Then their quarry swerved south onto a narrow lane. They followed. Cappen's car was stopping and McLellan halted his own machine in turn. There was no room to pass without danger of skidding into a ditch. The long machine in front of them began to back and twist in order to come about.

"They've taken the wrong turn," said Pursivant. "They're coming back."

"They ain't coming back because they've taken the wrong turn, but because we've taken too many right ones," answered McLellan. "If there's any hell in the air, they're gunna give it to us now. Are you heeled?"

"Yes, and you?"

"I wouldn't be dumb," answered McLellan, reaching into a side pocket of the car.

Then he drew to the side of the road to let Cappen go by, but the low-hung machine stopped with a little squeal of brakes just before them so that the full blast of its headlights streamed on them. Pursivant, staring out from under the brim of his hat, slouched low in his seat with the automatic ready, expecting a shattering hail of bullets. Instead, he saw the door of the other car open and the bending form of Cappen emerged.

He walked straight up to the hire-car, pulled the side door open, and looked in on Pursivant. The beard could not disguise a single line of that face, it was so printed in the mind of Pursivant, and the eyes he could have known, he swore, among all the bright danger signals in the world. He knew their smallness. He knew every wrinkle around them as they glared at him now.

"It had to be you," said Cappen. "You've won another trick, Pursivant, but this is the last one. Tomorrow—"

He stopped on that word, drew back, and slammed the

door. A moment later his car was trundling carefully past while McLellan began to turn his own machine.

He said nothing until they got out into the highway. Then he turned his head and muttered: "That all for tonight, Pursivant?"

"That's all—for tonight," said Pursivant. "Follow them back."

"That'll be easy," said McLellan. "Only, you wanta make sure that following is the thing you wanta do."

Pursivant said nothing, and they ran on easily towards the big city, while the glow of the town spread wider and wider before them and burned upwards into the rain. It was like approaching the open door of an oven.

Cappen went straight back to Number Twelve, Culver Square. Pursivant went on to pick up the wet draggled figure of old Gregory at the next corner and went straight back home.

His pay was enough to reward McLellan for ten nights of such work. Bigger pay would come, if McLellan wanted it.

But he surprised Pursivant by saying: "I turn in this bus at the shop where it belongs, and then I step back into my taxi job. I guess you gotta lot of influence, chief, but you better use it all on yourself. I seen the eyes of Cappen when he was talkin' to you. It cooled down my bloodstream a whole lot, as they say in a hospital. So long and good luck."

Pursivant went into his house and got on the telephone, to the police commissioner. There was the usual ten minutes of delay while he was being tracked down; and there is no lonelier sound than the whine and pause and whine of a telephone buzzer when one sits alone at night. Every door and every window of that house seemed about to open and let danger pour in on Pursivant. If he was at the telephone now, what was Cappen saying over the wires from Twelve, Culver Square?

At last he got the commissioner.

"Cappen's back," he said. "He's at Number Twelve, Culver Square. That's where his protegée, Jacqueline Leigh, is staying, too. Spot him there. Get the best men on the police force to work."

The commissioner was one of those fat men who lessen their bulk with the lightness of their voices. Now he almost sobbed across the wire: "What devil from hell persuaded Blane to pardon Cappen after he'd been put away by one of the neatest little pieces of work in the history of crime? Your work, Pursivant, put Cappen away. The devil doesn't like you! Are you sure about Culver Square?"

"I'm sure. He was there all day long. I should have tried to get the police on the job, but I thought I might do something single-handed. Let me tell you another thing."

"Fire away, Pursivant."

"The old partnership of Cappen and Merrill is probably broken up."

"I knew that before," said the Commissioner.

"How did you know?"

"Merrill didn't put up a penny to help out Cappen at his trial. Merrill simply got on board the next boat to come back to the States, and even a blind fool could see that Merrill intends to play a lone hand, now."

"That means," said Pursivant, "that both Cappen and Merrill are trying to get at the loot they've buried."

"That's what it means," said the Commissioner. "Merrill is somewhere in the country now."

"I'll tell you the direction the stuff is planted in. I don't know the spot, but out towards Duck Island is the direction. Get out all your spare men towards Duck Island. Put a good few of them on the Island itself. There are a lot of inlets from which men could put off towards the Island, and it may be that the loot is buried in one of those inlets or out on a peninsula, away from the roads."

"Pursivant, I'll cover the whole district. If a snake crawls over the ground or a bird gets into the air, I'll have a telephone report over the wireless inside of five minutes."

"If you'll do that, you'll embarrass them. You'll embarrass them a lot. Because something is going to happen pretty quickly."

"Damn quickly!" said the Commissioner. "Two like Merrill and Cappen bring on a flock of action in short order! Inside of twenty-four hours, if we put the brakes on them, the temperature of this whole town is going to be raised fifty degrees. Goodnight, Pursivant, and thanks for the tip. Don't worry. I'll cover that whole district with an army! You better keep out of this, Pursivant. You've done enough for the good cause, and if those fellows get a chance, they'll smash you. They'll take you to hell!"

"They can't do that," said Pursivant, bitterly, "because they don't know what hell is made of."

"What do you mean by that?"

"I mean that I'm going to bed. So long."

He rang off, and sat for a long moment until he heard a very soft whispering sound. It came from the yellow flowers in their bowl at the window. They were trembling in a draft that blew steadily under the sash of the pane, which was raised a trifle. Something in Pursivant began to shudder in sympathy with that trembling. He went to the window and closed it with a jar. And the sudden weight of the noise startled him.

There was a sigh behind him. He jerked around and saw Gregory entering in dry clothes, carrying a tray of food.

Pursivant sat down very suddenly. He had been on the brink, he knew, of pulling a gun as he turned.

And this was only the beginning. What would his nerves be made of before the morning came?

CHAPTER XXIX

HE went up to see Jerry Macklin and found Vasco asleep in a chair while Jerry lay in the bed with his eyes fastened on the ceiling. He sat up suddenly as he saw Pursivant. The sudden opening of the door seemed to have been like the pointing of a gun at him; but the sight of Pursivant started him smiling.

"I've been expecting some of 'em," he muttered. "Harmody. I've been waiting for Harmody to walk through that door."

"Why didn't you keep Vasco awake?" asked Pursivant.

"What's the good of that?" answered Macklin. "They'd hose him out of his chair with a flock of lead. He wouldn't count."

Vasco wakened with a start, at this point, while Macklin settled back among his pillows. Pursivant sent the chauffeur away and sat down on the edge of the bed.

"The other night out there at Oyster Point, what happened?" he asked, and watched Macklin turn shell-grey.

"You know. Just the old gag. A sock with a sandbag, and they haul me into a machine. When I come to, they've got me into a room. A cellar room with no window in it. Not even an electric torch. There's a candle burning and Jack Smith sitting beside it, reading a paper. He puts the paper away and pays some attention to me. I'm all tied up. I try to talk to Smith, but he just grins at me. His face is all busted up. After a while he says: 'Pursivant done this to me; what am I gunna do to you?'

" 'You got the first guess and the last guess, too,' says I to him.

"He just laughs at me."

" 'I ain't even gonna guess,' says he. 'I'm just gunna wait for Les Harmody.'

"That kind of sickened me. I knew Harmody."

"Who is Harmody?" asked Pursivant.

He watched the face of Macklin twist.

"Well, Harmody showed up, finally," said Macklin. "He came over to me and—"

His voice stopped.

"I'll have to be seeing Harmody, one of these days," said Pursivant.

"If you ever have to see him, God help you," said Macklin. "Are you fighting back at 'em, Mr. Pursivant?"

"I'm trying to fight back," said Pursivant.

"How did you ever buy me off of them?" asked Macklin. "My God, how they hated to let me go! You paid high to get me away."

"I paid high because you're worth a high price," said Pursivant. "Go to sleep. Stop staring at the ceiling and thinking."

"Am I gunna be in here—alone?" asked Macklin.

"No. I'm sleeping on the couch," said Pursivant.

A groan of relief came out of the loosening throat of Macklin. He slumped down off his pillows, smiling a little.

"Hell, I'm like a woman; I got nerves," said Macklin. "I'm a regular poor fool—of—a—"

That was how his voice trailed out. He was asleep in the instant. But when Pursivant left the room a moment later, he returned to find Macklin awake and staring, as at first. Pursivant came over and stood beside the bed.

"Easy," said Pursivant. "Take it all easy. Unless things

begin to break well for us, before long, we're going to take a boat for the other side of the pond. You understand me, Jerry? We're going to pull out."

"Any place with you, chief," said Jerry.

Pursivant went to his own room and swept the place with a glance. Literally, unless Cappen were brought to terms within twenty-four hours, it would be high time to jump the country and put both Cappen and Richard Franklin at a safer distance. It might be years before he could come back to continue his career. For that matter, it would be some years before the wretched hollowness left him whenever the thought of Mary Carthy came over him. Like a landlubber first at sea, a thousand nauseas and nostalgias beset him, and he had to keep his teeth set. The telephone rang; and he found the commissioner on the wire.

Said the commissioner: "Listen, Pursivant—I'm all falling apart. I've got the whole shoreland plastered with police. City plain clothes—and I pulled in the State police, too. They're filling all the nooks and the corners. But I have word from Franklin. He's pulled out of his fever; he says he's all right; but he talks like a crazy man. He says that you're through—that every time we can slap you in the face, we're to do it. Pursivant, what's the matter? I had to telephone to you, I can't believe my ears."

Pursivant merely said: "You'd better believe them, though. Something has happened, old man. That's all I can tell you. Better count me out, from now on. But—play your own game against Cappen for at least one more day. It's worth something to your reputation to get that crook, and if you keep plugging for one day you may get him—even if Franklin pulls you off the case to-morrow."

"Franklin? Pull me off the Cappen case? Pursivant, are you crazy?"

"I've said too much. So long."

He hung up.

If Franklin was back on his feet, it was time to jump. He considered the things he would take away with him.

There was not much. There was the ivory horseman and a couple of pictures. The grey flat of Oyster Point and the grey sea beyond it—that picture he could not take, because it would keep him thinking of Riccardo Francolini. Of all his possessions, how few there were that he would vitally regret putting up at auction? Out of all the life he had handled, how little had stuck to his fingers!

"Look up a sailing," he said to Gregory. "There's something going out to-day. The French Line, I think. You and I are going abroad. Not for a week or two. For the rest of our lives."

"Yes, sir," said Gregory.

"Get three tickets. I'll take Macklin, too. How is he?"

"Able to sit up, sir."

Gregory made a slow movement with his hand. "Is it all finished, sir?" he asked.

"Yes," said Pursivant, and went back to his study.

Everything was finished. Franklin wanted his blood and Franklin would soon have it, in this town. Riccardo Francolini was hearing a sacred call to duty and Pursivant had to die—unless he jumped quickly and jumped far. Everything was finished. But in the desk of the study there were things that had to be looked over.

He spent most of the day doing that, driving himself with his lips pressed together. There was nausea in him, as though he had drunk too much the night before, but when he traced the nausea to its source he always found the thought of the girl. Time washes us clean, but he would need to swim through a whole ocean of time, he felt, before his memory was cleansed of her. Perhaps, indeed, that blue stain of her beauty had penetrated him so thoroughly that time would have to rub him out before it cleared away all thought of her.

It was late in the afternoon before Gregory brought him a card that had on it: "Mr. Oliver Cutts Wentworth."

"Tell Mr. Wentworth that I'm out. Tell him I'm busy. Tell him that I can't possibly see him."

"Mr. Wentworth begs you to see him for five minutes," said Gregory. "He says it is something of the very greatest importance. Mr. Wentworth looks like a gentleman, sir!"

On this day when Gregory had been going about with a face stiffened by the sense of disaster, it would require a good deal to make him insist in this manner. Pursivant rattled his fingers on his desk for a moment and then permitted Wentworth to come in. He was a great big fellow dressed in rough tweeds in spite of the warmth of the season. His face was as big as the rest of him. Nose and chin and brows were all cut out on one huge scale, roughly fashioned. He was a good outdoors brown newly varnished over the red of a recent strong exposure. He was the sort of a fellow one connects with sailing and shooting rather than golf. His address was pleasant; in his speech he made haste slowly, using extra moments to get hold of the correct word.

"You have my card," he said to Pursivant. "I'm sure you've never heard of me because I'm an obscure fellow from up the country. Like most of us, I'm anxious to make money. I dare say you feel the same way about the matter. And I've come to you because I know that I can make a profit for both of us. The fact is that I've located the Weaver Trust loot and that I need your help to get it. The proof that I've found it, I'm unable to show you because I didn't venture to bring any of the stuff away with me. What I hope to gain is not money by stealth but the reward which the Weaver Trust has offered. It's a large sum. If it were divided into two portions, my half would still be worth a great deal in my life. The reason that I've come to you to ask your help is that the place is now guarded by police practically day and night and I know that you have enough authority to walk through them."

When he ended, Pursivant merely said: "If there are police near the spot, why don't you tell them what you hope to find? They'll go with you."

"I'm afraid they won't," answered Wentworth. "The police are perfectly capable of accepting what they would afterwards refer to as my 'hint,' making the search, discovering the loot, and claiming the reward for themselves only. If I press any claim, they're very apt to get me into hot water when I try to explain how I happened to discover the hiding place."

The speech was so entirely logical that Pursivant nodded.

"Will you tell me about finding the place?" he asked.

Wentworth nodded, but he hesitated just long enough to cause Pursivant to say: "Well, if this thing pans out, of course I'll go with you. You can have my word on that."

If, in fact, he could help to turn up the stolen funds, might not even the grimness of Franklin relent a little? He dared not believe that he would hear a thing he could believe; and yet the air of Wentworth was that of a man who could not waste his time on deceptions. Lies would appear trivial, compared with the real interests of the man, whatever these might be. And then, above all, it seemed to Pursivant that it was time for Fortune to smile on him. He felt that his luck was about to turn. That was why he sat in keen attention while Wentworth talked.

"I'm an ornithologist," said Wentworth. "I've been at it so

long that I don't think I have to apologize for claiming the title, even though I'm an amateur."

Perfect conviction now came over Pursivant. The think was too good to be a lie. If this burly brute of a man had declared himself to be an engineer, or a yachtsman, or an advocate, he might be suspected—but that he should turn out an ornithologist was too amusing to be a falsehood. It was easy for Pursivant to conceive of those mighty fingers caressing the exquisite feathers of a small bird. The picture burned suddenly into his brain as though he had actually seen the thing happen.

"People of my bent," said Wentworth, "are continually finding out strange places and queer nooks that are perhaps a little more secluded than most men care to visit. And I went out to old Fort Howard to study the nest of a certain gull. That was just the other day. You know the old fort?"

Newer and stronger surety came over Pursivant. He could remember how he had ridden over the hill with Verney and how he had looked out on the long, narrow, rough peninsula with the old road tossing about through the hills and the woods of it, and the sea creaming among the rocks at the bottom of the cliffs. Cappen had been at the Verney place at that time. Might it not be that he had therefore hidden the loot in the neighborhood—he and Merrill? Conviction grew greater every moment, and expectation swelled in the soul of Pursivant.

"I spent half the day on the rocks," said Wentworth, his big voice booming steadily along, well under that control which an educated man keeps over his speaking tone. "I took some pictures—I keep this little German camera in my pocket, most of the time—and I made a good many jottings in my notebook. Before I left, I sat down in a casement of the old ruins and looked over what I had written. Often while one is on a spot many obvious and important items slip by under one's nose, you know. And while I was scribbling in the book, the thing slipped out of my hands and dropped down inside the wall.

"It was getting on into the afternoon. When I looked inside the building, everything was so dark that I couldn't see the next floor.

"Well, I couldn't let the rats have my notebook without putting up a fight for it. You know that our jottings usually seem a good deal more important than our finished works. So I damned a good bit, told myself a way down into the lower portions of the fort. The night came on, while I was still trying one flight of steps after another, and always missing the corner of the fort that I wanted to get to. I used up most of my matches before I managed to make a torch out of some bits of good resinous pine. The place was very confusing, mind you, because so many walls had fallen and blocked up the passageway.

"I was beginning to think that I'd have to go back to the nearest house—about four miles, you know!—and get long rope or a ladder, when I made a last try and got down a long passage and a couple of flights of steps into a lower room—several rooms right over the sea. It was dashing and booming a good deal. There was a moon, and a white rag of moonlight lying on the floor. I thought at first that it was the open face of my book.

"But the book I found in a corner. I found the book and I also found a loose stone in the floor.

"This is where I come to the part of my little story which you will find it hard to believe. It was late. I'd had a hard hunt before I got to my notebook. I should have pocketed that notebook and hurried away as fast as I could, because that bit of torchwood was burning out in my fingers. Instead of that, when I stepped on the loose stone—well, I've never done such a thing before, and I can't explain it. But I pulled up that stone—and it came away easily in my hand. It had no right to come away so easily. The light from my torch shone down into the hole. And by heaven, Mr. Pursivant, the thing I saw there in the darkness was a very pretty thing —a hundred dollar bill face up, looking at me, I give you my word, like a living pair of eyes!"

He paused, here, and giving a strange look to Pursivant, with a gesture that asked permission and pardon he suddenly rose and crossed to the door with an oddly soundless step. The door he wrenched open, and Gregory was seen standing at the entrance with a loaded tray in his hands.

"Thank you, sir," said Gregory. "Your tea, Mr. Pursivant?"

CHAPTER XXX

WHEN Gregory put the tray on the table, Pursivant said, sharply: "You've brought only one cup, Gregory! But just a moment—will you have a Scotch and soda, perhaps, Mr. Wentworth?"

"That would do very well, thank you," said Wentworth.

He added, as Gregory left the room: "I think your man was listening at the door, Mr. Pursivant."

"Gregory?" exclaimed Pursivant. He shook his head violently and then laughed. "You don't know Gregory," he said. "Gregory is fitted to me like the muscles to my bones."

"Muscular rheumatism is a damned bad disease," said Wentworth, and failed to smile. "I didn't hear the pause when he came down the hall, but he was out there for some time, just outside the door."

"You may have overlooked his coming," said Pursivant.

"I heard him going, clearly enough."

"Ay, you were specially paying attention, then. How did you guess that he was out there, in the first place?"

"I don't know," said Wentworth. "Sometimes you can feel a shadow before you see it. And when a fellow has to deal with birds—you know how it is. You sharpen your eyes or the hawk will see you before you see the hawk. Gregory was listening at your door, though."

He was as calm as he was definite. Pursivant could hardly be angry, and he explained: "I suppose Gregory is a bit upset. As a matter of fact, a good many things have happened lately that he can hardly understand. It's just possible that he *may* have eavesdropped a bit. But not with any bad intention. If he listened—why, it's simply as though I heard with two ears instead of one."

He smiled, but still Wentworth was grave as he said in that deep, calm voice of his: "You trust him absolutely."

"Far more than I trust myself," said Pursivant. He thought of Richard Franklin and added: "He's the one man in the world that I'm sure of."

Gregory came back. Wentworth asked permission to fill a pipe; he had it loaded and lighted before Gregory left the room. As the smoke rose, Wentworth seemed to be gathering his heavy brows against the fumes of the tobacco as well as against a trouble in his mind.

"Your man knows that he's under suspicion," he said. "His upper lip is a little stiff. His eye moves a little too fast. There's too much cat-foot in his step, just now."

The minuteness of these observations angered Pursivant, frankly.

"And what of it?" he asked, rather sharply.

The big head of Wentworth lifted a little. "One has to take heed of degrees in all things," he observed. "A dollar's a small thing. Only a fool would stop to pick it up. A hundred dollars is worth a search. A thousand dollars lost will give a fellow a bad night. Ten thousand gone changes the plans for a year. A hundred thousand alters the entire inheritance; and for a million men do murder. You remember that two men already have been killed in the Weaver Trust removal. That's a little less than one man for each million. Perhaps there are some more killings in the air."

This quality of absolutely logical thought, this gradual adding up of units, impressed Pursivant, and not altogether in a favorable way.

"I've told you that I'd swear by Gregory," he said, and

set his teeth. "But at the point in the story where you left off, we'd only got as far as a hundred dollar bill. That was just the first page of the book, I suppose?"

"That was only the first page. I read the rest of the book through. It was the Weaver Trust loot, without any doubt. My infernal torch went out as I finished the business and I sat there in a sweat. Every beat of my heart was a footstep coming regularly towards me. I saw the glinting of guns in the dark, I give you my word. When I got over the panic, I worked the thing out this way: My job was to get the stuff away and hand it over to the Weaver Trust Company that had been robbed. If I could do that, I'd get the reward. You know how fat that reward is. With that in my capital account, I could do exactly as I pleased for the rest of my life. There are birds in other places than in North America. Well, I could go and hunt 'em! As much opportunity as I wanted would be in my hands. But if I took the stuff out and bundled it together in the tarpaulin it was wrapped in, the parcel would be big and I might be noticed coming or going. Men who hid a vast fortune like that, would hardly be without guards posted to watch it. They might have noticed a harmless fool of a bird hunter around the old Fort and let him go, but if I remained there much longer, they'd be after me. Mind you, I'm not telling you how I should have thought of it if my nerves had been still, but they were not still at all, then. They were on the jump. I was a frightened idiot. What I finally decided was to leave the stuff there for the night and come over the next day early—quite early in the morning, and have a horse to carry me. The horse would fetch back the money along with me. I'd hire an automobile and drive straight into New York. It would be a good moment for me and an unforgettable moment for the Weaver Trust when I walked into their office carrying my bundle.

Made my nerves tingle when I thought of that, I can promise you! I ought to beg your pardon for going all through this. My nerves are generally good enough, but as a matter of fact I re-covered that stuff as well as I could. Then I fumbled about on the floor till I found the fag end of my torch. After that, I got down on my hands and knees and brushed the floor all over to rub any marks that my feet had made. Finally, I fumbled my way out of the place. The next morning, I saddled my horse and rode across country and out across the peninsula. It was very early. But at the neck of the Howard peninsula, I was stopped by three police. No, not in uniform, but they had their badges. They wanted to know why I was there and where I was bound. I had to tell them that I was simply out on a morning canter and they advised me to go in another direction. Well, I took their advice. Since then I've been beating my wits to pieces, trying to make out how I could get onto the peninsula. Tell the police about the find, I would not. I didn't trust 'em, as I explained to you before. Nine chances out of ten, the rascals would find some way of attaching me to the commission of the crime. I've heard of their dodges. I thought of getting a small boat and working it in towards the foot of the cliffs and climbing with ropes. But the cliffs are set about with reefs and sharp rocks, and people told me that no boat could live through that sort of water. There was nothing for it but to get across the neck of the peninsula, and there was no way of managing that except by handling the police. I thought the thing over and wondered who would be capable of that. Of course the first man that popped into my mind was Richard Franklin. Honest—so they all say—and certainly able to deal with the police like a grandfather. But Franklin might be too busy to get away. So I thought next of Charles William Pursivant because everyone knows that you had a sufficient interest in the business. It was you who caught Cappen and jailed him. Then there was your disappearance. Most people seemed to think you had slipped out of sight to search for the loot. At any rate, you can see how my mind worked. And that's why I'm here."

He had spoken, throughout, without the slightest hurry, pausing now and then to pull at his pipe and quietly find the next word. When he had ended, he had filled the mind of Pursivant with the picture of the truly honest and somewhat clumsy-minded ordinary citizen whose wits are too clean to be rich in dishonest expedients.

There was a justice in the fate that had brought Wentworth to the man whose advice had caused Franklin to send out police towards all the districts near Duck Island. Moreover, it made Pursivant smile contentedly when he considered how the great Cappen must be grinding his teeth in a passion, blocked away from the treasure by that chance police guard. There was still another figure to be thought of, and that was Merrill, who probably by this time was in the country and about to break his teeth on the same problem of the guarded peninsula. In any case, the thing for Pursivant to do was to get out to the spot quickly.

"Cappen must be battering his brain with both fists, trying to get into the place," said Pursivant. "Perhaps Merrill is back on the job, also. And yet they can't get by the police. It's amusing, Wentworth. We'll go out there to Fort Howard as fast as my car can take me."

Wentworth sighed out a great breath.

"I've been waiting for you to say that the whole thing is a daydream," he remarked. "That car can't take me out any faster than I want to go!"

Vasco slid them through the city traffic, out over the suburban hills and, at Pursivant's directions, right into the Verney place. Wentworth looked a little askance but Pursivant explained: "There's no road for an automobile between this spot and the Fort. And if we go it on foot, we'll be more than an hour on the way. Verney is a friend of mine. He'll give us a paid of horses. Do you ride?"

Wentworth was glad to ride, he said. And so Pursivant got hold of Verney and made his request.

"Go pick out what you want," said Verney. "I'm going to give up the whole outfit. I'm sick of the place and I'm sick of living."

"Is it the girl?" asked Pursivant.

The fat face of Verney puckered all over.

"Damn a female who looks on money as though it were dirt!" he exclaimed. "I'm going into the South Seas and buy an island that has a harem on it."

Pursivant escaped from that sad story and went out to the barn.

CHAPTER XXXI

THEY got a pair of big Irish hunters, as strong as cart horses but full of gallop. The stableman gave them leggings which would keep their trousers from working up, and they rode out into a confusion of twilight and moonlight, of mist and bright starry openings in the sky. Pursivant led for a time down the old road that wandered out from the mainland into the peninsula. It was still barely possible for an automobile that was willing to go at a walking pace, wavering over the ups and downs, but even though it was free from brush, better time could be made across country. So Pursivant pulled out into the open fields and got the wind of a hard gallop in his face. He kept the tail of his eye on Wentworth who rode without skill but with a very capable determination. Horse and rider looked like two in the air when they went over a jump but Wentworth kept up well in spite of that, and Pursivant did not pull up until they were on the last hill overlooking the peninsula.

Over the sea, the horizon opened up, with the narrow tongue of land pointing like the hand of a compass at some infinite direction. The air was warm. The night was struggling to be fair and whole continents of stars appeared now and again but clouds would close in once more and the squalls of rain kept moving about like tall ghosts between earth and heaven. They were dark ghosts towards the moon, but away from it they had a sheen and their trailing skirts raised a glimmering dust over the water. The landscape, too, was tarnished wherever a shadow fell, but big patterns of trees and shrubs and grass were always in high relief, polished by rain water and moonshine.

In the uncertainty of this light, sometimes they could make out the jags and lifts and dippings of the old road towards Fort Howard, and the shoulders of the ruined fort itself, but again the peninsula was a featureless arrow that pointed at the unknown. Now and then they could make out the white margin between the cliffs and the ocean but through moonlight or shadow they could always hear the waves booming and shattering on the rocks.

Wentworth stretched out his arm. There was something about his gesture rather than his size that made his horse seem much too small for him. "Something is coming on," he said.

"What do you mean by that?" asked Pursivant.

"Well," said Wentworth, "you think back through your life. Whenever the stage is set for a big effect, the big effect appears."

Pursivant was silent, as a man generally must be when a good deal of meaning has been clothed in simple words. He led the way down the slope and out to the narrow neck of the point of land. It was flat, slippery rock and so narrow that one sentinel could easily command it. No wonder that the police, when they had been scattered out towards Duck Island, chose this as one post. At this moment the sky opened; the moonlight fell far away on the long, low outline of Duck Island across the water. When Pursivant looked back from that, he saw two men coming out from under a tree; the moon fell on them; their black oilskins crinkled into lines of brightness and shadow.

"State troopers. Nobody can do anything with those devils," said Wentworth, gloomily. "Why the devil didn't I think of that before?"

"What do you fellows want out here?" asked the leader of the pair in oilskins. He came closer and showed a neat, official looking pair of moustaches, the sort that only a sergeant can produce out of his grizzled pride of place.

"We're looking for frogs," said Pursivant. "Seen any out here?"

"Look for them some other place," said the man of authority.

"Hey, Wally, it's C. W. Pursivant!" said his companion, straining the whisper.

"He can be C. W. God, for all I care. He doesn't go by here," said Wally.

However, he had been impressed. He took a half step forward and remained like that, braced. Every brave man knows that the best way to shrink the enemy's fire is to attack it at the source.

"Hold on," said Pursivant, "I think I know you. I saw you—when was it?—being decorated—"

"Last year? I didn't know you were up there. But a lot of the big guns were there with the governor. I'll tell you what, Mr. Pursivant, I don't know why you want to ride out here, but it's our job to close the way. I'm sorry. But you know how it is."

"I understand," said Pursivant. "It's not important. But why should you poor fellows be put here to guard what's left of Fort Howard?"

"I don't know," answered Wally. "And there's another man back there with a machine gun."

"We'll go along," said Pursivant. "But I hate to give up the joke. I've driven all the way to the Verney place and ridden all the way out here for the sake of a practical joke. That's why I'm a fool."

"For a joke?" said Wally. "Nothing but rats to play jokes on in Fort Howard."

"But suppose a light flashes out of the old fort and someone sees it across the water. Suppose that a very high gentleman in the government of this great state should have that signal reported to him—"

"You mean out there on the Farnham yacht?" asked Wally. "You mean the Old Man himself?"

"He's not too good to be laughed at, is he?" said Pursivant.

The trooper began to chuckle.

"You go ahead, Mr. Pursivant," he said. "I'll take the responsibility of letting you pass."

Pursivant thanked him and rode on, the horse slipping a little on the greasy brightness of the rocks. Wally's companion exclaimed in a voice that was not sufficiently subdued: "The big fellow, Wally! He looks like—"

Pursivant did not hear the name; he only heard Wally telling his associate not to be a damned fool. Then through a winding or two they followed the old road.

Wentworth said: "That fellow back there seemed to think that I looked like somebody else."

"You look like a snapshot of someone or other," said Pursivant. "You've got the facial strength to be a politician."

Wentworth chuckled. His powerful voice resounded as though they had been in a small room.

"You did that well, back yonder," he declared. "Is the governor really out there in the Farnham yacht?"

"He might be," answered Pursivant. "A little mystery is what charms an honest fellow like Wally."

He left the slowness of the road and sent his horse galloping across country again with Wentworth like a knight in heavy armor keeping in labor beside him. That was how they drew close to Fort Howard. The ground swayed down. From the bottom of the hollow the sea seemed to be about to flow over the land from either side while the time-moldered walls of the fort still seemed lofty above them. A great portion of the peninsula had wasted down the cliffs into the sea but the prow of the ship, so to speak, retained its high, clean outline. It was easy to understand why the place had been selected for the building of a fort a hundred years ago.

When they mounted the slope, the ruin was more apparent. It looked as though Fort Howard had been destroyed by a great explosion not many years ago. Lumps and hummocks of green at a distance from the abbreviated walls might be the portions of battlements that had been hurled to a distance and rounded over with green turf. There was still the central cleavage of the entrance gate which led them into the big square where double lines of troops in brass-buttoned jackets of blue had once been paraded every morning while officers with swaggering swords paced here and there, looking for trouble. That square was now darkened and a broken pile of masonry in the very center was afloat in the shadow. For the moon was westering rapidly. In the blackness of the ground there was no token of the puddles through which the horses splashed.

They dismounted and tied the horses to a convenient stump of stone. Wentworth stretched himself.

"I'll be sore in the morning," he said. "Why don't they have springs in those English saddles? Let's see. That's the door over there. Yes, that's the one."

He began to whistle, as he strode across the parade ground, and the music took hold of Pursivant more than the jigging strains of a military band when he heard:

"Charlie is my darling,
My darling, my darling,
Oh, Charlie is my darling,
The young Chevalier!"

But when they stepped into the wide black mouth of the door, the whistling penetrated a deep passage and confused the sound with thin echoes, far away. Wentworth fell silent and pulled out an electric torch. He swung the widening glare of it across the outer square. The little pools of rainwater flashed like eyes. The opposite wall kept its big doorways of darkness yawning. Then the cone of light wavered on the passage in front of them. The stonework had simply been roughed out by chisels; one could count the infinite strokes. For wars or pyramids men would build like mighty little ants and disregard the pain of labor.

They went along the hall. The echoes of their steps walked towards them from the distance but never arrived. Drifts of leaves had piled up in corners and rotted. Colorless growths, like fungi, came out of them. They turned a corner. Instantly they were dangerously lost to the outer world. Pursivant was breathing more quickly and getting less of the vital air, as though the place were sealed to the winds and the fungi had been sipping the precious store of oxygen these many years.

They went down a stairway, stepping with caution because little rivulets of water ran like bright, living things over the steps beneath them, and slime made the stones dangerous. Down two flights, they passed into another corridor. Even at this distance below the surface, time had leaned its elbow so hard that the ceiling of monstrous joined stones was broken, here and there. The place was a hive which the bees had deserted because the old quarters threatened to collapse, it seemed. At any moment the place might go to wrack,

Pursivant thought. There would be a deep grinding sound of stone on stone, and coughing, wheezing noises of air expelled from the flattened galleries. The picture grew very vivid and he had to think back to the view of the fort from the outside—green hummocks in which the years could no longer get a toothhold. Still his nerves were a little ragged and the vast shoulders of Wentworth, the heavy, echoing step of the man, made him feel young and incapable of judgment.

They came to a door still firmly fixed on its hinges. Wentworth said: "This is the one, I guess." His voice growled like that of a beast in a cave. He pushed the door open. A gust of fresh air sweetened the very soul of Pursivant and brought to him the good, sour smell of the sea. When he went in he saw a white rag of moonlight on the floor and knew, somehow, that this was the room into which Wentworth had dropped his notebook—this was the room where the treasure was buried.

The room was two stories high. One ceiling had fallen; the wet ruins of it were scattered on the floor, and two rows of windows let the night look into the chamber and the sea sound through it. It was strange that even soldiers with guns in their hands dared to live year by year so close to the melancholy voice of the ocean.

Wentworth stood there in the middle of the room shining his light steadily into one corner.

"Go over there and pull up one of those stones, Pursivant, will you?" he asked. "By thunder, I'm afraid to find the stuff gone!"

Pursivant went, obediently as a boy. The fact that Wentworth was behind him walled out the fear that had kept peering at him through the windows and the doors. The stones in that corner seemed solidly laid but when he gripped at one of them the cement proved to be dust. The burden came away readily in his hands. Something slid out of the hole and scampered across the floor. All his nerves shrank with disgust.

He took up another stone, and another. The hole widened. He laid his grasp on the folds of a rough tarpaulin that appeared. The thing had a good weight. He had to give a heave to drag it out onto the floor. It was made into a bale with wrappings of strong twine that looked very new. A strange horror came over him as he smelled the tarpaulin. It was as though a mutilated body were packed inside the folds. For that matter, two men had given up their lives to get this stuff; and Wentworth had suggested that it was in the cards for still others to die, before the game had ended.

Wentworth himself was leaning over the tarpaulin, now, breathing at his work as he unknotted the cords. He pulled the loosened twine away and unfolded the wrappings. Inside lay a heap of paper, stacks of greenbacks in brown wrappings, small folders of paper that must be negotiable or it would not be here. But after all, the entire heap was just paper; the flame of a match, touched to this mass, would soon turn the whole into nothingness. But in another sense, it could be transformed into wide acres, mansions, factories, ships strong enough to sail the sea. It was like great poetry locked up in the silence of a dead language, waiting for a translating voice.

Wentworth straightened. The light from his torch looked straight into the eyes of Pursivant, blinding him.

"Well, there's the stuff," said Wentworth. "There's the whole of it! Two million and a good whack over. By God, it's boiled-down bit of beauty, that!"

His voice had changed. The torch and the light from it trembled in the big hand.

"Turn the light away, will you?" commanded Pursivant, angrily.

"Excuse me," said Wentworth. "It just occurred to me that I wanted to see what a man looked like when he had his first look at a treasure. If money's the root of all evil, the devil ought to have been somewhere in your eyes."

He laughed, as he said this, and the sound moved off to a distance and mocked them with a crazy rumbling of echoes that kept turning corners and fleeing away. Pursivant made no answer. The laughter stirred him even more than the shining of the light in his eyes. A very unreasonable passion was growing in him, and a desire to fight.

Wentworth, on his knees, commenced to split the loot into two parts. Inside the tarpaulin were a pair of sacks made of strong cloth. Pursivant widened the mouths of the sacks one by one, while Wentworth dropped in handfuls of the treasure. He treated it casually. He began to whistle "The Young Chevalier" again.

"I beg your pardon," said Pursivant. "But will you please stop making that damned noise?"

Wentworth looked up at him, raising his head slowly like a man who has thought his thought before he uses his eyes. Pursivant could see the glint of the teeth as the big fellow grinned.

"I'm sorry, Mr. Pursivant," said he. But he kept on looking up, while his hands were busy tying up the mouths of the sacks; and he kept on grinning, also. It was plain that he had reached an amusing conclusion about his fellow adventurer. Pursivant was shamed and angrier than ever.

"On the way back, you'd better ride ahead," suggested Wentworth. "When they see Charles W. Pursivant again, they won't use their eyes. And these sacks won't be so very large.

We're going through with this, and we're going to split up the reward."

He was still amused, particularly when he used the word "reward."

"I'm not taking a split in the reward," answered Pursivant, stiffly.

"No?" said Wentworth. "Not taking a split in the reward?" He began to laugh softly, again. "Well," he said, "perhaps the newspaper headlines will be worth more to you than the hard cash."

"Do you know," said Pursivant, "that that's offensive?"

"Offensive? My dear Mr. Pursivant! I'm sorry about that. You know that a fellow sometimes is carried away a little in a high moment. But—"

It seemed that a new and grim thought had come over him. It brought him to his feet and Pursivant saw that he rose from crouching on his heels without touching a hand to the floor. The torchlight spilled away to the side. Out of the moonshadow the eyes of Wentworth probed Pursivant's mind, as it seemed.

Then he said: "Do you hear it?" and Pursivant realized that the mind of the big fellow was absent from his eyes, intent with listening. Then in turn he heard or thought he heard a sound like the rapid tapping of heels on stones. It seemed to descend the stairs. Lightly and quickly it came down the hall. There was no doubt about it, now. Someone was walking towards the door which they had left open, like two fools!

CHAPTER XXXII

MARY CARTHY, on that evening, had finished putting on a gown of filmy green, and now, turning gravely before the tall glass, she passed a judicial eye over the image down to the red-heeled slippers. The red-heeled slippers, and the red-gold hair, made her smile a little. She was still smiling when Helen Leigh came breaking into the room, wild-eyed with excitement.

"The poor, one-witted dummy!" said Mrs. Leigh. "He's done, and I'm laughing! Oh, Jacqueline, he's finished and out of the picture!"

Mary Carthy, instead of turning, studied the wonderfully evil face of Helen Leigh in the mirror.

"Who are you talking about?" she asked at last.

"The man who knew other men so well. The hero—the man's man! He's gone. He's wiped out! He's sold by his own valet, by a man he had saved from stripes. Sold! And we've got him in our pockets!"

"What in the world do you mean?" asked Mary Carthy.

"Look at me!" commanded Mrs. Leigh. "There's no use. I can see your sick look there in the mirror. You know perfectly well whom I mean. And high time that he should go down the shoots, because he was beginning to get under your skin. Don't tell me that he wasn't. You were forgetting Mary Carthy and turning into Jacqueline Leigh even off the stage, because of him. You brainless little ape, you would have been in love with him inside another ten days. By heaven, Jacqueline, you slanged him so frightfully just because you thought that you weren't *worthy* of him. A pretty mess he would have made of my work and Cappen's money."

"You're talking of Pursivant?" said Mary Carthy, turning at last. "I don't care a whit about him. He's a dull cluck, to me."

"Is he?" said Helen Leigh. "That's why you're smiling with white all around your mouth, is it? I know how dull a cluck he is to you. You're half in love with him this minute. And now I'll show you that it pays to keep on the road that I lay out for you and not go rambling up by-alleys where you don't find dividends in hard cash. Do you know what's happening to Pursivant now? He's being passed out of the picture!"

Mary Carthy put one strong hand on the back of the chair that stood before her dressing table, and when Helen Leigh saw how profoundly the news had affected her protegé, a fury came over her.

"It's true!" she cried. "You're dizzy about that second-rater! You red-headed little fool, Cappen's bought him—Cappen's bought Gregory the valet, and Gregory has sold his master right into the middle of hell. That's the only place you'll ever see him again. And if—"

Mary Carthy, without a word, ran to the closet at the corner of the room and snatched from it a beret which she jerked over her hair, a cloak which she flung over her shoulders.

"Mary, darling!" gasped Helen Leigh. "What are you going to do? What do you mean? What would—"

She gripped the arms of Mary Carthy. Her savage anger made the cords of her neck thrust out wide as she screamed: "Are you going to let me down, and nine years work, for the sake of a—"

She was flung aside. She stumbled against the little chair,

almost fell, heard the slamming of the front door of the apartment, and the thin, distant ringing of the elevator bell.

She could not pursue. The silence with which Mary Carthy had flung her aside was enough to convince her that mere words would never persuade the girl. A nightmare incredulity made the face of Helen Leigh such a frightful thing that the glimpse she caught of herself in the mirror frightened her into action.

Nine years! She had given nine years and all her hopes to the creation of this picture of gentle beauty, and this sublimation of real inward vice, and now it struck her, with a frightful shock, that the creation of the picture might have become the reality—that indeed Jacqueline Leigh had been brought into existence and that Mary Carthy was the stage property, the illusory image.

That was why she was presently babbling into a telephone: "Helen Leigh—Yes.—Find Cappen—Don't tell me you can't find him, but get to him—Tell him the girl has gone.—You fool—*the* girl—*the* Jacqueline Leigh!—Yes, she's gone.—Oh God, I think she's gone forever!—Ten years of my life—Get Cappen! Get Cappen! Get Cappen!—I don't know where. She's gone to Pursivant's house, I suppose! Tell Cappen! And send somebody here to me—or else I'll go crazy—"

Mary Carthy had seen the front of Pursivant's house before; now, as she paid her taxi and ran up the steps, it seemed to her that the face of the place was empty as the features of an idiot. As she pressed the bell, she looked back at the hugeness of the city, the amber glow of it in the sky, and a bitter sense of futility came over her. She never would be able to find Pursivant in time. And she would have to remember him, the rest of her life, as she had last seen him when he had listened, with a sick face, to her filthy tirade. Even then, through the words, he had seemed to be searching gallantly for a finer truth than that which met his ears.

The door was opened by a man with a grey beard and grey moustaches and a sort of weary nobility of face.

"Are you Gregory?" she asked.

"Yes, Miss Leigh," said he. "Will you come in? Mr. Pursivant is out, but if there is anything that I can tell him—"

She went past him into the dimness of the hall. A front room was lighted; she waved Gregory before her and, as he entered, closed the door behind her. Now that she had a better light, she examined him more deeply, and what she saw made her despair. The man was rock—old, grey, impenetrable rock.

"Gregory," she said, "you've sold your master! You've sold Mr. Pursivant."

"You are in a position to know," said Gregory, smiling a little. "Perhaps you bought him?"

"It's no good trying to brazen it out," said the girl. "The police would be glad to have you, if they could know everything about you."

"Ah, Miss Leigh," said Gregory, "they would want most people, wouldn't they, if they could know everything?"

"You have a last chance," said she. "You can tell us where he is. It isn't too late to undo what you've done. I don't want to turn you over to the police!"

Gregory looked at his watch, calmly. "I'm afraid that it's too late," he said. "About the police—the Commissioner has special instructions to be useful to me in all possible ways. I shall have no trouble in this city, Miss Leigh. Mr. Franklin will see to that!"

Her little bluff had been so feeble, it had failed so utterly, that the moment she found herself stripped of that small weapon, despair and a sort of screaming weakness came over her. She put both hands on her throat to keep back the working of the muscles; and she saw Gregory lift his eyes to something above her and beyond her.

"If that's all, Miss Leigh," said Gregory, "I'll show you out."

Still he did not look at her. A queer shadow of apprehension was in his eyes and, suddenly, she knew what it was. He was afraid of a scene. No matter what rock-like impenetrability defended him, he was afraid of something that she might say to him. And suddenly she knew what the thing was. She slumped to her knees and caught the hands of Gregory before he could draw back.

The hands of Gregory were cold and there was a tremor in them. He would not look down at her.

"Gregory," she said, "help me! I love him! I love him!"

"Madame," said Gregory, "there is nothing to be done! What is started must be finished. It is perfectly useless to make a scene. Nothing can be done. Madame, if you will not stand up, I will have to raise you."

"They're killing him, Gregory!" sobbed the girl. She let the sobs come and fight in her voice. They might help her. They might draw down his eyes to her. "They're murdering your master, Gregory. And I love him! I love him! Help me, Gregory!"

"He was lost before I sold him," said Gregory. "There was no way for him to escape. They were closing in on him. They had a thousand heads against him. There was no hope."

He looked down at her, suddenly, and then made a vague effort to free his hands from her grasp.

"And he loved you and trusted you!" said the girl. "Even now, he's wishing that he had Gregory with him—"

"Madame—" said Gregory.

"He's told me that he could put his life in your hands. He *has* put his life in your hands, and you've thrown it away. But you'll give me a last chance to fight for him. You can tell me where he is. If I can't help him, I want to die with him. Gregory, I love him, I love him!"

"God, God Almighty!" whispered Gregory. "But it's too late. We can't help him, I tell you. He's between Cappen and Merrill. I sold him to Cappen—and Merrill is with him under a false name. They're at Fort Howard—it's too late!"

Fort Howard? She saw the picture of the green old bastions that moldered on the end of the narrow point, over the hills from the Verney place. And she had her own car, not big, but it would go like a witch; in two blocks of running she could be at the garage—

She got out of the house in an instant, with the vague, dull voice of Gregory calling after her.

A good, stiff wind was blowing. She leaned into it. The thin fluff of her skirts washed about her knees as she ran. The cloak flapped and snapped over her shoulders. As she reached the first corner and turned with it, a large form that pursued, clumsily, made her wince away. Then she saw that it was Gregory, running at her side with the wind blowing the grey hair high on his head.

CHAPTER XXXIII

AS those footfalls came hurrying lightly on the ear of Pursivant, while he waited at the side of big Wentworth, the electric torch snapped beside him. From under his coat, Wentworth produced a long gun, faintly shimmering. Pursivant followed suit, gripping hard on the rough handles of the automatic. The weight of the gun came more and more delicately into balance.

"Take him hip high," said Wentworth. "I'll shoot below the shoulder."

And, as the whisper ended, the footfall paused—exactly in front of the door to the room. He steadied his gun on the mark of the black square. He could see a picture of the stranger edging little by little across the threshold. It must be Cappen, then, who had devised a way through the police guards—a note from Franklin would be enough to give him easy passage.

Or was it the other partner, Merrill, who had come to the hiding place.

Then he heard the voice of Mary Carthy, half whispering, half vocal as she called: "Charlie! Charlie! Where are you?"

Perhaps she had called like that at every open door.

Wentworth damned softly—in relief, and in irritation.

"Here!" called Pursivant.

He snapped on his pocket torch and the flying wedge of it showed the girl just inside the doorway, her wet cloak glistening in the dim cone of light; and he could see the wide, frightened shining of her eyes, also.

"Here!" said Pursivant, and ran to her with his arms out. She was laughing, with the sound breaking into many keys. She put her hands up against his face.

"I've been seeing you dead—all the way out, I've been seeing you dead—but they haven't reached you yet."

"What damned business is this?" muttered Wentworth.

She was exclaiming: "You're sold, Charlie! Your man Gregory sold you to Cappen. Cappen's coming! He's on the way. Be quick! Be quick!"

"Gregory? Not my man Gregory!" groaned Pursivant.

"It's true, Charlie!" she answered. "Be quick, or they—"

"Ay," said Pursivant. "We'll hurry."

But he wanted to laugh.

For his whole soul was in labor, scenting happiness, trying to breathe it in like sweet air. Even with Cappen on her heels, even with the great Cappen opposed, she had come out to warn him; and that reckless, savage tirade with which she had driven him from her place in Culver Square—why, all that was an illusion. The truth was here under the beret that the wind had pulled awry on her hair.

"Something was up. Cappen wouldn't tell me. I only knew that he'd gotten something through Gregory and that had to be something against you. I knew he'd been trying to buy Gregory for a long time, and at last he'd won. I went to Gregory—Charlie, can I talk like this?"

"Wentworth is all right. This is Jacqueline Leigh—"

"No, no! Mary Carthy! Mary Carthy, Charlie. Come with me. I'll tell you on the way. Cappen—I went to Gregory and got on my knees. Finally he crumbled and told me what he'd done. He'd told Cappen you were coming out here with another man. I got him outside and made him drive the car with me. We came out here. The police stopped us. I hoped I could rush by them, but the ruts and the rough of the road stopped us. They closed on poor Gregory. I got into the brush and came on. Charlie, why do you stand there like a man in a dream? Cappen is coming! Cappen himself is coming with Les Harmody and Jack Smith."

"They'll be stopped by the police," said Pursivant.

"The police won't stop them. Because they've got Richard Franklin with them."

The name took hold on Pursivant like an hypnotic. And again, it was something that he had foreseen in a chamber of his brain that was only now opened. Franklin would be at the death, of course. He heard the girl saying:

"Charlie, what's the matter? Don't you hear me? Will you come?"

Police? Why, what policemen, what troopers in the state would dare to question for an instant the orders of the big boss? They would come to heel at a gesture from him; he would sweep them from their place and come on with Cappen and Smith and the great Les Harmody.

But all of that seemed a small matter compared with the hands that pulled at his coat, trying to draw him forward. Wentworth strode by him, bearing a double burden of the sacks, merely growling: "Has the heart run out of you, Pursivant?"

The girl, pointing over her shoulder, pulled closer to Pursivant, drew into the thin moonlight so that he could see the rain glistening still on her face.

"Merrill!" she whispered, and that name, like a potent solvent, dissolved the cold numbness of body and brain. He could move and breathe and think. On the heels of "Wentworth" he turned into the outer hall with the girl running beside him. He had been witless as a child, he felt, in not realizing from the first that only Merrill was apt to know the hiding place. He had been less than a child for not learning, first, the exact description of Cappen's partner.

With a flash of his torch he lighted the dripping stairway. Merrill had halted at the bottom step, staring upwards.

Then, like a delayed reflection cast from that ray, as he put out the torch again he saw a brief glimmer of light above him. It went out, but he heard the sound of descending footfalls like the muttering of heavy rain.

CHAPTER XXXIV

MERRILL turned with a gesture that swept the others into motion. One of the sacks he flung to Pursivant and went on with the second, flashing his light now and then like a firefly as he led the way across the hall and through a door so low that Pursivant had to bend double to get through. The ceiling of the room was low, also, and the winking of the light showed cobwebs hanging loose-bellied like old wind-worn sails. Perhaps this had been a magazine of the fort. They went through half a dozen of the cramped little rooms while Pursivant wondered what insects could have flown through this darkness in such numbers as to tempt the wise, fat spiders to build their traps. He dreaded touching the webs for fear lest a loathesome thing might drop down on him. But when he flashed his own light, he could see the great shoulders and hat of "Wentworth" cloaked with dusty filaments. The girl moved between the two men, her feet hurrying to keep up with their long strides. The winkings of Pursivant's light showed, beneath the edge of her tweed waterproof, the trailing green silk of an evening dress, with the red heels of her slippers visible now and then.

Imaginary fragments of the scene kept sweeping up in his mind. She had been dressing for dinner, perhaps, when she heard from Helen Leigh—or perhaps through the door a word from Cappen—that Gregory had been bought at last and had delivered his master into their hands. She cared enough to be here, now, crawling among the cobwebs of old Fort Howard; but she must have received the news with a calm face in order to leave no loophole through which the evil eyes of Helen Leigh could look in on her soul. Perhaps she had gone on doing her hair, putting up the heavy coils of it, her brown image bending and turning in the mirror, her smile reassuring her from the glass of the excellence of her acting; while Helen Leigh took a swig of her favorite gin, straight. After that, the girl had found a way to get out. She must have moved quickly, snatching up the beret and pulling it over her head, swinging the coat about her shoulders, still buttoning it with rapid hands as the elevator dropped her to the street. A taxicab would take her swiftly to the house of Pursivant and there she had encountered the solemn, grey-whiskered face of Gregory. It would be harder to budge him than to dissuade a hungry old owl from a house-hunt, but she had found the words. She had gone on her knees to Gregory, she said. He tried to see that picture but it kept slipping out of his mind: she on her knees and old Gregory with his hands hard shut, fighting against her beauty and her voice. And now she had for her reward a few moments to struggle through the dark corridors of Fort Howard and an excellent chance to die, a little later, with half an ounce of Cappen's lead in her heart. She knew too much, she *was* too much for Cappen to let her live. They would throw her along with the rest off the cliff and into the surf that was grinding up the boulders on the beach. Perhaps no other man in the world would have the resolution to put out such a light, but Cappen was a surgeon who loved the knife.

Out of the little, cobwebbed chambers they came, now, into a rounded tunnel. Merrill let the torchlight glance once up and down the passageway. Then he stood silently in the darkness, until Pursivant could hear the sound of the sea increasing through the walls and a tremor either of the ground or of his nerves went upward through his body.

In the distance, something boomed, like the slamming of a heavy door. The voice of Merrill sounded immediately afterwards on the same resonant note: "They're fighting themselves or shooting at shadows. This way! We've got two-thirds of a hope."

His torch gleamed down the dripping walls of the passage to the lower steps of a flight of stairs. Up this they climbed and turned into a long chamber that had once been used for the stabling of horses—the iron rings were still fitted into the wall and the stone had been grooved and hollowed by the stampings of armed hoofs. Strange to say, the horses had been placed on a seaward side of the fort instead of where they could be most accessible for any use. Through the deep casements the moon was shining and the voice of the ocean seemed to be coming with the light rather than the wind.

Merrill paused with all of him in shadow except his huge feet and the bulging laces of the leggings which were far too small for his calves. He had covered plenty of ground since the first alarm, but yet he always seemed to be pausing, deliberating, as now for an instant in front of one of the windows.

"This is the one," he said at length. "Here, Pursivant. Come here and I'll hand you up. There's a ledge up there."

Pursivant leaned out the window. There might be a ledge above him, but there was a frightful chasm beneath. A gull flew by him so close that he saw the eyes and heard the whisper of the wings as the bird dodged away. Far down, made small by the distance, he saw the flash and shadow and white breaking of the waves and the wall of the fort trembled or seemed to tremble with the blows. When he glanced up, he had a dizzy impression that the top of the fortress was reeling back through the sky, toppling. No, that was merely the movement of the clouds.

"Well?" said Merrill. "Well? You're not afraid, Pursivant?"

Afraid? Only a half-wit would have failed to be afraid, Pursivant thought. A cloud slid like a dark shutter over the moon; a burst of rain came through the shadow—heavy drops that jogged the brim of his hat and stung his neck. But Merrill was hardly likely to attempt a treacherous move —not at this stage of the game, when an outcry from the girl would probably bring Cappen to the spot, or before the two sacks of loot were secured.

So he stood up on tiptoe and barely touched the rim of a ledge where the masonry was set back a step from the lower face of the wall.

Merrill picked him up beneath the knees and lifted him. It was like being raised by a machine. He got his hands and elbows on the ledge and hauled himself up. The wall continued to rise without a break for another twenty feet; the ledge appeared now as a dangerous path which ran straight around the fort. Off to sea, he saw one end of Duck Island silvered by the moonlight, the other half of it lost in rainmist. A ship was out there, its line of lights curving at the bow and stern.

"All right," called Merrill's voice.

He lay over flat on the ledge and gripped the money sacks as they were passed up to him with the anxious hands of Merrill spread out in the air until each batch was safely put away. Then the girl appeared. There was such strength in the grasp of Merrill that he lifted her with his hands alone, thrusting her up high so that Pursivant had little to do in drawing her onto the ledge. She pushed herself right back against the wall and sat still. She made him think of a frightened child.

Then came Merrill in turn. He was so tall that he could get a finger hold to the second joint. Pursivant lay flat again and took a wrist lock to steady the hold. He felt the big wrists bending out; the tendons under the curve turned into hard ropes that shuddered under the strain. Then the head and shoulders of Merrill swung up above the ledge. Pursivant caught him by the shoulder and dragged him strongly in. They were all three on the ledge.

"Make your girl get up. Shake the frost out of her nerves," said Merrill. "She's frozen up all at once. We have to make time. We're not out of hell!"

Pursivant leaned over her.

"Go on!" she said. "I can't stand the height—and the sea under it. I can't move. Charlie, go on—and come back for me afterwards!"

"That's a woman," said the calm, unhurried voice of Merrill. "Nerve enough to get herself into trouble but not enough to take herself out. Well, come on when you can."

He picked up the two sacks. As he shouldered them the wind rammed its fist into him, hard. He had to lean forward for an instant, without taking a step; then he strode on. Even with that double burden, he would manage to get away from everyone if he had a tithe of a chance. Perhaps that was what got the girl to her feet even more than the hands of Pursivant. She tried to tell him once more to follow on, alone, but no matter how frightened, she had too much sense to argue the thing. When she was standing, the first glance downwards at the sea made her slump towards the wall. She kept a shoulder brushing against it but she dragged herself forward. Pursivant followed, keeping a grip on her elbow and a steady pressure. That was how they rounded the slow turn of the wall and saw big Merrill again. He had the two sacks in a monstrous heap upon one shoulder. The wind hammered him and swayed him a little so that he made the ledge seem to shrink and narrow with his danger; and he had halted because the way was broken in front of his feet.

It was a new break. The moon came out and showed the whiteness of newly exposed, unweathered cement, and the crystals of fractured stone where thirty feet of the outer wall had sliced away and taken the ledge along with it into the sea.

Merrill turned. Pursivant felt like an infant, facing that bulk.

"I've got half a mind to throw the stuff into the sea," said Merrill. "But that's no sense. We've got to go back through that same window."

There was no other way, of course. Pursivant turned and stepped along the ledge. There was a constant pull on his coat where the girl was gripping it. However, now that he had to go back into the old danger the mere height of the cliff and the pull of the wind became insignificant fears. He kneeled on the ledge and looked down towards the window from which they had just climbed. Light slashed across it from the inside at that moment; he heard the voice of Cappen and the wind fell away so that he could make out the words clearly.

CHAPTER XXXV

THE three of them crouched back on the ledge. The girl kept looking up at Pursivant, and Pursivant at Merrill, and Merrill down at the sea, thoughtfully. They could hear everything, because the rounded ceiling of the stable room was a sounding board that projected every sound with a fine vibrancy. Jack Smith was down there, and though Pursivant had only heard it once before, he recognized perfectly the husky voice of Les Harmody because of the peculiar animal whine that mixed into it, now and then.

Cappen had been saying: "They sneak through the lower hall; they climb the stairs; they turn into the stables; they come right up to the windows."

"Do they step into the sea, then?" asked Les Harmody.

His voice came out into the open air.

"There's only the straight wall over these windows," he said. "The only place they went to was into the sea."

"There's got to be a place up the wall, there," said Cappen. "Stand up and you can feel the face of it. I'll steady you."

"What could there be? Have you got the idea of a secret door in your head, Arthur?"

"I don't know. Merrill was here more than I was. He used to climb all over the place. Wherever a bird was able to light and nest, Merrill could find a way to get to the spot."

"Hold me hard," said the voice of Les Harmody.

The moon, at that unlucky moment, chose to show the full brightness of its face, and Pursivant saw the tips of fingers sweep along the ledge. Merrill waited with a ready gun and in that same attitude of thoughtfulness.

"Nothing up there," said Harmody. "Steady me, Arthur. I don't like these perches in the middle of the sky."

His voice reappeared in the hollowness of the room below.

"Not even a bird would be at home out there," he was saying.

"Look here!" called Smith from a distance. "Here's a side door they might have gone through."

"Follow them then," said Cappen dryly.

"Follow Pursivant and Merrill all by myself?" exclaimed Jack Smith. "What kind of a dummy do you think I am?"

As he heard his name pronounced, Merrill looked up, without haste, and right into the face of Pursivant. And Pursivant, looking back, smiled a little. Merrill stared down again into the sea.

"Here's where the trail ends, and here's where it has to begin again," said Cappen.

"One of us ought to get back to the automobile," declared Harmody. "The three of 'em may be getting into the yard again, by this time."

"Maybe," said Cappen. "But look over this room, first. There's a broken place in that ceiling. Jack, hoist me up and let me take a look into it. I know Merrill. He knows how to be simple. The easy trick is his trick whenever he can play it."

Merrill looked up again, not at Pursivant but at his own thoughts, and this time he smiled at the golden face of the descending moon. He had appreciated the compliment paid by his old partner.

However this affair turned out, Pursivant knew that the two had both been wrong. Millions could hardly be worth to them what they were worth to one another. He thought of many comparisons, but none were right. Hawk and tiger hunting together would never go hungry; that was the nearest way of thinking of the pair. It seemed to Pursivant an absurdity that he had been able to jail Cappen and so, by a devious chance, bring Merrill the opportunity to double-cross his old companion.

"Nothing here," said Cappen.

Feet dropped with a jar to the stable floor.

"Well, they're gone by this time," remarked Harmody. "There's no use hurrying. They're gone and they've taken the stuff with them. They can drive off in our car and lead the horses behind them. No need for them to worry, now. You're doing yourself proud tonight, chief."

"Don't bother me," answered Cappen. "I have to think a bit. Brain work is faster than footwork, Harmody. And I've been upset, tonight. The girl, Harmody. I thought I understood her. I thought she was the best link in the steel chain. This morning I heard her jeer Pursivant off his feet. This evening she's out here with Merrill and Pursivant."

"You may be wrong," commented Jack Smith. "We got the mark of a woman's shoe on the floor. That's all we've got."

"When I telephoned back to Helen Leigh, she told me Jacqueline was gone. She has to be the one. No other woman in the world knows what's up, at old Fort Howard."

"For God's sake," shouted Harmody, "are you going to waste time on the girl? They're sneaking away from you every minute, now!"

"You can't be so sure. They may be sitting close by and listening to what we say," answered Cappen. "Besides, the big fellow is out there with the car."

"What's he stack like against a Merrill and a Pursivant?" demanded Jack Smith.

"They'd wipe him out in a second!" said Harmody.

"He stacks up very high against anyone," answered Cappen. "But suppose they do manage to down him. We hear the shots. So do our men down the line, and they wait to bag the birds that try to fly. I won't be hurried, Harmody. Thoroughness will do a lot more than speed against Merrill. Try that next room, will you? I still have to think things out."

Footfalls drew away from the stable. A light step began to move up and down across the windows where Cappen must be pacing with his thoughts. What would he devise? What could he in fact accomplish by a mere process of thought?

A chilly hope began to live in the mind of Pursivant.

The "Big Fellow" of whom they spoke—that would be Richard Franklin, who had made a way for them through the guards who watched the peninsula. They would have to retreat to him, before long, and confessing failure they would draw away towards the town.

However great the hope might be, Merrill showed no token of a light heart. With his arms folded and his chin on his breast so that his head was lifted by his breathing, he continued to contemplate the sea. Pursivant shut out the sight of him by turning to the girl.

It seemed to him that Mary Carthy was gone. Twelve Culver Square and the lantern-light of the open-air café held her. This was the girl he had found at Verney's place. She had turned a little and she was smiling at the moon. One hand lay palm up on her knee. The wind that had fallen so suddenly was beginning again. It lifted and dropped the broad lapel of her coat and across her throat it threw quick movements of the thin chiffon. Then he looked nowhere but down at her hand, seeing all of her in that. It was hard to approach her with words.

"There's one thing that I have to know," he told her. "That is why you did all this tonight."

She kept staring at the moon and the smile was dying.

He said: "I don't want to try to read your mind. Women and men speak a different language and the women a man can talk to easily have simply picked up a way of chattering. But if you can get at the truth in your mind and speak it, I want to hear. What I said to you this morning about coming away with me—I meant that. I ought to say that to you, if it helps you to talk back."

"Do you still mean it?" asked the girl. "About going away?"

He leaned over her, but since he could not see her entire face, he straightened again.

"I mean anything that will make you happy," said Pursivant.

He had to wait for a long time, until he thought that perhaps she would not speak. But the wind no longer seemed to blow on them; instead, it was as though they had been given movement towards the western sky.

"When I was Jacqueline Leigh," she said, "the only person I was happy with was you. And this evening, all at once I was terribly tired of being Mary Carthy."

He grappled at this idea. He touched her hand and she closed her fingers over his, absently.

"Jacqueline Leigh," she said, "had to work hard at languages and books. She had to learn how to read poets and how to look at pictures, and how to see the best things in a temple or a statue. It was a lot of hard work and it nearly killed Mary Carthy."

She had to speak so softly that he leaned closer and felt the physical presence of her voice all through his body.

"Mary Carthy used to be dusty and dirty; her finger nails were broken and stained. She used to pick at them as she sat in her dingy little room and read cheap magazines and stories about guns and lovers. But Jacqueline Leigh had to keep her body strong and clean. She had to dress her hair a touch at a time, and every touch had to be perfect. A girl can't ride well unless she loves the horse she's riding; I had to learn that. I had to learn a lot of things like that. Finally—this evening—all day long I'd been Mary Carthy. She sent you away this morning. She said such frightful things to you that you went away. She tried to tell herself that Cappen or no Cappen, she liked the savor of what she had said. She drank some cocktails and smoked a good deal. But then, this evening, she heard that Gregory had sold you and all at once she knew that she never wanted to be Mary Carthy again. I want to be Jacqueline to the last breath I draw."

She took her hand from him, suddenly, and for the first time faced him.

"If I'm stained in your mind so that you'll always be looking for Mary Carthy's face and listening for her talk," she said, "perhaps you'll find what you look for; but if you want the other girl, I think I can be that for you. But however you want me, I'll go with you. I knew that this morning when I drove you away, because something went out of me and flew after you. That's what brought me out here tonight."

The moon put its chin on that highest hill of Duck Island and the thin rain that blew across the disk made it seem to be turning. Pursivant smiled at the sight.

"You've gone so far," he said, "that you know what you'll have to do?"

"What?" she asked him.

"Teach me how to catch up."

The quiet murmur of Merrill came to them: "You two will do very well—if you live 'till morning. The long-winged hawks are the best game birds. They make the fastest flyers."

It was like the materialization of a spirit to find him suddenly added to them.

"Poor Cappen!" said Merrill, looking down at the joined hands of Pursivant and the girl. "What do they say about building better than we know? Why, Cappen took such pains with her that he never would let me see her. He took such pains to teach her how to fly high that now she's gone up into the sky and she'll never come down again!"

He began to laugh, silently, of course, and the slant moonlight painted his huge face with yellow gilding and black jet. When he was able to speak again he said: "But I don't see a happy ending for your story, Pursivant. You owe something to the devil. So does the girl. And the devil always collects. You can lock up the past in the best safe in the world, but the devil is a yegg who breaks in through armor plate."

It was just on the heels of that that the voice of Cappen sounded beneath them: "Well, what have you found?"

"Mr. Richard Franklin," said Les Harmody. "That's all we've found. He got restless and came to investigate."

"Ah, that's too bad," said Cappen. "Franklin, you shouldn't have done that! They're probably in the car already. Move, now, all of you. Straight back to the yard of the fort. Here, I'll lead the way because I know it best. Show your lights!"

And there was a rush and a rattling of heels on the floor. The arching vault of the ceiling received the sounds, softened them, gave them out through the windows into the night until the sounds of running died out.

Merrill was instantly on his feet.

"I'll climb down—we have our first real break of luck, here. You can pass me the stuff, Pursivant—"

"I'll climb down first," said Pursivant, coldly.

"All right," said Merrill. "Just as you please. But you're wrong to think that I'd let down a friend in the middle of a job. Over the edge. I'll hand you along. And I know how we can double up our trail for Cappen, now!"

CHAPTER XXXVI

PURSIVANT hung by his hands from the ledge. Then the capacious grasp of Merrill crushed his wrist and let him slide down until his dangling feet found the sill of the casement. He hooked his right arm under the upper rim of the window. The dizzy height meant nothing to him now. The sea was black. Over Duck Island only the red-gold brow of the moon was peering and the clouds seemed to be sweeping lower. When he looked up, there was that former illusion of the wall falling through still air. He received the two sacks one after the other and dropped them through the window. The girl came next. He made so sure of her that the breath went out of her with a gasp, and he held her for an instant, angling out over the drop of the cliff with a tumult in his mind. Beauty was the strength that ruled the world for good or evil, nerving us or betraying us. Cappen for the sake of three small rubies had entered the death-house. Now Pursivant was on a threshold and could not tell what the door would open on.

The girl slipped past him into the dark of the room. Merrill swung down. To grasp him was like surrounding the round, hard bulk of a barrel; but he steadied that weight of bone and muscle through the casement, dropping down immediately behind him into the stable. After the wideness of the outer night, the air seemed warm and stale and an odor of foul animal habitation reeked out of the masonry.

Merrill's voice was saying: "Take one sack, Pursivant. We

head through that door on the right. Then follow me back to the room where we found the stuff."

From the very door towards which Merrill had made the first stride, an eye of light opened at them. There was a sound of rapid fire like the tearing of treble bolted sailcloth in the fingers of some giant storm. Merrill seemed leaning to run. He kept on leaning till his whole great body rushed down to the floor. His head bounced with the impact against the pavement. Like the whole van and center of an army, he was subtracted from Pursivant before the battle began.

For his own part, he had started moving the instant that eye of brightness shone at them. Machine guns or automatics are apt to cut a straight line with their fire. He ducked low and with a sweep of his arm knocked the footing from under the girl. She went down sidelong.

"Lie flat!" he yelled at her.

That was as he saw Merrill dropping like a tower, and he hopped towards the wall like a slow, clumsy kangaroo. He wanted to put all the bullets from his automatic into the eye of that light but he had to treasure his lead as a thing more priceless than breath.

His own electric torch, with the switch snapped on, he skidded out on the floor, for there had to be light to answer light, one spot of brilliance to make the rest of the long stable seem dim.

Something plucked at the shoulder of his coat and struck the wall behind him at the same instant. They had turned loose with many weapons. The uproar had a strange effect of dimming his eyes. In the air there was an acrid smell of stone dust.

To shrink the enemy's fire, attack it at the base. Well, even a cornered beast knows that much. Pursivant knocked the light in the doorway into darkness with his first lucky shot and sprinted across the room.

He fired as he ran, hoping to get his bullets through the door. No other lights were in there for that vital second. Then a screech from the blackness splintered like red lightning across his brain. He heard a body fall.

One of them was gone. Cappen, he prayed, knowing all the while that even bullets could not pump screams out of the throat of Arthur Cappen. Franklin, Smith, Harmody all remained, at the best, and all good fighting men.

He got to the doorway, striking one shoulder heavily against the jamb so that he lurched sidewise. Another cone of electric light slapped him in the face. He dodged, leaping with all his strength and shooting towards the torch. Then a blow as hard as a good straight left hammered against his left shoulder. His feet tripped on a fallen body. More lights caught him in a quick weight of brilliance. Everything combined at once against him. He thought that as he toppled. He saw a face very long and lean and pale and the flash of a swinging gun across the face. That was Harmody, of course; but the blow he had aimed glanced from the head of Pursivant instead of crushing the skull.

Pursivant, falling, tried to throw out his left arm and jerk Harmody down on top of him, but his left arm would not work. That hammer stroke on the shoulder had been a bullet tearing through. He twisted about. Harmody simply stepped on his right wrist and pinned the automatic to the floor.

"That's about all," said Harmody. "Go get the skirt, one of you. I've got this baby, all right. Have I got you, kid?" he added, leaning and staring his flashlight into the eyes of Pursivant.

The brilliance was so close that he could see the thin

twist of burning filament with the silvered reflector behind it.

A brave man should never stop fighting in order to think but Pursivant was thinking that Harmody had him, surely enough. The girl was lost, too. The thought of her and the image of her was somehow enclosed within the twist of burning wire in the electric torch.

Harmody pulled the automatic out of his nerveless fingers. Someone else leaned over him. That was Franklin. His face was all bright with sweat but his expression was wonderfully calm and still.

The girl screamed out in the next room. Cappen was there. Cappen might be cutting her throat, now.

"Oh, God!" said Pursivant. And the sound of her cry thrust fingers into his shoulder wound and struck another blow on the bruised, torn scalp of his head.

"You see?" said Harmody. "It's the gal. That's the way to get at him. I told you that, Franklin. Stand up, Pursivant. Here's some twine, Franklin. Tie his wrists behind his back."

Richard Franklin tied his hands together so hard that there was an instant pressure from the constrained blood. Cappen stepped through the doorway not thrusting the girl before him but holding her back. When she saw Pursivant standing, a cry came out of her throat that took the pain from him as though all the suffering of the world were in her alone.

"Charlie, what have they done to you?"

Cappen held her back.

"I'm only nicked. I'm not broken," said Pursivant.

"Now, that's funny," said Harmody. "I never thought she'd give a damn. Not about anything. Did he get Jack Smith for keeps?"

Jack Smith lay on his back with his head and shoulders propped stiffly up against the wall. Across his stomach there was a lake of blood damned up inside the wrinkles of his coat. Harmody leaned over him and said: "He's not dead. But he's dying. The tap on the head when he whanged the wall has knocked him silly. He'll be out for good before he comes to."

Cappen had released the girl enough to let her face him. She put her arms around him and kept straining herself closer and letting her head fall back so that she could look up into his face.

"What are you going to do with him, Arthur?" she said. "For God's sake tell me what you're going to do with him!"

Cappen simply kept smiling, now at Pursivant and now at the girl.

A sickness of horror barely left Pursivant enough breath to call out: "Stop it! Jacqueline, stop it!" But Cappen kept on smiling and moving his pale, bright eyes from one face to the other.

"I'll go back and begin again," said the girl. "I'll go through with everything you want, Arthur. I'll forget tonight. I'll forget *him,* if you'll let him go. You can trust him. He won't talk. He'll give you his sacred word of honor. His word of honor *is* sacred. Arthur, I'll make up for everything—"

Cappen had lifted his arm without haste. Now he struck her across the face, deliberately, first with the palm and then with the back of his hand. He kept on smiling while he put her away from him. She slumped up against the wall with the white of the blows marked on her face.

And Franklin, who had always stood for everything that is fair and right between men and men and men and women —Franklin stood in the room while this was going on. But then Pursivant saw that it was not going on, for Richard Franklin; he was entranced by a single thought and that thought centered with a vast and calm hunger on Pursivant.

Cappen said: "Keep your eye on them, Harmody. Better herd them in the next room. Wilbur Merrill is dying!"

His voice lowered on that name. Someone might have said, in such a tone as this: "Abraham Lincoln is dying!"

Harmody took Pursivant by one arm and the girl by the other. Franklin followed. Cappen led the way, his torchlight lifting up and down along the floor.

Merrill had been turned. Cappen must have done that, and settled the head of his former partner on one of the sacks of loot. It seemed as though the big man had simply lain down for a rest. There was no mark of his fall on his face. His hair was not even discomposed, and the little ribbon of blood that kept rippling slowly across his body and gathering on the floor seemed a matter of no importance. Only when Pursivant looked closely could he make out the slight alteration in the color of the lips. They were growing pale.

CHAPTER XXXVII

OF course there was no moon, but sometimes through the movement of the clouds Pursivant could see beyond the windows the gleaming and whirl of the stars. The wind kept low; it uttered a vain hushing above the deep sound of the sea. And these things, but above all the reverent attitude of Cappen, set the stage for the death of a hero, a Hamlet with his Horatio beside him.

Cappen was on one knee with a flask of brandy to offer Merrill.

He said: "You know wounds, Will. If there's a ghost of a chance, I'll have a doctor here inside an hour."

"There's no chance," said Merrill. "It got me through the liver, and you know what that means."

"Much pain?"

"Not much. Just where the bullet cut the skin going in and out. I'm tired and there's a good bit of air hunger. You know what that means, too. I won't last very long, now."

"What made you go through, Will? I mean, after you'd come back and found that I was pardoned, why didn't you try to get in touch with me?"

"My promise was to keep out of the country. Once you knew that I had landed, you'd never forgive me. It would be dog eat dog, after that."

"You're wrong, Will," said Cappen. "I would have forgiven you."

Merrill smiled.

"You think so now," he declared, "and it's not so hard to

forgive a dying man for things he can't repeat. But what's done is done. Let me have another taste of that brandy."

It was pressed to his lips. His eyes closed under the shaggy brows as he swallowed a stiff dram.

"Are you in pain, Charlie?" murmured the girl. "Are you bleeding?"

"Hardly at all," said Pursivant; for the blood that wasted from his body, the small, cooling trickle that ran down his breast and back, was far less to him than the anguish which kept her turning her head a little from side to side as she watched his face. It seemed strange to him that the old primitives, so praised for the direct force with which they painted emotion, should have used contortions of the mouth and weeping eyes, for high grief is as noble as high joy and as calm; he could see it now, glassed in the eyes of Jacqueline Leigh. Perfect hatred is calm, also; for when he looked away from her he saw the look of Richard Franklin and found it almost mild.

"Be quiet, everyone!" said the hushed, impatient voice of Cappen.

Merrill was speaking, now. The mere closing and opening of his eyes seemed to have brought death near to him. As always, he was unhurried, and in attempting to save breath he so lowered his tone that sometimes it seemed as sonorous and distant as the sea, or again as though the noise of the sea were entering the room and trying to utter syllables of human meaning.

"Colfax has my last will," said Merrill. "Everything goes to you, of course. The key to my safe-deposit is with him, too. You'll find one of the diamonds in the safe."

"Never mind for all that," said Cappen. "Think of yourself, Will. Think of—"

He kept his speech soft, so that the least whisper might interrupt him as he was interrupted now.

"But this is one of the Duchess' diamonds," said Merrill. "The big center one. You remember that we turned the first ace to see who got it? I want to laugh when I think of the Duchess; but laughing takes breath. I remember the three fat wrinkles on the back of her neck when I was unhooking the string. It was hard to work the catch, too. You remember that?"

"I remember the look of her afterwards, when I'd managed to get the string of paste imitations around the fat of her throat. But to think of Leon Criquot being taken in that night and stealing the paste after we'd stolen the real things!"

"I went to his trial," said Merrill. "You know it wasn't till the day of the trial that the experts discovered the ice was faked."

"Ah, I'd forgotten that!" said Cappen.

"You'll remember that and a lot else when you see the big center diamond. As long as you hold it, Arthur, every sparkle of it will remind you of some day we've had together."

"I'll keep it," said Cappen, softly, "to the last day of my life."

"Will you?" asked Merrill, wondering a little as he lifted his eyes.

"To the last day!" said Cappen. "Now, there are things you want me to do. There's the boy in England."

"I've arranged a trust for him. Five thousand a year is enough for him. That will let him follow his ambitions, if he wants to be something that doesn't pay a cash return. I don't want him to have any more. A big income lets fat gather on the brain of a young man."

"It's true," said Cappen.

"If you want to know how he's getting on, you can look up old Markham, but—"

"No," said Cappen. "I'll never come near your boy, Will."

"Sorry," said Merrill. "But a fellow with your talent as a promoter and exploiter, Arthur, couldn't be with the lad without finding some new way of using his wits."

"I'll never be near him," said Cappen. "Markham will tell me if he's ever in need. There's the mother, though?"

"She took to roulette," said Merrill. "That was the end of her. So long as she kept with baccarat, she was modest, serious, temperate, charming. She never cost me more than I was glad to spend on her. But roulette speeded her up too much. She passed from Bordeaux to Burgundy in a month or two, spoiled her digestion, ruined her eyes, and three months ago she decided that life was not worth living. I was going to visit her grave when I got to the other side of the water."

He began to smile. His face was now so pale that the smile seemed to be worked in stone forever.

"I'll visit the place for you," said Cappen.

"Tush! She was nothing. She was a mere nothing," said Merrill. "I got a good foal by her, and that was all she amounted to. You take women too seriously, Arthur. There's this girl Mary Carthy. You were going to make her into a key that would unlock the best bank accounts in the world. But she stayed in the first strong hand that touched her."

"I've damned her and I'm done with her," said Cappen. "But I'll remember your advice."

"Remember this, too," said Merrill. "Very active men ought to retire early."

"Now?" said Cappen.

"Now," answered Merrill.

"I'll close the book with to-day," said Cappen.

"Then there's another matter—let me have the brandy again."

Cappen put it to his lips. When Merrill had finished swallowing he was breathing rapidly, his pale, leaden-colored lips constantly parted.

"Listen to me, Arthur, because the bucket is smaller than I thought, and the leak has drained it. Listen: In my safe you'll find a folder of papers on the Urinatoridae. Never mind writing down the name. Take that folder to Professor Oscar Thomas at Oberlin. Ask him to look at my drawings, particularly. I think when he reads my stuff through, he'll think that I've seen some new things in loons. And if he can clean the thing up for publication—pay him what his time is worth, will you?"

"I'll give him twice what he asks."

"No," said Merrill. "The thing has to stand on its own merits. But after the magazine publication, Thomas will give you some other small contributions I've made to ornithology. Gather them together and get the whole out as a small book. Bind it in brown cloth—brownish red buckram. Letter it in gilt. You understand?"

His whisper was hardly vocalized at all. The life was panting out of him in words instead of empty breathing—that was all. The big vibration of his voice no longer matched the booming of the waves but rather the faint rushing of the withdrawing waves and the thin whispers of the wind.

"In brownish red buckram," repeated Cappen. "The lettering in gilt."

Merrill had begun to gasp a little for air.

"Well," he murmured, "this is about all, Arthur, till we—"

He put his hand in that of Cappen and a quick little shudder ran through his body. His mouth remained open, so that Pursivant kept expecting more speech till he saw Cappen lay the limp arm of Merrill across his breast. He drew the other one over it. With the cautious tips of his fingers he closed the eyes of the dead man.

Cappen stood up.

"Except for you, Pursivant," he said, "none of this would have happened. Get out of the room! Mr. Franklin, take him back in there, if you please. Harmody, stay here with me. I'll need your help about Merrill for a few minutes."

That was how it came about that Franklin marshalled Pursivant and the girl into the next room. His electric torch, shining between the two, glinted on a slender batch of old straws that hung from a crack in the wall. Loose hay, apparently, had once been stored here for the horses.

They were through the doorway before Pursivant had sight of big Jack Smith who had risen to his feet with his hands spread out in front of his stomach. The pool of congealing blood had flowed over those hands and was still dripping towards the floor.

CHAPTER XXXVIII

"LOOK at it—look at *me!*" said Jack Smith. "Mr. Franklin—my God, look at all the blood! Why ain't somebody done something for me? Who's going to bandage me up? Why don't you answer me? Where's Cappen? Where's Harmody? My God, what does it mean?"

His voice kept going up the scale. Franklin closed the heavy door between the two rooms. He merely said: "Cappen is in there with a dead man. Don't trouble him with your noise. Don't trouble me, either. Doctors can't help you, Smith."

Franklin went over to the opposite side and stood in the doorway, occasionally playing his flash across them. In his other hand he held that old gun of Pursivant's that had killed Alberto Francolini ten years before. Only by the reflection of that light from the walls was the face of Franklin visible, but Pursivant could make out the familiar features well enough at all times. Merrill and Cappen, and Harmody the brute, they were soft as putty compared with the iron of Franklin.

Jack Smith turned towards Franklin, slowly. What he had heard had not come readily into his unwilling mind.

"Doctors," he said. "That's what I need. I need a doctor, Mr. Franklin. Look where I was plugged. I tell you, it's serious, sometimes, when a bird gets ripped through the belly like this. I gotta get to a doctor quick."

"It's too late for that," said Franklin, with the most perfect indifference. "You've had your teeth in plenty of other men. Now you're getting your turn at the music. You'll never hear the end of this tune, Smith."

Jack Smith embraced his stomach with both of his big hands. He gaped on Franklin, incapable of utterance.

"What's up in there?" asked the voice of Harmody, from the stable room.

"Smith has come to. He's walking around," said Franklin. "But he'll soon be through."

"Keep your head up, Jack," said the cheerful roar of Harmody.

That brought the power of speech back to Smith. He kept one hand pressed over his wound but the other, dripping red, went out in a wide gesture.

"Mr. Franklin, tell me true! A man like you, a gentleman like you would tell me the truth, sir. What you mean by never hearing the end of this tune?"

"Don't you see that you're dying?" asked Franklin. "You're staggering already."

"Staggering?" breathed Jack Smith. "Dying! Is this some kind of a gag? I'm only scratched, I tell you. No more pain than a cut on your finger, hardly—"

"There's very little pain with body wounds," said Franklin. "There's chiefly thirst and the lack of air. You'll be dead in five minutes, Smith."

Jack Smith began to sway a little from side to side. Franklin went on: "You've done killings for hard cash, and murder is your game to-night. Now that you've lost your trick, try to lose it like a man. Don't gibber at me like a baboon."

Jack Smith went slowly down on his knees, as though he were praying to a god and that god were Richard Franklin, or death that stood beyond him. Pursivant closed his eyes to shut out the sight of the loose, quivering face, but he could not help hearing the voice groan: "You mean that I'm going to die? You mean I gotta die?" Then, in a scream: "I can't die! There ain't no priest! I gotta have a priest before I die."

Said Les Harmody from the other side of the door: "Tap that bum on the head, Mr. Franklin, will you? Cappen wants a bit of quiet."

It seemed that that voice subdued Jack Smith to such a point that he feared to speak loudly afterwards. Perhaps his terror weakened him. At any rate, all the strength and stiffening went out of his body and made him spill over so that he rested on one elbow, with his hands over his wound.

He began to cry in a shrill whisper, a falsetto; it was like the weeping of a woman; it was the most horrible sound that Pursivant had ever heard. Jack Smith slobbered out words through his tears, in his new, weak voice: "I gotta have a priest. If you won't let me have a doctor, oh God, lemme have a priest! It ain't askin' much to have a priest."

He threw back a hand into the short bristle of his hair and made it a clotted red blur. Jacqueline Leigh gasped and ran over and kneeled by him.

"There's no priest here," she said.

"I gotta have a priest—I done things that'd send me to hell, without a priest," sobbed Jack Smith.

Then he pawed at her with his bloody hand.

"Lemme talk to you!" he begged. "Lemme talk to you, Miss Leigh. You're better than no priest at all!"

Self pity turned him limp. She slipped down beside him so that his head rested on her knee, and bracing herself on one hand, she leaned over that mumbling, blood-stained, tearful face.

"Talk to me, Jack," she said. "I'll listen to every word. You haven't been as bad as you think. You've been a little wild, but you've been not so bad. And they've punished you. They've had you in prison. It's going to be all right, Jack."

"You're educated. You oughta know," said Jack Smith. "Have I got an even break?"

"I hope so. Yes, you have!" said the girl.

Pursivant came a little closer. He looked at the pair on the floor and then he stared at Franklin. There was the same calm in the face of Richard Franklin, with only a slight accenting of the sneer that had been freezing on his lip. And still nothing existed for him except Pursivant. A foolish impulse rushed up in Pursivant to call out to Franklin that a miracle was being performed there, under his eyes, for if there was purification by fire there was purification by blood, also; and he had a ghostly sense of insight that told him that the girl was not befouled but cleansed by the wet hands of Smith. His begging gestures kept maundering about her but not a shadow of horror was in her face, and she never winced.

"I wouldn't care except for Squeeze Malone," said Jack Smith to his priest. "To hell with the rest, but Squeeze thought that I was his friend."

"Perhaps it doesn't matter. It's a long time ago," said the girl. "Don't think of it, Jack."

"Maybe it don't seem long ago to God," said Jack. "But the truth is that I tried to stop myself while I was swingin' the axe. The best I could do was to turn it in my hand. He only got the flat of it. You wouldn't think it would bust in his head. You wouldn't think nothing would bust the head of Squeeze Malone. It went all in. His eyes popped out like the eyes of a crab. But I only gave him the flat of the axe."

"It may not—I don't know," said the girl. "Be quiet, Jack. You have other people to think of. You told me about Nelly—she has a pretty face. Think of her, Jack!"

"To hell with her!" groaned Jack Smith, feebly. He began to gasp out his words in whispers, as big Merrill had done and something crumbled in Pursivant as he listened. He glanced at Franklin, but still the dying man did not exist for him and the eyes of Franklin were pondering only one thing. "To hell with her," breathed Smith. "She's started running around with that runt of a Mooney. She's no good. She never was no good except to sop up my cash. She ain't like you. She's like him—she's like Franklin, there, sneering at me."

He took a hand away from his wound and stretched it out dripping towards the big man whose flashlight held the scene. The strength of his normal voice came suddenly back to Jack Smith. He began to shout.

"You sneer, do you?" he yelled. "I can wipe the sneer off your face, you fat fool. I'm gunna wipe it off, too. I'm gunna show you *what* a fool you are. You come out here to smash Pursivant. You dirty Dago, you ain't fit to lick his boots. You come out here to play your cards, but you're only playin' Cappen's hand. You come out here to fix Pursivant for murdering your brother. You dummy, Pursivant didn't murder him! Cappen and me fixed the lie, and we bagged you with it. Laugh that off, will you? Why don't you sneer now? I got your eye now, have I? Look at him, will you? A damn dummy, is all he is!"

Franklin came a step out of the doorway and stopped again, saying nothing.

"Suppose he did sock Alberto?" said Jack Smith. "Why not? What was Bert good for? Only to get stinking on vino or tequila. He'd of been stuck in the gizzard a hundred times except Pursivant stuck with him. What did Bert want but trouble? And he'd of got plenty except Pursivant was always ready to put his hand in. He put his hand in again, that night when he run the gang of Chinks over and Bert wanted to go on to town and get stinko, the way he always got. He was no good. He was the dirtiest rat I ever seen. He couldn't please nothing but a brother. Bah! He even had to buy his women. I can't have no doctor or no priest, eh? I'll give you your slice of hot hell, then. Your Alberto was a lousy bum. Pursivant tries to keep him out of town and the hoozegow, and he pulls his gun without no warning and opens up on Pursivant. Yeah, on Pursivant, and knocks him down with a slug. I heard the sock of it as it went into him. And Pursivant lies there and pulls his own gun, at last. Even then he don't shoot to kill. He just tries to knock that murdering dummy of a Dago off his feet, and the bullet happens to hit inside the hip and glance up into the soft of his belly!"

He paused to gasp for breath, his head bobbing back and forth, his mouth biting at the air.

In that small interval the voice of Cappen called from the next room: "What the devil is loose in there? Smith is talking. Harmody—go in there. I'm on your heels!"

Franklin sprang across the room, jarred the door home with the weight of his shoulder, and pulled the rusted bolt into its pocket in the stone. The screech of the iron against its guard made Harmody shout: "Open up! Open up! Franklin, where are you?"

Franklin flung the bright cone of the flash back on Jack Smith in time to see him lift on one hand and exclaim: "To hell with you and all the dirty Dagoes! To hell with you; I wouldn't give a damned nickel for a whole hell-full of you! I wouldn't—"

An invisible hand throttled him. He pitched over on his face and began to kick himself around in a circle with the last mechanical flurry of his strength. He looked like a headless thing, like a butchered chicken struggling beside the chopping block.

Les Harmody banged against the door.

"Franklin! D'you hear me?" he shouted. "What's happening in there? Open the door!"

"Franklin! Oh, Franklin!" cried the voice of Cappen. "What's that lying fool of a Smith been saying?"

That lying fool of a Smith was saying nothing. Not that human ears could ever hear, at least. He lay in the midst of a vast red blur on the stone floor. Franklin jerked the light away and rubbed that picture out. He came straight up to Pursivant, putting away his gun and snatching out a small pocketknife.

Over his shoulder he called: "It's all right, Harmody. I have everything in hand."

Two brief tugs of the knife blade freed the hands of Pursivant. His numbed arms swung forward; there was no feeling except a vague tingling below the wrist.

"Open the door, then!" called Cappen. "What's the matter, Franklin?"

And Harmody said: "It's strange! It's damned strange."

"Wait a moment. It's worth waiting for," said Franklin.

He said to Pursivant, rapidly, through his teeth: "Take this gun. I've got another. We're going to open the door and walk through them."

"I can't use my hands," said Pursivant. "It's no good. And Harmody—he's a trained tiger. Break for the yard of the fort, Dick!"

"It's too much for me," said the obscure mutter of Cappen. "Put a few bullets through that lock. Smash the door down, Les."

Franklin was already through the door. Pursivant was held back for an instant as the girl unbuttoned his coat, pulled his wounded arm across his breast, and refastened the buttons to hold it in place. The light of Franklin's torch drove back at them so that Pursivant could see she had been looking up towards his face while her swift hands worked for him.

The strong hand of Franklin now thrust him forward. The girl was in the lead, Pursivant next to her, and Franklin running last, as they got through the farther door of the storeroom into a big corridor that bent smoothly, like a huge leaden pipe. Behind them, they heard a sudden thrumming of rapid fire. Harmody was blowing the lock out of its strong wooden frame.

CHAPTER XXXIX

THE girl carried a flash that showed the first quick face of every bend, the well-like darkness of the stairway they reached, the veins of seeping water that crossed the ceilings like bright steel chasings. Out of the looseness of her coat she slipped with a single twist, though the flashlight was in her hand. She kicked off the red-heeled slippers but she seemed no smaller, she was running with such airy lightness with the wind of her speed blowing the green chiffon closely about her. Pursivant could see her by the swaying light of Franklin's torch as the big fellow ran behind them. And often Pursivant's own shadow obscured her, swallowing her with blackness, letting her emerge again for a swift instant. It was marvellous that she could set a pace almost as fast as he could follow.

They came to that long stairway which led straight up towards the yard at the fort. That was where Pursivant felt himself failing. The heavy swaying of his shoulders pulled horribly on his wound. The pain of it flashed in electric currents downwards through his arm, upwards through his brain and as the mouths of the torn flesh opened, the blood began to run hot on his back and breast. In his knees his strength failed him. He was stepping wide, straddling, leaning far forward when he heard a shout behind him. It had a metallic ring as though it echoed through a brass tube. Then the strong grip of Franklin caught him under the pit of the arm and gave lightness to his feet again.

He saw the girl swerve as though to slow her running and wait for him.

"The horses!" gasped Pursivant. "Untie them!"

And she raced on again, quickly drawing away. The beret was off, and the pitching light in the hand of Franklin showed the red and the sheen of her hair, by glimpses. Then she was gone before them, and they came out after her into the dimness and the broad uproar of a steady rain. A big automobile with its hood back lay open to the downpour. They saw the headlights like great round eyes under water and the body of the machine was sketched in dimly. Just beyond it were the horses, tail to the wind and head down, the girl already working at their heads.

She had them free as Pursivant came up. The cold beat of the rain was helping him. Franklin panted out orders as he arrived. The girl was to get up with Pursivant because with one hand he could hardly manage a plunging horse over such terrain as that which lay ahead of them. And Franklin was too great a weight to take Pursivant up with him.

He helped Pursivant into the saddle on the biggest of the two Irish hunters and then tossed the girl up before him. She slipped on aside. He wanted to yell to her to sit astride in order to have a grip, but sidesaddle was all she was used to, probably. So he pushed as far back in the saddle as he could and reaching across her gripped the pommel. She sent off the big gelding with a rush that let him skid with a stagger over a bit of sleek mud. The grip of Pursivant saved them both but she did not need much help. She had a light and perfect balance and the rigid bar of his forearm pinned her down. Franklin came with them. Hoofs of his horse struck out dim splashes of white. From the tail of his eye, Pursivant saw the bulky figure swaying through the rain.

They passed the automobile as two forms lurched out of the

hollow mouth of the doorway from the fort. Two guns spat angry, rapid little tongues of red fire. Franklin, half turned, was answering. Now only one automatic pounded; the other man was leaping into the machine. Neither of them carried any burden. In fact, they could never have come so swiftly if they had paused to bring the loot of the Weaver Trust away. To stop the flight was the great objective and Cappen was the fellow to understand that.

The headlights flared. All about Pursivant the air filled with crystal pencil strokes of the rain and there was an illusion of bright mist rushing upwards as fast as the drops fell. He saw the head of the girl, darkly rusted over with water but still faintly shining. He saw the way her hands gripped the reins, working back and forth with them. She held them low. She held them hard. She steadied that plunging monster like a little sprig of a jockey when it sweeps a long-gaited steeplechaser over the jumps. He had a ridiculous impulse to loose his grip on the saddle in order to feel the hardness of her forearm.

He looked back. Franklin was there, riding very well, with his overcoat flying out like the wings of a clumsy bird. And right down the narrowing funnel of light he could stare at the two eyes of brightness.

The beat of the rain blanketed down all other sounds, whether of wind or sea or even the jarring explosions of the guns, but he could hear the thrilling whine of the self starter. Then the ragged spluttering of a machine gun began from the car.

They dropped down out of the headlights as though the ground had disappeared beneath them. That was merely the dip of the slope that led to the fort. His own weight lurched forward and thrust the thigh of Jacqueline against his right arm. If his grip failed them on the greasy pigskin she would be shot from her place. His own position was insecure enough, for pushed far back as he was, his feet thrust the stirrups awkwardly forward. In his handhold on the leather lay the only security for them both. And he managed to keep it, though he groaned with relief when the good gelding crossed the bottom of the hollow and rushed the farther slope.

They got into the field of the headlights again, of course, at the crest of the rise, but no machine gun opened on them. The lights themselves pitched and danced like two one-eyed devils as the automobile came out of the old gate of the fort, staggering over the bumps and the stones.

The lights were snatched away from the fugitives; the machine was lurching on the downslope and the darkness, thickened by the kind rain, closed deeply in around Pursivant.

"They've lost us!" said the girl. She did not turn her head, and the wind of the gallop blew the sounds raggedly back to him.

"They'll head straight for the neck of the peninsula," he told her. "If they can get there first, they can walk back and eat us up on the way. They can water every inch of the ground with the lead out of their machine gun, and all we have is a few rounds in a pair of revolvers. We've got to get past the narrows before they arrive and put us in their pocket. Ride all out, Jacqueline!"

She rode all out, but there was a vast disadvantage in that she could not risk the horse at a big jump while there was a clumsy double burden on its back. She had to search out through the dimness of the night the low spots in the fences. She had to slow the good gelding and let him nose and crush his way through the wild hedges.

Off to the side, they could see Franklin commence to fly

the obstacles in splendid fashion. But when he saw they were not keeping up, he pulled gallantly across to them.

"Dick, you fool!" shouted Pursivant. "Go on! Go on for help! Get out of this and bring help!"

Well, that was a clumsy device, perhaps. At least it would not catch Richard Franklin. He stayed on, unmoved, close beside them.

"He loves you! He'll die with us!" cried the girl.

It meant that, perhaps, since there was no talent in Franklin for dividing his mind. There was his hand for his friends, his fist for his enemies, his heart for Charlie Pursivant; and if he had taken Pursivant back into his soul again, then there was nothing in the future for either of them to fear except that pair of headlights which bobbed on the high places and swayed suddenly down into the shallow hollows.

They had an extra eye to fix on the fugitives, however: a big high-powered searchlight that first threw a ray across the rain mist and picked out the wet green of a patch of shrubbery. After that it pulled back by leaps and starts, wavering across the narrow land until it laid its ghostly hand on the three riders.

It clung to them, and the whir of a machine gun sent a stream of bullets through the light. They knocked up an unexpected clangor out of tin cans, invisible in a grassed-over mound. They kept Pursivant's head ducking. Shame could not keep him erect though he saw the girl as straight as ever with the wet green ruffles of chiffon blowing about her neck.

They could not avoid that searchlight. It followed them like a thought, like a spirit, and now and again the bullets were in it.

Pursivant could give his wits for an instant to the whirling confusion that must be in the mind of Cappen. For even after the narrows of the peninsula had been reached, the manhunt had to be organized and pushed through. It would take time, and Franklin, at least, was still able to put up a battle.

When that battle ended, there was the necessary return to the fort to get the loot; then they must return once more. And by that time, might not the police guard which had blocked the way be again at the old post, even though Franklin had dismissed it earlier in the night?

Those were the desperate reasons why Cappen was firing from the jogging automobile whenever the searchlight touched on the target. From such a platform no gun could fire with a true aim but every chance had to be taken now.

Then luck took a hand against the three. The rain that had befriended them proved no more than a clearing shower which was passing, now. Out of the east the stars appeared, higher and higher. No downpour was streaking across their faces and the piled rearward of the storm tumbled over the zenith and rolled more rapidly towards the west, leaving all clean behind it.

They neared the narrows of the peninsula. On their right, they saw the headlights leaping on a piece of higher ground. The searchlight staggered between heaven and earth, finding the target, losing it, whipping across it again and again.

Cappen would be at the wheel, his head thrusting farther forward than ever as he scanned the road, probing at the depths of the ruts through the water that was gushing in them. No doubt it was Les Harmody whose hand worked the searchlight, his long, pale face twisting as he tried his snapshot bursts with the machine gun.

The horses were behind, at this point. Their goal would be that small cloud of trees at the side of the narrows. If they could reach that shelter first, then even revolver fire would be enough to stop the automobile and turn it back.

"Now for it!" shouted Franklin, beside them, and waved towards the comparatively smooth sweep of ground that extended before them. The girl cried out an answer that Pursivant could not make out distinctly for suddenly he was aware that his teeth had been set so hard that they were as brittle as glass. His strength had been running out. He remembered what big Merrill had said about a small leak draining even a great bucket; and though his wound was far less vital, he was by no means such a reservoir of life as Merrill.

After that, he began to see things with the deadly clarity of one about to topple from a height.

Off to the right, the automobile was struggling across the pitches of that outworn road, flinging its headlights here and there, catching at the fugitives with mere glints and flashes, and futile bursts of fire. It was following the road straight towards the trees which were the goal of the riders; it seemed to have an equal chance of reaching the vital point; and then again luck struck at the heads of the three.

No, not Franklin, for he had seen the thing fairly as he ranged ahead, and his horse had flown the danger. He was trying to pull up, now, turning in the saddle, shouting, pointing. And that was how they saw a ditch worked by the rainwater, opening its funnel wider and deeper as it extended towards the sea. They had missed it by fortune on the ride out to the fort, because they had followed the other side of the peninsula for some distance.

The girl straightened a little. For a sick instant, Pursivant thought she was pulling on the reins. Instead, a fine 'haloo' came ringing from her. They swayed their bodies at the same time forward; the honest Irishman, as one who knew right well what lay ahead and the perils of it, gathered himself with pricking ears. Whip and spurs could not have put more heat in him as he started his run.

Something stopped inside Pursivant. His heart, perhaps. Then the ground dipped away beneath them. The searchlight, by an odd chance, looked down the ravine at that very instant to show the riders what manner of rocks lined that ditch like teeth in the mouth of a shark. But the Irishman was lifting as he ought to lift under such a burden, as high as for a wall. The stars blurred into thin streaks on the eyes of Pursivant. The air came cold against his teeth. Then the hoofs of the horse thumped into the yielding earth beyond. His quarters sagged as a mass of the ground gave way under the impact. They were falling back for an instant, then clambering, then wading, as it were, forward onto the level.

But they had lost the vital moment of the race, for the headlights of the automobile were drawing well ahead of them into the throat of the narrows.

ꕥ CHAPTER XL ꕥ

NOW, with a slight turn, the full force of the headlights and the powerful searchlight combined in a sharp focus on the riders. The automobile itself almost disappeared behind this brilliant dazzle, dissolved as completely as in deep shadow; but Cappen was there, with a savage riot in his heart, and the grin of Les Harmody would be twisting up one side of his face.

"Go to ground!" shouted Franklin, suddenly, and started to swing out of the saddle before the inevitable final hail of bullets began to sweep over them. All the ground about them would be pelted with lead also. They had no more chance of life than a bit of dust has of remaining dry when the garden hose is turned on it. Quite distinctly, Pursivant heard Cappen shout: "Now! Harmody!"

And as he heard it, instead of flinging himself out of the saddle and onto the ground, Pursivant chose that they both should die in a finer attitude. The girl had started to free herself, but the first moment his arm checked her, she understood and slipped back against him with her face raised and her hands drawn back against her breast as though she wanted to shield that part of her from the bullets.

He had a tenth part of a second to look at her before they died and something divinely great, beautiful and assured, ought to flower in that moment. He ought to kiss her; the first and the last kiss. But all he could do was to wonder where the bullets would strike her. One of them might smash through the chin bone and mushroom upwards, ruining that beauty with a frightful red furrow. He kept looking down at her, calmly, and nothing in him would react and no emotion would blossom. Nothing that he saw was more important than his own soiled right hand as it appeared grasping the round of her shoulder, the crooked fingers sinking deep in the wet chiffon.

In his tenth of a second before the machine gun fire would begin, he had a chance to see and to note these things, and to be shamed by his insufficient humanity, and to understand that love may come behind thought, slowly trailing.

Then gunfire hammered at his ears, but not from the direction of the automobile, and the crashing of glass and the clangor of beaten iron from the car of Cappen.

Out of the trees which had been their goal he saw Gregory running straight on towards the automobile, his figure growing more distinct as he advanced into the cone of light, so that the grey fluff of his hair was like a mist of white flame. He was firing a revolver which he held far before him.

The machine gun from the automobile answered with a sudden roaring; but the bullets did not sing in the air about Pursivant. Instead, they merely caused Gregory to stop his charge. He stood up straight, like a duellist, with his left arm across the small of his back and his gun carefully on his mark. And the figure behind the machine gun slumped suddenly back.

The automobile twisted its headlights away. It ran with the whine of gears in second, then the thumping and crashing of the body battering against the running gear as the driver took his way headlong in spite of broken terrain. The gunfire from the trees had ceased but the speed of the flight did not lessen. Once or twice, Pursivant saw a body fling up loose arms and aimless head above the top of the car. That was a dead man's dance, he knew; but whether it were Cappen or Harmody who jounced on the pitching seat, he could not guess. Then a twist of the old road from Fort Howard snatched the machine from view, though they could still hear the battering of it and a clattering as of tin cans.

Some vital center of perception had been deadened in the brain of Pursivant, for although he knew that Cappen's car was gone, still he could not join the picture with the meaning behind it: that Cappen at last had turned his back and run from his quarry and from the stolen treasure that lay yonder with the dead men in Fort Howard.

He heard Franklin say something; he heard the girl speaking; but all the meaning of their words was scattered like dust in a wind as the voice of Gregory came to him, saying: "Mr. Pursivant! Are you safe, sir?"

"Gregory, you smashed them up!" shouted Pursivant.

He slid down from the horse into the anxious flurry of light that Gregory threw over him with an electric torch.

"Give me that light," commanded Pursivant. He took it and flashed it straight into the face of Gregory. It was perfectly immobile except that the lips were parted a trifle and the panting breath stirred the grey of the moustaches.

"You damned scoundrel!" said Pursivant.

"Yes, sir," said Gregory.

"Do you thank God that you changed your mind?" asked Pursivant.

"I thank Miss Leigh, sir," said Gregory.

"Are you hurt?"

"They smashed the pocket flask in my coat, sir. I am bleeding nothing but brandy. If I may ask—your shoulder—"

"There had to be a little paying," said Pursivant. "And that's the nickel in the slot."

They got across the hills to the Verney place without any hurry for if anything was certain it was that a certain automobile with broken springs and shattered glass and the loosely flopping body of a dead man on board it would not turn back towards Fort Howard again, on this night. From the Verney house they sent the telephone messages that brought police sweeping across the country, their motorcycles bouncing and bucking along the narrow bridle paths. They found Richard Franklin at the Fort to show them the dead men and the recovered loot of the Weaver Trust Company and to greet them with a silence which was often characteristic.

But at the Verney house, Pursivant refused to go to bed. Gregory and Jacqueline Leigh cut away his coat and shirt and probed and cruelly cleaned the wound through his shoulder. Christopher Verney came in and tried to wave the girl out of the room but she smiled at him in such a way that even Verney suddenly understood.

Pursivant, sitting up in a chair, watched the doctor who had come panting in from White Forest put on the elaborate bandage. The medical man was only excited by the haste in which he had made the drive. As for the wound, he thought so little of it that he seemed to carry over some of his contempt and add it to Pursivant.

As for Pursivant, he saw his image turn its head in the mirror across the room and he found a certain dignity in the reflection, for it was all white and black, like a Rembrandt; all thinned and hollowed and aged; it would have served as the head of one of those cadaverous cavaliers.

Weakness kept bubbling up in him like a spring and there was a dimness of mind like that which comes with a fever. He would be pretty thoroughly knocked out on the morrow, he knew, but he refused to shorten his present moment and afterwards walked out onto the terrace, leaning on the shoulder of Gregory. Verney had dug up some of his sister's clothes and the torn, rain-ruined green frock of Jacqueline was replaced with white silk.

It was an evening for white. The rain had washed clean the deepest reaches of the sky and all the stars were bright across it except as they descended into the dullness towards the western horizon. A south wind was blowing warmer and warmer until Verney declared that it was the exact moment for a mint julep and went to see to the crushing of the mint because he said that only a loving hand could do the thing properly.

That left the girl and Pursivant with old Gregory on the terrace.

Pursivant said to his man: "Is there anything you want to say to me, Gregory?"

And Gregory considered for a long moment before he answered: "Not in words, sir."

Pursivant felt a smile pull at the grimness of his face till his own sour look was mastered, and he waved to Gregory to dismiss him. The girl had been watching, saying nothing. She looked almost as dark as an Indian, in that white dress, but with the turn of her head sometimes he found the blue stain of her eyes again. She was not smiling, but always brightening towards it, as on that evening when he had first seen her in this house.

He started to speak, but every word that came up in his mind and his throat dissolved before it reached utterance, and new thoughts formed and soundlessly gave way to others; yet all the while happiness sang in a louder voice near him, somewhere, happiness breathed into the south wind from the garden and from the wet earth.

Franklin came striding from the house. He stood behind the chair of Pursivant, leaning his elbow on the high back of it, as he said, quietly: "The police have everything. They were glad to see Merrill—dead. On the road they've picked up the dead body of Harmody, and they say that Cappen can't get away in that car. I've said nothing but a few words to the police, and I'll say less to the reporters. I advise you to do the same."

After a pause he continued: "I hope I'll be able to get in touch with you before long. That is, if you think that you'll want me to."

"I've left the door open all the time," said Pursivant. "Come in whenever you please, Dick."

He heard Franklin breathing for a moment before the deep voice went on: "I ought to thank God that there's one such man as you in the world. After a while, I'll be able to. When that time comes, I'll ask to see you. Goodnight, Bill."

He went off the terrace without speaking another word, without even noticing the girl. And Christopher Verney came out with a tray of mint juleps trailing fragrance behind him.

THE LIBRARY OF CRIME CLASSICS®

THE BEST IN MYSTERY—PAST AND PRESENT

BACKLIST

George Baxt
THE ALFRED HITCHCOCK MURDER CASE $5.95
THE DOROTHY PARKER MURDER CASE
"I!" SAID THE DEMON
A QUEER KIND OF DEATH
A PARADE OF COCKEYED CREATURES
SWING LOW, SWEET HARRIET

Anthony Boucher
NINE TIMES NINE

Caryl Brahms & S.J. Simon
A BULLET IN THE BALLET
MURDER A LA STROGANOFF
SIX CURTAINS FOR STROGANOVA

Christianna Brand
CAT AND MOUSE

Max Brand
THE NIGHTFLOWER

John Dickson Carr
BELOW SUSPICION
THE BURNING COURT
DEATH TURNS THE TABLES
HAG'S NOOK
HE WHO WHISPERS
THE HOUSE AT SATAN'S ELBOW
THE PROBLEM OF THE GREEN CAPSULE
THE SLEEPING SPHINX
THE THREE COFFINS
TILL DEATH DO US PART

Carroll John Daly
MURDER FROM THE EAST

Lillian De La Torre
DR. SAM: JOHNSON, DETECTOR
THE DETECTIONS OF DR. SAM: JOHNSON
THE EXPLOITS OF DR. SAM: JOHNSON, DETECTOR $5.95
THE RETURN OF DR. SAM: JOHNSON, DETECTOR

Carter Dickson
THE JUDAS WINDOW

Dashiell Hammett & Alex Raymond
SECRET AGENT X–9, 6″ × 10″, $9.95

Paul Gallico
THE ABANDONED $5.95

James Gollin
ELIZA'S GALLIARDO
THE PHILOMEL FOUNDATION

Richard Hull
THE MURDER OF MY AUNT

Victoria Lincoln
A PRIVATE DISGRACE $5.95
LIZZIE BORDEN BY DAYLIGHT

Barry N. Malzberg
UNDERLAY

Margaret Millar
AN AIR THAT KILLS
ASK FOR ME TOMORROW
BANSHEE